AVIELLE OF RHIA

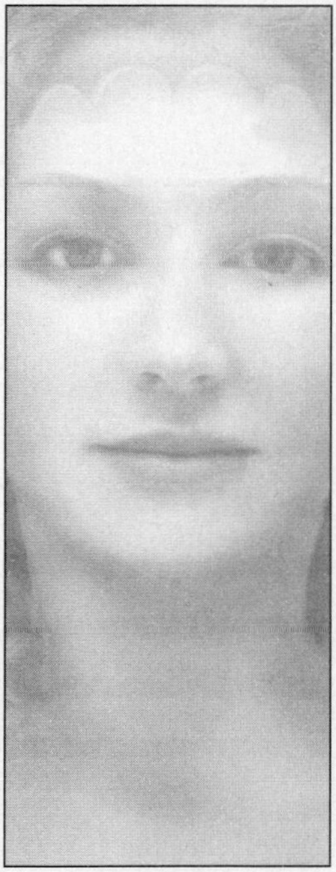

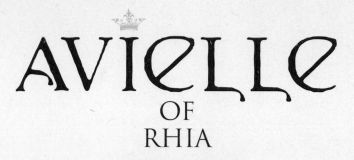

BY
DIA CALHOUN

MARSHALL CAVENDISH

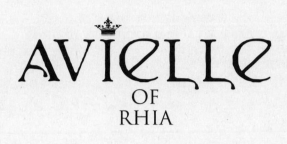

AVIELLE
OF
RHIA

Marshall Cavendish Corporation
99 White Plains Road
Tarrytown, NY 10591
www.marshallcavendish.us
Library of Congress Cataloging-in-Publication Data
Calhoun, Dia.
Avielle of Rhia / by Dia Calhoun.
p. cm.
Summary: Taught to hate and fear the heritage that sets her apart from most people of the kindgom, fifteen-year-old Princess Avielle of Rhia must finally embrace the magic of her Dredonian ancestors to save the very people who scorn her.
ISBN-13: 978-0-7614-5320-8
ISBN-10: 0-7614-5320-2
[1. Magic—Fiction. 2. Princesses—Fiction. 3. Weaving—Fiction. 4. Prejudices—Fiction. 5. Fantasy.] I. Title.
PZ7.C12747Avi 2006
[Fic]—dc22
2006005630

The text of this book is set in Cochin
Book design by Alex Ferrari/ferraridesign.com
Printed in China
First edition
10 9 8 7 6 5 4 3 2 1
mc Marshall Cavendish

OTHER BOOKS BY DIA CALHOUN

Firegold

Aria of the Sea

White Midnight

The Phoenix Dance

ACKNOWLEDGMENTS

I would like to thank Diane Bunting, Steven Chudney, Margery Cuyler, Kathyrn O. Galbraith, Lorie Ann Grover, Joan Holub, Laura Kvasnosky, and Lorna Dumont Shinkle for their help with this book. Special thanks to my husband, Shawn R. Zink.

Living under the shadow of terrorism
calls for a special kind of courage,
a courage that does not come easily for some.
This book is for them.

TABLE OF CONTENTS

THE CHAMBER OF WINGS
CHAPTER ONE

As Princess Avielle raised her candle, a white swan woven on cloth of gold shone out from the darkness. She stood alone in a cold stone chamber far beneath the High Hall, where her father and mother, King and Queen Coroll of Rhia, reigned. She touched the woven white feathers; the thread felt bumpy beneath her fingers. The chamber was round, and weavings and tapestries of birds covered every inch of the stone walls. There were herons, eagles, ducks, geese, owls, meadowlarks, and more. All in flight.

She called this secret place the Chamber of Wings.

Avielle closed her eyes. She imagined she was being lifted into the air by the beating of all those wings, carried aloft on a current of wind. She rose onto her toes, held out her arms, and whispered, "Take me with you," even though she knew it was a foolish thing to say.

Nothing happened, of course. Avielle sighed and moved on to the next weaving: blue herons rising from a pond with their necks outstretched.

She had come here many times, fled here to hide from her dismal life up in the High Hall. She had first found this place when she had been running away from something, clutching a candlestick; sobbing; racing down one staircase after another until she had reached the cellar beneath the cellar. There she had stumbled through a warren of boxes and crates that twisted and turned until at last she found a door, flung it open, and shut it behind her. Avielle could not even remember now what she had been running away from.

Running away from looking Dredonian, she supposed, from looking Dredonian when all her brothers and sisters, though they had the same amount of Dredonian blood as she did, looked Rhian. Or perhaps she had been running from Edard, her eldest brother, the crown prince.

Avielle bumped against a locked chest. Thick with dust, fastened with leather straps and brass buckles, it stood against the wall. She had once tried to open it but the lock had defeated her. In the center of the room was a round oak table. Strewn across it was a black stone bowl; a tarnished silver goblet; a mirror; three bronze bells of varying sizes; a gold five-pointed star on the end of a golden chain—a necklace of some sort; leather packets of dried herbs which had lost all their fragrance; a soot-dimmed lantern; metal tools of various sizes and shapes that were unfamiliar to her; and stoppered vials—one stained with the dried remains of some kind of orange liquid. Some of the vials had labels with odd names written in a bold, elegant script—*tears, storms, essence of rain.* The golden candleholder in the center was fashioned in the shape of the Goddess. Everything was scattered across the table in great disarray, as though whoever had been using the objects so long ago had suddenly thrown them down.

Avielle had never asked anyone about these things or about the weavings hanging on the walls, because she did not want to give away her hiding place. But she suspected the weavings had been made by her great aunt, Princess Trisarna, who had been a renowned weaver, and who had loved birds with such passion that she had commissioned poets, musicians, and artists to create works of art about them. Though why Trisarna had hung some of her weavings here, and why they had long since been forgotten, Avielle did not know. Avielle was a weaver, too, and she knew how exquisite the weavings were.

In the year Avielle had been coming down here, no one had discovered her. She had never stayed long enough for anyone in the High Hall to notice her absence. But then, probably nobody would miss her anyway, except her little brother, Rajio.

Today Avielle had fled here because of what was going to happen tonight. Embarrassment—no, worse—utter humiliation. She pressed her hands together, every muscle in her body tensing. What was her mother thinking? Did she not see? But no, she did not see anything, as usual; that was the problem. Avielle turned toward the door. She had better go up and get it over with. Instead, she turned back and stepped toward the weaving of the white swan.

"Fresar." She spoke her name for the swan. "Rastart, Melilee," she said to the herons. She had names for all the birds; they were her only friends. She took a deep breath and touched her head against a woven wing, wishing she could tuck herself beneath it.

Later that night Avielle stood outside the ballroom, her long silver hair covered in a purple net dotted with winking crystals. She wore a purple brocade dress embroidered with bunches of grapes, as though she were a fruit about to be plucked. The dress was so stiff it could have walked into the ballroom, bowed, danced, and made meaningless polite conversation all by itself. For a brief moment, Avielle thought of slipping out of it and sending it in her stead. But she knew Prince Graedig, seventh son of King and Queen Pathsaur of Imsethia to the west, had come to see her face. Her Dredonian face with its silverskin, pointed ears and, ugliest of all, the scallops of faint bony ridges along the top of her forehead. Dredonian Rhians like her were called silverskins. True Dredonians lived in the Kingdom of Dredonia, to the south of Rhia.

Avielle heard the music stop in anticipation of her entrance, and she knew the dancing was stopping, too.

When the footman swept open the door, Avielle felt her knees shake. Why, why had her mother insisted she come in late in order to make a "grand entrance?" But there was nothing to be done about it now.

"Her Royal Highness, Princess Avielle Reginnia Coroll," the footman announced with a flourish. Avielle walked forward. A blur of light bounced off the crystal chandeliers, making shiny shifting patterns on satin skirts, bows, breeches, and waistcoats. Cascades of white lace spilled from the men's throats. And all the eyes were turned toward her, reflected a hundred times in the mirrors that lined the ballroom walls.

When she saw her mother, dressed in royal blue lace over gold satin, her face slightly pinched with anxiety, Avielle walked toward her. Like her sisters, Avielle had had lessons in deportment, and she could walk as gracefully as any princess in the world. But she knew no one cared how she walked. She knew exactly what everyone in the room was thinking, what, indeed, they had been thinking about, gossiping about, and waiting for from the day she was born. Since the blood of her Dredonian great-great grandmother, Dolvoka, had sprung up in Avielle—because she looked Dredonian—would Dolvoka's evil magic spring up in her, too?

The members of the court, the ministers, the servants, and everyone else—even the members of her own family—were always watching for signs of it, the first signs of evil magic breaking loose. In spite of her anger, Avielle wanted to laugh. What did they expect she would do with two hundred eyes turned upon her? Suddenly make someone's teeth fall out? Turn the candles black? Poison the plate piled with baked ham in Lord Pritherly's greedy hands? Did they expect a demon to spew from her mouth and swing like a monkey from the chandeliers? Never was she just Avielle to them. Never was she free of her great-great grandmother's shadow.

She reached her mother and curtsied. To her mother's left stood Avielle's beautiful sixteen-year-old sister, Ismine, snapping her pale pink fan open and shut.

"I have consulted the stars, my Lady Mother," Ismine was saying. "The planet Hycath the Hunter and the red planet Demord the Demon are in conjunction in the sign of the Arrow. You must believe me, the time is perilous! It is a time to protect and guard the kingdom." Ismine was an ardent student of astrology and had decided opinions about everything.

Avielle had five brothers and sisters. First came Edard, her oldest brother, the crown prince, who was eighteen and who had plagued her since the day she was born because she looked Dredonian and so dishonored the royal family. He strode across the ballroom pulling on his gold turban—all the men wore turbans; it was the fashion. Next in age to Edard was Mildon, seventeen. After him were Ismine and Cerine, who were twins. After them came Avielle, fifteen, and last came her little brother, Rajio, her darling, who was only five.

Ismine smiled at the man who stood to the queen's right; he stared back, and what man—or woman for that matter—

would not? Ismine's skin was as white as snowdrops, with roses so soft upon her cheeks it seemed as if the Goddess had kissed them. Her hair, bound up in ringlets and braids, was as gold as the betrothal ring around her finger.

Avielle judged the man to be at least twenty years older than she was; that would make him thirty-five. His nose slid on and on, down and down, into regions more properly occupied by lips and skin, but alas, these regions appeared to have been vanquished by a marauding mustache that shot out hairs in every direction. Avielle thought of kissing him and shuddered.

"Avielle," her mother said brightly, "I would like to introduce you to His Royal Highness Prince Graedig Pathsaur. Your Highness, allow me to present my daughter, Her Royal Highness Princess Avielle Reginnia Coroll." The prince bowed and Avielle curtsied.

Avielle wondered what was wrong with him that he had come seeking the hand of a fifteen-year-old girl who looked like a full-blooded Dredonian. Several possibilities occurred to her—besides his having a gut sagging nearly to his knees. First, of course, was that he was a seventh son of a minor king, and so his inheritance would be small, and he would have little chance of acquiring a 'normal' royal wife who would bring him a substantial dowry. And Avielle's dowry was substantial. The second possibility was that because Prince Graedig was so dreadfully ugly, his parents thought that only someone as ugly and as seemingly desperate as she would consent to marry him. And third—this was her favorite—he had a turnip for a brain and they wanted someone of rank so grateful to find a match that she would put his boots the right way on for him. But in this she was disappointed when she glanced surreptitiously at his boots. They were the right way on, though not shined to perfection. Perhaps it was his nightshirts that were the problem?

"Good evening, Princess Avielle," said Lord General Maldreck, who was standing to the queen's left. He commanded all her parents' troops in Rhia. He had no hair, no waist, and no neck—his chin pressed into the medals of honor lined up in rigid rows upon his chest. The medals and the top of his head both shone, as though both had been freshly spat upon and polished. "You rival the moon in beauty tonight," he added.

"You are too kind," Avielle said. How she would like to flick one of his medals with her fingernail. She had never liked him. Rumor had it that he wanted her sent away because she was an embarrassment to the royal family.

After an awkward silence, while Prince Graedig kept glancing at Ismine, the queen cleared her throat. The prince started.

"If I may suggest, Prince Graedig," said the queen, "perhaps this would be a good time for. . . ?" She looked pointedly over his shoulder at the footman hovering a few steps behind the prince.

"Oh yes, of course," Prince Graedig said. "Very good.

Come here, man." He beckoned to the footman, who stepped forward holding a red pillow with a black velvet box on top.

"Excellent," the prince said, lifting the box. "Brought something along with me from home. Something I thought you might like, Princess Avielle. What you'd call a present—though just a token, really. Precious, though, extremely delicate and precious! We do have fine craftsmen—really fine! In Imsethia. Quite proud of them I am. They do what I tell them sharplike."

Avielle tried not to laugh. Imagine being married to this bumpkin and having to hear him chatter all day long. She would certainly go mad or her ears would drop off in protest. One of the crystals on her hairnet was digging behind her ear, and she was longing to reach up and scratch it, but princesses did not scratch in public.

Prince Graedig turned the box in his hands so it faced her, and then opened it.

Avielle froze. Nestled on the black velvet, shining where the light caught it, was a crystal bird.

THE CRYSTAL SWAN
CHAPTER TWO

As Avielle stared at the crystal bird, a swan, she heard her mother's inrush of breath. Ismine stopped snapping her fan. The people who were close enough to see fell silent. Then, quick as the cook with his cleaver, whispers ran through the ballroom.

Avielle's breath came hard and fast. She was thinking a hundred things and wondered whether she was going to faint.

Prince Graedig looked bewildered. "Don't you like it, Princess? I had heard you had no birds in this country. Thought you might like to . . ." His voice faded away.

She looked up at him. Surely he knew; *surely* he knew. But as she looked into his flat pale blue eyes she realized that her third guess about him being a turnip was not so far off the mark. He was not being cruel, merely stupid and completely oblivious.

"Yes, Prince Graedig," she said, her voice dull. "I like it very much."

"Pick it up," he urged. "Turn it round. You can see how the crystal catches the light. It's something to see."

Avielle took a deep breath and clasped the bird in both hands—though it easily fit into one. She held it carefully. She must not drop it. She must not. Slowly, she turned it and light glittered on the folded wings. The neck was a long, delicate fluting of glass, for the swan was fashioned as though swimming on a pond.

"It is lovely," she said. "Thank you, Prince Graedig."

After Avielle put the swan back in the velvet box and closed the lid, a sigh traveled around the ballroom, and she thought, for a moment, it made the candles in the chandelier flicker. But was it a sigh of relief or of disappointment? And even if Prince Graedig had not meant to insult her, someone in his government had. The story of Dolvoka was legend, and certainly known far beyond the borders of Rhia.

"Keep this for me." She gave the black velvet box to the footman. Prince Graedig's duty done, he immediately went back to staring at Ismine.

"Let the dancing continue!" proclaimed the queen. The musicians began to pluck their harps, slide their bows, and trill their flutes; and soon the room was full of skirts whirling like upside-down umbrellas spinning in the wind.

As Avielle watched them, she thought of the Presentation Ball she had never had and of the events of her life that had led up to it. When she was five, after her mother had sent

Avielle's favorite nurse, Kesel, away, Avielle and her twin sisters had begun formal instruction. Tutors taught them history, literature, music, art, drawing, and languages. Governesses taught them etiquette, royal deportment, and conversation. They learned the art of dressing appropriately for different functions. They learned how to treat those of lower birth. They learned to ride horses and to participate in the hunt. Avielle's sisters were interested only in these lighter subjects. Avielle alone pursued more academic matters; not only did she love the ideas revealed in books, but she loved the whisper of a page as she turned it, the smell of the leather bindings and glue, even the dust on those volumes long unused. By the time she was fourteen, she was more learned than anyone in her family, excluding her mother.

Avielle also had an artistic flair. She loved to draw, especially anything with a pattern. Her sisters, whose taste was questionable, were always asking her advice on how this hat or that bit of ribbon looked with a particular dress. Only last week Avielle had saved Ismine from the calamity of a red dress with a puce hat. Avielle was grateful to be needed, even in this small way.

When her sisters turned fourteen they each had Presentation Balls, where they were presented to the kingdom as princesses ready to participate in the affairs of court. They began to attend royal balls, court dinners, entertainments, and similar functions. But when Avielle turned fourteen, there was no such ball for her. No one even mentioned it. At the time she had felt a peculiar mixture of anger and relief. She had attended only one ball before this one tonight, a sumptuous ball celebrating Ismine and Cerine's sixteenth birthday—and only because Ismine had begged her to come.

Avielle watched the dancers. Although her parents knew she hated balls, nonetheless they had insisted she come tonight so they could parade her before Prince Graedig and his retinue, and assure them of her royal breeding.

"Prince Graedig," the queen said. "Do you enjoy dancing?"

"Sometimes," the prince said. "When my knee is not bothering me. Hurt it on the hunt last year. Damn horse. Killed him for it." He stood on one leg and swung his other knee back and forth. "Appears to be working fine. So, all right then! Let's give it a go. Would you care to dance, Princess Ismine?"

Avielle recoiled as though she had been slapped.

Ismine looked at her sympathetically.

"Thank you," she said, snapping her fan. "But I am not inclined to dance at the moment."

"Then perhaps," the prince said as he turned, hesitated, and looked at Avielle. "Then, well, perhaps you, Princess Avielle?"

"I . . ." Avielle wanted to refuse, but she glanced at her mother. Her mother raised her eyebrows. "I would be delighted, thank you, Prince Graedig." He is a turnip, she reminded herself, a turnip. How can I be hurt by a turnip?

The prince pulled out a pair of white gloves from the pocket on his waistcoat and, with a great deal of tugging and flexing, put them on. Then, taking her own bare hand—it was not the custom in Rhia to wear gloves—the prince led her out onto the dance floor of polished parquet where they began to waltz. However, it did not go well at all. Avielle, who had been trained by the best dancing masters in the kingdom, was puzzled. Then she realized that the prince was holding her as far away as possible, his arms stiff. She looked around and saw to her horror that none of the other members of the prince's retinue were wearing gloves. Then she understood, and her cheeks flamed. He did not want to touch her. He did not want to touch her because she looked Dredonian.

Then how could he possibly want to marry her?

Every minute or so the prince let out a heavy sigh that made the long hairs of his mustache fly up and wave like the legs of a centipede. Avielle felt ill. Would the music never end?

At that moment Edard whirled by with a lady in white crushed in his arms like a grub. He smiled at Avielle, enjoying her discomfort. When the dance was over, Prince Graedig led her back to the side of the dance floor, and bowed slightly.

"Well," he said, "perhaps that sister of yours is ready to dance now. Don't want to neglect your family! Come along." And to Avielle's astonishment, instead of escorting her, he simply waved one hand at her to follow along behind him—as though she were a dog—and left her.

She did not follow. Indeed, she could not move.

Avielle knew that every eye was on her, that every eye had watched the incident with Prince Graedig. All of them knew, of course, why he had come. And she was certain all of them were delighted to see her demeaned. She wanted to run from the ballroom, but if she did, everyone would know she had tasted humiliation. Instead, her head held high, Avielle walked toward one of the curtained alcoves that was set aside for people to rest and converse in. There she could hide for a few moments and regain her composure.

She longed to wash her hands, which were slightly damp from the sweat that had seeped through Prince Graedig's gloves. Even if he were a toad, no princess would ever kiss him to transform him back into a prince. And as a frog he would probably still have that horrible fluttering mustache, no doubt sweeping in flies.

When she reached the alcove, it was already full. She turned to go to another when she heard one word: "Dredonian."

She froze. Were they speaking of her? Or of someone else? There were many others in Rhia who were part Dredonian—perhaps a tenth of all Rhians. Indeed, even here and there in the ballroom Avielle could see Dredonian Rhians who had pointed ears, or the bony crown of scallops at the top of their foreheads, or even silver hair; but very few had silverskins. Only Dredonian Rhians with silverskins were called silverskins; the term was not applied to those with the other Dredonian features. And all silverskins had all the Dredonian features. So one could not really tell the difference between a silverskin who was a Dredonian Rhian and a Dredonian. Though there was some prejudice against silverskins, they were not hated and feared as Avielle was, because they were not descended from Dolvoka.

Dredonians had strong gifts for magic power, though not all among them had it. Now and then a magic gift popped up even among the Dredonian Rhians. But again, they, unlike Avielle, were not descended from Dolvoka, so no one suspected them of having the latent ability to do horrendously evil magic. As they suspected her.

Avielle stepped closer to the alcove, then turned her back toward it as though looking out upon the ballroom, but she could still hear every word that was being said.

"The Dredonians—or rather the Brethren of the Black Cloaks—have sent a deadline for their demands," a man's voice said. "The news arrived in a letter today."

Avielle tensed. What new tidings had come from those evil wizard-priests?

"What did they say?" asked a woman.

"We must agree to give them a yearly tribute of five thousand slaves, as well as our gold and silver mines in the Heart

Mountains, in the next two days. If we do not, they say, and I quote, 'we will unleash death and destruction upon you.'"

Avielle took a deep breath. Of course, she had heard before about the demands the Dredonians were making through the evil wizard-priests, the Brethren of the Black Cloaks, but not that the threat of retaliation was imminent. It made her feel even worse about being part Dredonian. She knew her parents would never agree to send a single Rhian citizen as a slave to Dredonia, nor give up the gold and silver mines, which contained much of the wealth of the kingdom.

"It means war," someone said.

"The king and queen have been mustering troops; they'll be ready."

"That's right. The king and queen will prevail. Haven't they protected us and kept us safe all these years? Even now they have our own wizards working to put a ring of power around the city to protect us."

"And," someone added, "the queen is learned in the arts and stratagems of warfare. Without their majesties, we'd be lost. With them, we're safe. They will never give in to the evil Brethren."

"But the Dredonians may not attack Tirion. They may attack another city."

"Tirion is the capital. If they attack, they'll attack here. You can be sure of it."

"I say let them come! We will never be defeated."

Avielle withdrew. She walked down the length of the ballroom, no longer caring who saw her leave.

Her mother and father stood talking to one of the lords of Imsethia across the room; they did not notice her departure. But then, they seldom noticed anything she was doing. It was not that they did not care for her, which they did, in a distracted, distant sort of way; it was that they never paid much attention to her. They did not seem to notice that she rarely attended court functions—state dinners, dances, parties, excursions, even family gatherings—or that she spent much of her time alone either weaving on her loom or curled up with a book in the library. They were too busy managing the realm, and that, she thought, was probably as it should be.

They would be disappointed, she knew, when she refused the match but not surprised. She did not think they would resort to forcing her to marry against her will. But how would she ever find someone she liked who was also blind enough to marry her? Who would want to marry her when she was a perpetual reminder of the terrible magic spell that Dolvoka, the Cursed One, had cast over Rhia? But Avielle had one small comfort: although she was part Dredonian, she had no hint of any kind of magical power at all. She clung to this. For without magical power she could not do the kind of great evil that Dolvoka had done.

After Avielle retrieved the black velvet box from the footman, she walked out of the ballroom, down the long hall—its stone floor covered with carpets, its vaulted ceiling carved with stone arches—up three wooden stairways, and down two corridors with wooden floors, toward her room in the south wing.

She passed the Gallery of Ancestors. The door was open, as it always was; and candles burned inside, as they always did. On the walls hung the portraits of many generations of the royal family. Rhians greatly revered their ancestors. Indeed, they believed that traits were passed down from one generation to the other, and that each person had an ancestor who was largely responsible for who they were. It was called the Creed of Ancestors.

For example, everyone believed that Avielle's mother's skill at scholarship had passed down from her great grandfather, Periclodor. And so her mother paid homage to him, bringing flowers to leave before his portrait. Avielle's Aunt Rolina, who was old and ill and kept to her bed on the fourth floor, had been a skilled painter, and everyone thought this derived from her great-great aunt. Every member of the royal family had some trait passed down from their ancestors; sometimes, the trait was a bad one. Avielle's Uncle Seyna, who had died five years ago, had been a scatterwit, and this, it was said, had passed down from Avielle's twice-great grandfather.

Dolvoka's portrait did not hang inside the gallery. All images of her had been destroyed. Avielle passed the gallery without going inside; she never did.

As she walked, she thought over the conversation that she had overheard. She wondered why she was not so certain as the others that her parents—good and wise rulers as she knew they were—would keep them all safe. Maybe it was because they had never kept her quite safe.

They had turned a blind eye toward Edard's cruelty toward her, and a blind eye to the way everyone else treated her as well. She had always excused them, always thought that this, also, was because they were too busy.

Avielle turned a corner and her breath caught in her throat as she saw Edard lounging against the door to her room.

THE SHADOW OF DOLVOKA
CHAPTER THREE

Avielle looked at Edard, who was regarding her with amusement, his head pillowed languidly against his raised arm leaning against the door. How had he slipped past her? He must have noticed her leaving the ballroom, then had run around and used the servants' stairs. Very dignified for a crown prince. Avielle clutched the black velvet box and braced herself for whatever was coming.

"So," Edard began, "even the ugly seventh son—who, by the way, cannot even speak in complete sentences—even the ugly seventh son of a minor king of an impoverished kingdom—I've heard their major export is pig snouts—does not want to touch you. And who can blame him? For who can abide to look at you, oh Cursed One?"

"You are a Dredonian Rhian, too," she said. "The blood came through you from Father just as it did to the rest of us. You were even born with one of the features. Your ears were pointed. Mother and Father snipped the points off and had them reshaped when you were born. Kesel told me all about it. That's why Mother had her sent away."

Edard stood straight up. "She was a liar and you are one, too!"

"Then why do you always wear that turban if not to hide your mangled ears? The fashion came in just after you were born. Father began it."

"Shut up!" Edard said. "You are only trying to lessen your own filth by attacking me. Give me that crystal bird the lump-head gave you."

Avielle did not move.

He plucked a bit of lint off his blue waistcoat; a stain ran down from the bottom button. "I would enjoy making you."

Avielle knew this was no idle threat. He would not hesitate to resort to violence. She opened the box and showed him the crystal swan.

He threw back his head and laughed. "How appropriate! But the lump-head is not so subtle. One of his ministers is behind this. What a superb insult!"

Avielle's fingernails dug into the black velvet.

"Ah," said Edard, "I can see from the expression on your face that you are wondering why they should insult you if they want you to marry him."

She could not help nodding.

"Are you so dense? All they want is your dowry. Then they will lock you away somewhere, and the prince can keep on with his hunting and hawking, and never have to see you again. Some clever minister suggested Graedig give you the bird to show they know exactly who and what you are."

She stared at him. A smile hovered about his lips.

"Did you think he would hold you in high esteem? Honor you? Strew your path with roses?" He paused. "I know what would be entertaining. Let me see you dash that thing to the floor. You cannot let this chance to follow in our dear great-great grandmother's footprints pass. Come! Come, let me see you do it!"

"Keep away from me."

He made a grab for the black velvet box, but only caught the edge of it. Avielle grabbed the crystal swan and turned to run. But Edard was too fast. He ran up behind her, slipped his arm around her ribs, and squeezed until she gasped.

"Throw it!" he shouted. "Throw it!"

"No!" she cried.

He grasped her arm, drew it back, and then forced it forward as he pried open her fingers. The crystal swan went flying. It spun, arcing like a brilliant thought in the air. Then down it went and shattered on the floor.

"I will inform the servants that there is a mess to clean up," Edard whispered, his breath hot upon her ear. He laughed. Then he let her go and walked away.

Avielle fell to her knees. Something hammered at the base of her throat. She wanted to run after Edard and kick him and beat him. But she was too afraid. She had to get up. The servants would be here soon; she could not let them see her like this. But she could not move.

"Your Highness?" said a familiar voice. Avielle looked up and saw Salulla, her maid, holding a candlestick, looking at the fragments of crystal on the floor. Avielle's shoulders sagged. Salulla would tell the servants, who would tell those who brought goods to the High Hall. Then like the plague, the tale of the broken bird would spread to tradesmen, merchants, masters, mistresses, and on and on it would go until by tomorrow evening it would be discussed by every urchin and lord in the city. "Bad blood calls to bad blood," they would say, nodding, delighted that they had been proven right. "They ought to lock her up."

Her hands cold, Avielle stood.

"I'll get a broom," Salulla said. Then she hesitated, looking at Avielle's stricken face. "But first you'll need help getting that dress off."

Inside Avielle's room, Salulla moved about with her candlestick and lit the white candles in the sconces on the walls. A soft golden light spread over the room, shining on the tall canopy bed. Sheer white silk shot with silver thread hung in graceful swoops across the frame and tumbled down along the tall beech bedposts on all four corners. So light the drapes looked, so diaphanous, as they were stirred by the wind coming through the window, that they seemed to be the cloak of some fairy being. The bed itself had a cornflower blue spread and white lace-edged pillows. The candle glow also flickered over a rosewood desk with two neat stacks of books, and a painting hung in a gilt frame.

In silence Salulla helped Avielle off with her dress. Avielle sat down before her dressing table with her eyes closed so she would not have to look in the mirror. Hairpins clicked in a small silver bowl as Salulla took off the purple hairnet and brushed out Avielle's hair.

"Like a waterfall it is," Salulla said suddenly. Then she clamped her mouth shut.

Avielle, surprised, looked up at her in the mirror. Like the other servants, Salulla treated her with a mixture of disdain and fear, but every once in a while a streak of kindness flew out of her mouth in spite of herself.

"Will that be all, Princess?" she asked coldly, setting the brush down. "I'd best be cleaning up that glass."

Avielle nodded, and Salulla left, eager, no doubt, to impart the story of the crystal swan's destruction.

Avielle stood up and went over to the candle on the table by the window. Pure white, the candle was two feet tall and carved with the image of the Light-Bringer, who carried the sun in one hand and the moon in the other; her hair of stars swept out behind her. The Light-Bringer was Avielle's sun sign, one of the signs of the zodiac. The sun had been in the constellation of the Light-Bringer in the month of Mara, the first month of spring, the pale, wet month when Avielle was born.

The light gleaming on the gilt picture frame caught her eye, and Avielle walked over to look at the painting. She had loved it the moment she had seen it gathering dust in one of the unused drawing rooms, and brought it up to hang on her wall. It showed a busy street in a village at sunset. Snow lay upon the ground, and the lamplighter was just beginning to light the lamps. The shops were lit, and shopkeepers and customers smiled at each other inside, passing bundles back and forth. People smiled at each other in the streets, too, and waved to each other out of shop doors. A boy greedily ate a string of sausages; a girl huddled in her muff; and another girl held a pair of ice skates as though she were heading for a lake. All of them looked happy. All of them looked as if they knew one another.

A warm wind poured through the arched windows of Avielle's room—it was the middle of the late summer month of Aukim—and the candle flames wavered. Avielle went and opened one of the windows wider. The sky was a swathe of black velvet. The stars scattered upon it were like the broken fragments of crystal that had been scattered in the hallway. She could see the Hunter rising, his arrow drawn. Outside the window, to the left, hung a bird feeder full of seeds. Every mansion, shop, and house in Rhia had at least one feeder to encourage the birds to come home. A handful of seeds were cast into the wind every morning and every night.

Avielle thought of what Edard had said. Had Prince

Graedig really planned to marry her and then lock her away somewhere? She shuddered. It was too similar to Dolvoka's fate.

A hundred years ago, when Rhia had defeated Dredonia in war—long before the evil wizard-priests of the Brethren of the Black Cloaks had come to power—King Ithwel of Rhia, Avielle's great-great grandfather, had demanded Dredonia send one of its princesses as a captive to ensure the peace. They had sent Princess Dolvoka, who came against her will. It was said her shining silver hair spilled to her knees, her silverskin gleamed like moonlight on beech leaves. Her beauty enchanted King Ithwel, and though she did not wish it, he forced her to marry him. They had two children, and so Dredonian blood found its way into the Rhian royal family.

Although Dolvoka was queen, wife, and mother, she was still a captive, and never allowed to leave the High Hall. Many cold winter days she stood on the highest tower with her gray cloak blowing back behind her in the wind, watching the birds fly across the clouds. Sometimes she would call them to her, for calling animals was her magic gift. She pined in her captivity, in the knowledge that she was not free. At last, so the story went, in her longing to be free, in her despair and grief over her captivity, she grew twisted and evil. She became a creature of nightmare. Her eyes ran with blood. Her hair grew ratted and tangled. Her fury grew until she hated all things free, especially birds.

Finally, one terrible day, Dolvoka unleashed a magic spell that killed every bird in Rhia. Death rained from the sky as the birds fell to the earth, where they lay smashed and shattered. Dolvoka died that night, some said from despair, others said from the force of the spell; and still others said the king killed her for her crime.

And her cursed spell did not abate. From that day to this, no birds had come to Rhia. Oh, there were some each year that flew in from neighboring kingdoms, but they always either left or died. There were no chickens, no ducks, no geese, no robins, no jays, no larks—and no eggs. Sometimes birds were brought to the kingdom in cages at great expense—but only royalty were allowed to own them. Avielle's mother had a meadowlark that did not sing, kept in a gilded cage with a ruby-studded base. But the caged birds always died after six months or a year had passed. Bird feathers brought from other lands were precious—the queen and king had robes made of white feathers that they wore only for the highest court functions—coronations, marriages, christenings, and funerals.

But the most devastating loss of all, Avielle thought now, was that of the birds in their role as messengers of the Goddess. Indeed, in the images of the Goddess, a white swan soared up from her left hand; it was her Messenger, called the Quasana, promising transcendence, promising a link to the divine. Now that was lost.

Avielle leaned out into the night. All her life she had

been fighting to be free of her great-great grandmother's shadow and curse, and it suddenly struck her, like a blow to the stomach, that she would never be free of it. Never. And now she had broken the crystal bird and everyone would say that was a sign of the bad blood rising up in her, that she, too, was a killer.

A wheel of fire flared up inside her. She seized a handful of birdseed and cast it into the darkness.

GAMALDA AND THE TOY SOLDIERS
CHAPTER FOUR

Alone in her workroom late the next morning, Avielle shot the shuttle across the loom. She pressed the thread in place with the beater. She shifted foot pedals, changing which warp threads were raised, and shot the shuttle back the other way. Then the beater again. Then the foot pedal . . . and on and on until her mind grew blank and nothing existed except the belt she was weaving. Kept at bay were the thoughts of the war, the disastrous ball, the struggle with Edard, Dolvoka, the crystal bird in a thousand fragments, and the rumors its destruction had surely caused.

Earlier that morning Avielle had sought solace in the Chamber of Wings, but even the sight of the beautiful birds had not stilled the tumult of her thoughts.

A shadow crossed the loom.

Avielle started.

"I see you've nearly finished it," said a shrill, disapproving voice.

Avielle turned her head and saw Lady Kipferd, a pasty-white woman whose eyes were so goggly she needed only scales to make her look exactly like a fish. When she spoke she sounded as though she were rolling a nut around in her mouth. Most unwillingly, and only because commanded by the queen, she had taught Avielle to weave.

"I don't know what possessed you to weave a pattern of *insects*," Lady Kipferd said. "It is most unseemly. And a shocking waste of time. I am certain the queen would not approve."

Avielle looked down at the belt. On a brilliant blue background was a pattern of golden fireflies—not shiny gold, but the softer burnish of antique gold. She had only the final inch of blue border left to weave.

"I don't know who you imagine will wear such a disagreeable thing," Lady Kipferd said.

"I will," Avielle said, rubbing the wooden shuttle with her thumb. She rarely made things for herself, but this had appeared in her mind whole and complete, and she had felt compelled to make it.

"At least now you can return your attention to Princess Ismine's tablecloth." Lady Kipferd looked over her nose at the big loom.

There were two looms in the room, a large one for weaving big pieces, and a small one for weaving belts, mats, handkerchiefs, and other such items. The big loom held a half-finished ruby red tablecloth with a sanguine diamond pattern that Avielle was making for her sister's wedding gift.

Lady Kipferd did not approve of it either—too bright, the pattern too original—but it was preferable to a woven belt of insects.

Avielle wished Lady Kipferd would return to the fourth floor. There, at the far end of the north wing, was a long, sunny room full of looms, where many of the ladies and ladies-in-waiting spent their days weaving, stitching upon tapestries, making lace, or embroidering. They gossiped and chattered as they worked. Sometimes musicians played softly in the background, or poets read aloud. But three years ago, when Avielle had asked to learn to weave, her presence had cast a pall over the room. Every time she entered it all chattering ceased. After a month of enduring this, Avielle had asked for her own workroom. Her mother, trying to hide her relief, had granted this request.

Lady Kipferd examined the tablecloth, looking, Avielle knew, for a mistake.

"You will never finish this before the wedding," Lady Kipferd said at last. "It is far too ambitious for someone with your limited skills. You should never have attempted it."

Far too ambitious for you, Avielle thought. At times like this, she almost wished she had magic powers. It would give her great pleasure to turn Lady Kipferd into a fish, or better yet, a rabbit with a twitchy nose.

But she merely said, "Thank you, Lady Kipferd. I need no further assistance today." And indeed she did not. Lady Kipferd, though loath to admit it, had not only grudgingly taught Avielle everything she knew, but was now enraged to watch Avielle surpass her.

Lady Kipferd's mouth pinched. "As you wish."

Avielle noted that Lady Kipferd had not once called her "Your Highness" or "Princess."

"Would you be so kind, Lady Kipferd, as to have a maid bring me tea, toast, and cheese?" Avielle asked. "I had no breakfast this morning."

Lady Kipferd dropped a whisper of a curtsey, walked to the doorway, then turned back.

"Shall I have the maid bring you up some preserves for your toast? Perhaps in a *crystal* dish?"

Her cheeks hot, Avielle dropped the shuttle. Lady Kipferd smiled and then left.

By the time the maid brought up the tea tray, Avielle had almost finished the belt. As soon as she finished eating, she planned to visit Rajio, who would be playing in his nursery.

"Here's your tea, Your Highness," the girl said, curtseying with the silver tray in her hands. "Want it on the table here?"

"Please," Avielle said. She walked to the table as the maid was setting down the tray. On it was a teapot with a chipped spout, a tea cup patterned with roses that had tea stains inside it, a plate with a piece of yellow cheese with a fuzz of blue mold on one edge, and two pieces of nearly burned toast scraped with the thinnest bit of butter.

The girl, who had the short whirly hair of a shorn sheep,

did not look at her. "It's what they give me, Princess," she said. "It's not my fault. Not a bit of it."

Avielle nodded. It was quite clear that the kitchen servants were telling her exactly what they thought of her. She put one hand on the teapot. Cold. Of course. She wanted to throw it across the room.

"Cold is it?" the girl said. "Well, I can fix that at least." She put her broad, reddened hands—the nails bitten down to the quick—on either side of the teapot. Avielle took one breath, two, four, six. Then the girl stepped back. "There," she said, a distinct note of triumph in her voice.

Avielle touched the teapot; it was now quite hot. She glanced at the girl. Though she did not look it, the girl had a strain of Dredonian blood and had a magic gift: the ability to heat liquids.

"What is your name?" Avielle asked.

"Griot, Your Highness."

"Can you do anything besides heat liquids, Griot?"

Griot shook her head, then blurted, "And I don't never use it for nothing evil! Not like some as might!" Then she turned scarlet. "Oh, I'm sorry, Princess. I didn't mean it. Please don't say nothing on me, I might get dismissed . . ."

"Leave at once!" Avielle exclaimed.

After Griot left, Avielle stared down at the steam curling out of the teapot's chipped spout, but it blurred before her eyes.

She turned, leaving everything on the tray untouched,

and returned to the loom to finish the belt. When it was done, she stood up and ran it through her fingers; it felt soft and nubby, and was so long the ends would fall nearly to her knees after it was tied around her waist.

Sometimes she thought she had really wanted to learn to weave, not only because she loved color and pattern and texture, but because it was something she could hide behind, just as she had hidden behind the great tapestries and weavings on the walls when she was little, to escape from Edard.

"Good day to you, my lady."

Avielle glanced up and saw a large black woman standing in the doorway.

"What do you want?" Avielle asked, still upset by her encounters with Lady Kipferd and Griot.

The woman seemed startled by her rudeness. "I apologize for intruding, but I took a wrong turn somewhere, and I'm lost. This maze of halls goes on forever! I thought I should be a little mouse, finding my way crumb by crumb until I came at last to the kitchen door." She laughed, and her laugh was as warm and cheerful as a fire on a cold night. "I thought all the weavers were upstairs, so I was surprised to see looms as I was passing by. I am a weaver myself, you see. My name is Gamalda Calima."

Avielle stopped running the belt through her hands and looked at the woman more carefully. She had heard of Gamalda Calima, who was reputed to be the best weaver in Tirion and held in high esteem. She was part Dredonian, though like Griot she did not look it, and it was said she used magic in her work. Her skin was ebony, her hair gold, and the contrast—like the sun shining in the night sky—was striking. She was not fat, but big-boned, and was as straight and graceful as a column in the Temple.

"I am delighted to meet, you, Mistress Calima." Avielle at last remembered her manners. "You are very welcome here."

"Please, call me Gamalda. Are you a weaver? Did you make that belt?"

"Yes."

"Might I have a look?"

Avielle thought the request rather bold. She looked down at the belt, slid it through her hands, then looked up and nodded, though she knew she was probably setting herself up for more humiliation.

Gamalda walked into the room. Her white linen dress fell straight down from her shoulders in folds to the floor—an excellent choice for a large woman. A simple border of sun rays woven around the hem rippled as she walked. She was perhaps forty years old.

She picked up a pair of gold-rimmed spectacles that hung on a chain around her neck, put them on, wrinkled her nose to shove them upright, then took the belt from Avielle's hands.

Gamalda held it up to the sunlight streaming through the window. Her rolls of golden hair were unruly, in spite of being swept up haphazardly here and there by numerous golden combs. They looked, Avielle thought, as though they were battling for territory on her head.

"Well, this is a sight to see," she said. "And no mistake. The golden fireflies look almost gossamer. And the way the wings interweave makes them seem to be flying. I half expect one to fly out right now and dart about the room." She laughed. "The palette is perfect. And all well crafted. Let me tell you, my lady, this is fabulous!"

Avielle could not speak. A bud of light unfurled in her heart.

"May I take a peek at the big loom?" Gamalda asked.

"Yes, of course," Avielle managed to say.

Gamalda, still holding the belt, bent over the loom, wrinkled her nose again to keep her spectacles from slipping, then rubbed one edge of the cloth between her thumb and forefinger. "Yes, yes, this is fine, too! A bright color subtly enhanced by a darker hue, which in contrast makes the brighter red almost luminescent. Marvelous." She dropped her spectacles, which fell on their chain and clinked onto the buttons on her dress, then she looked at Avielle with a puzzled expression in her pale green eyes. "Who are you, my lady?" she asked.

Avielle braced herself. Now it would come. Now it would change. Approval would turn to derision.

"I am Avielle," she said, "Princess Avielle."

An expression flitted over Gamalda's face, but it was so quick that Avielle could not make it out. Gamalda curtsied deeply and gracefully in spite of her size. She could have been a statue come alive, or a great tree bowing in the wind.

"Your Highness," she said. "Forgive me. I'd heard you were a weaver, but not that your work was extraordinary. I should have guessed who you were." She was standing beside the table. She touched the white tablecloth, her eyes fixing on the dismal items on the tray. Her eyebrows drew together in a puzzled frown.

Then Avielle noticed that Gamalda's hands were always moving—across the tablecloth, across the top of the chair, across the loom, across the chain on her spectacles, as though her fingertips were another sense, like hearing or seeing.

"Why have you come to the High Hall, Mistress Calima—Gamalda?" Avielle asked.

"The queen wants three new woven panels for the conservatory. Scenes of meadows—grasses, wildflowers, and birds, of course."

Avielle looked Gamalda straight in the eye. But she saw no dagger meant to wound, no hidden meaning, no fear. Avielle wondered if Gamalda were the only person other than Rajio who had ever said the word "bird" to her without hesitation.

"Is the belt for you?" Gamalda asked. "Have you just finished it?"

Avielle nodded.

"Then may I have the honor of being the first to tie it round you?"

"Ah . . . certainly," said Avielle, though she was not at all certain she wanted this queenly stranger to come so close to her. But Gamalda's hands, which had surprisingly long fingers, were as gentle as they might be with a child. And she smelled faintly of cinnamon. Avielle felt herself relax under the woman's touch.

"There," said Gamalda when she had finished. "Isn't it a great joy that such loveliness can be created by our own hands? And be enjoyed by all who look upon it?"

Avielle did not know exactly how to respond to this. But then she found she did not need to.

"May I make a suggestion, Princess?" Gamalda's hand still held one end of the belt, and she kept rubbing it between her thumb and forefinger.

"Of course."

"I'd be honored if you'd come visit my shop—perhaps one day next week? It's not far from here—near the corner of Postern and Luxora Streets. My sign says *Wind Weaver*. I'd so much like to show you my work. And perhaps you'd honor me further by joining me for tea. A proper tea." Her fingers swept over the abysmal silver tray. "Do say you'll come, Your Highness."

But the bud of light in Avielle's heart had not opened far enough for her to trust a stranger. Even a friendly one who had kind hands and smelled of cinnamon.

"You are very kind," she said, pulling away so the belt slipped out of Gamalda's fingers. "But I prefer not to leave the High Hall." She stood with her eyes lowered.

"I understand," Gamalda said. "Then would you please tell me how to find my way out of here? So I don't wander until my hair turns gray and my teeth fall out?"

Avielle smiled and gave her directions. After Gamalda left, Avielle walked to the door and watched her turn the corner in a wave of gold, black, and white, leaving a faint scent of cinnamon in the empty hallway.

A few minutes later, Avielle, still thinking of Gamalda, walked down the east wing of the High Hall toward Rajio's rooms. She wondered how Gamalda used magic in her weaving. Did she touch the cloth to enchant it? Did she weave the cloth with magic threads? Did she use magic when she wove upon her loom? Or possibly all three?

Avielle reached the door of Rajio's nursery, which stood open, and was about to go inside, when she heard Edard's voice. She stopped.

"I have brought you a present, Rajio," Edard was saying. "A wonderful present."

Avielle pressed herself against the wall outside the door, where she could not be seen, but could still hear what transpired.

"A present!" Rajio exclaimed. "For me?"

"Of course, for you. You are my favorite little brother, aren't you? Now take your present out of the box."

Avielle heard the sound of paper rustling.

"People," Rajio said, his voice puzzled. "Hard wooden people all straight and stiff."

"They are toy soldiers," Edard said. "For playing battles and war."

"But they are not soft, like Dumpkins."

"I know you love Dumpkins, Rajio. But you are five years old now, too old for stuffed lambs and other such toys. It is time for you to start becoming a man, and to do that you must leave baby toys behind."

Avielle had never heard Edard speak so gently.

"Come!" Edard said gaily. "Let us set them up. Then you will see how much fun they are to play with."

Avielle could hear little clunks as they set each toy soldier on the floor.

"Some are painted green and some black," Rajio said to Edard. "Why?"

"The green ones are Rhians and the black ones are Dredonians. We will play that they are trying to kill each other in a great battle. The Dredonians try to kill us, so we kill them."

"I do not want to kill anyone!" Rajio exclaimed. "Or get killed. I want to play with Dumpkins."

"No, no—listen to me, Rajio. You are a prince of Rhia. We are at war—your country, Rhia—is at war with Dredonia. Really and truly, not just in a game. The evil men we call the Brethren of the Black Cloaks are trying to kill us."

"No!" Rajio cried.

"Yes!" Edard was growing impatient. "You see? You see now why you must grow up and learn how to be a prince and a man? So you can learn how to fight the evil Black Cloaks! Playing battle games with toy soldiers is one way to start."

Rajio began to cry. "Don't let them get me! Those black cloakmen. Don't let them kill me!"

"Oh, come now. You are too big to cry and be a scaredy-cat."

Rajio's sobs grew louder. Avielle ached to go in and throw her arms around him and scream at Edard for frightening him. However, she knew from past experience that that would only make everything worse.

"Do not be afraid, Rajio," Edard said at last, his voice gentle again. "I will never let the black cloakmen hurt you; I promise."

Rajio continued to cry. "Dumpkins. I want Dumpkins."

"There now," Edard said. "There. Do not cry, my little brother. You do not need Dumpkins. Here, I will hold you on my lap instead."

"Dumpkins!" Rajio screamed.

Avielle could stand it no longer. "It is all right, Rajio!" she cried, running into the room.

"Avi! Avi!" Rajio ran to her and hid his face in her skirts.

Edard stood up slowly and seemed to swell, as though he might burst through his elegant blue shirt. He pulled his golden turban down so it fit more snuggly over his ears.

"You are not wanted here," he said to Avielle. Leave." Then he turned to his brother. "Come here to me, Rajio."

"You have frightened him," Avielle said. "Leave him alone."

"Rajio!" Edard raised his voice. "I said, 'come here.' I am your older brother and your crown prince. You must obey me." Then his voice softened. "Do not cry, Rajio, please. We will have fun with the toy soldiers. I promise."

Rajio turned his head, tears on his cheeks. "Can Avi play, too?"

"No." Edard's face became a stone. "She is a silverskin. She is nothing—I have told you that many times before. Come to me at once!"

When Rajio continued to cling to Avielle, Edard came over and picked him up. "You shall not have him," he said to Avielle. "He loves me, not you." Then, carrying Rajio on his hip, Edard stalked out of the room.

Avielle stared down at the toy soldiers in their rigid rows, then kicked them over; they flew every which way across the room and clattered onto the floor. She would come back later and comfort Rajio after nightfall, when she could be certain that Edard would be feasting, entertaining his loathsome friends, or bothering some poor woman.

And she would burn the toy soldiers.

THE FIREFLIES
CHAPTER FIVE

"Begging your pardon, Princess Avielle, but I thought you might like a look at this."

Avielle turned a page and tried not to be annoyed. It was later that same night, and she had just managed to lose herself in a book—an epic poem about Padrad, a legendary king of Rhia who had overcome his fear of a giant monster and led his people into battle against it. As she shifted, the old leather chair creaked beneath her; it was just large enough to curl up in and had the advantage of being in an obscure corner of the library. Avielle had once again managed to shut out her problems. And now she was being interrupted.

"Yes?" she said, looking up. And then she saw Esilia, the librarian's daughter, who assisted her mother in her duties. Esilia sometimes brought Avielle unusual books. Indeed, she had a book in her hands now, a large one with a zigzagging crack along the brown leather spine. She also held what looked like an envelope made of parchment paper.

"I found this book in an old chest in one of the storerooms," Esilia said. "We've been clearing and sorting. You can't imagine the dust." She held out the book. "It's about weaving."

"Thank you," Avielle said, taking it.

"How did you like the last one I gave you?"

Avielle leaned forward "It set me upon a treasure hunt!" Esilia had given her a book that analyzed the work of a famous painter, Master Kalioram, long dead, whose paintings hung here and there in the rooms of the High Hall. Some of the pages had been torn out. Esilia knew Avielle was a weaver, and had surmised from this, correctly, that she would like books on art.

"I was running around the rooms trying to pick out his paintings." Avielle found herself smiling, then stopped. Treasure hunt! Esilia, who was about her own age, would think her a simpleton.

But Esilia smiled back. Her skin was tawny, her face shaped like an upside-down pear—wide at the top and tapering to a rounded curve at the chin. Though a red ribbon pulled back her hair, which was the color of almonds, tiny ringlets had escaped, and in the light from the candles made a fuzzy halo around her head. She wore a huge white apron streaked with dust over her brown dress.

"Anything else interesting in the storerooms?" Avielle asked, leafing through the book.

"Mouse droppings."

Avielle laughed.

Esilia grinned. "We've been able to salvage a few things. Some books by Mayanar on philosophy, a few by Loran on mathematics. But I also found this." She held out a large envelope made of parchment. "It was in a chest crammed with old letters from the royal family—just personal letters—nothing that would have been carefully preserved. Pretty dull stuff, frankly—no offense to your royal forbears." She bowed playfully.

Avielle smiled. "What kind of dull stuff?"

"Oh, someone named Duke Frik rambling on and on about a 'bully' new horse for the hunt. A Princess Sephrina's snippy congratulations to a 'rival' on the success of a charity ball—that sort of fluff. But then I found this." She gave the parchment folder to Avielle.

Avielle untied the string fastening the envelope and opened it. Inside was a heavy scrap of paper, yellowed with age. All the edges were charred; one large corner piece was all that had survived the fire. The only words she could make out were: cobalt; vermilion; black; *The Book of the Sorrowful Queen*; Power to—the rest had all been burned away.

"There's no *Book of the Sorrowful Queen* in the library here," Esilia said. "I checked with Mother. But I thought you . . . I mean since you've studied the royal dynasties and all, I figured maybe you'd know of a sorrowful queen."

Avielle shook her head. "I have never heard of a sorrowful queen. Sounds lonely doesn't it? Lonely and sad. 'Power to'—how intriguing. I wonder what that means?" She slid the scrap of paper back into the envelope, tied up the string, and was about to hand it to Esilia, when something—the curl of the charred edges of paper? the allusion to power? the loneliness of some age-old queen?—made her change her mind. "I will keep this for a while," she said. She slipped the envelope into the book on weaving. "Perhaps you will find something else in the chest that explains it."

Then, as Avielle fingered her belt of dragonflies, she realized that Esilia was standing with one foot hooked behind her leg. Avielle wondered if she was waiting to be dismissed.

Esilia said suddenly, "I'm leaving next Thursday."

"Leaving?"

Esilia nodded. "I'm going to the Temple to become a damada."

Esilia leaving? Avielle turned her head sharply to the left and looked down at the wooden floor. She ran her eyes across one board over and over again. There were three knots in the grain. Three knots, three knots, three knots. Esilia leaving? But she was—not a friend, exactly—rather, Avielle realized suddenly, she was the only person in the High Hall besides Rajio who did not treat her as a shadow of Dolvoka.

"I did not know that you . . . ," she said, still looking at the knots, "that you . . ." She stopped, unsure of how to express her thought. "That you honored the Goddess" was what Avielle almost said. But everyone was supposed to honor the Goddess. However, though she had once been worshipped with great reverence, she was now largely neglected. Her Temples were crumbling, few went to worship, and even fewer became damadas and damads. Avielle herself only sporadically went to worship, though the royal family was supposed to be deeply religious. Indeed, when Avielle did pray she only rarely felt a flicker of something inside her. Sometimes she thought it was comfort, sometimes longing, sometimes exhortation. Perhaps it was the Goddess. She did not know.

"You have never mentioned your wish to be a damada," Avielle said at last. Then she felt like an idiot. Esilia had told her nothing about her life beyond the library. Indeed, Avielle had never thought to ask.

"I've wanted to be a damada ever since I was a little girl," Esilia said. "Since my grandmum told me the story of the Great Hunger."

"But many blamed the Goddess for that," Avielle said, "for all the famine and death two hundred years ago. That is when people stopped going to worship. Why did hearing the story make you want to be a damada?"

"On every high holy day my grandmum brought in a beggar to share the feast with us. 'Feed the hungry and you'll feed your soul,' she always said. This might sound strange—but I don't think the Great Hunger was the Goddess' fault. I want to be a damada to help her feed the hungry. Their bodies, their spirits."

"Do you feel . . . close to the Goddess?" Avielle asked.

"You mean in a personal way?"

Avielle nodded.

"Yes and no." Esilia patted her frizzy hair down but it immediately sprang up again. "I feel her as—as a presence for goodness and love—at the heart of everything. The way I can serve her is to be a servant of that."

"I see," Avielle said, trying to imagine it.

There was a silence.

For a moment, Avielle thought of commanding Esilia to stay. After all, Avielle was a princess; she had the power to do it. She could wave one arm and proclaim magisterially, "You are to stay and bring me books at my leisure and discuss them at my whim." Like a pet dog.

"I'm so terribly sorry you are leaving." Avielle stood up, clutched the book, and dashed out of the library.

She hurried toward her room, which was a long way from the library. Why did one of the few people in the High Hall who did not dislike her have to leave? For a wild moment she thought perhaps Edard had found out she liked Esilia and had dismissed her. But he would have sent Esilia somewhere unsavory, not to a Temple.

Avielle turned a corner and let her fingers trail over a mahogany table with a curved edge that sat against the wall. Only Rajio was left to her now. But he was so young.

As Avielle passed the hall that led to her mother's chambers, she longed to confide in her; however, she knew from past experience that her mother, though she loved Avielle in her distant way, preferred to remain oblivious to her pain. Ismine? Ismine would merely laugh and call her a fool and ask whether this or that dress looked best with this or that hat. Her father? He was too busy with the wizards and ministers preparing for war. There was no one else.

Then another face appeared in Avielle's mind, an ebony face with golden hair swept up with golden combs. The weaver. Gamalda Calima, who had sun rays on her dress.

When Avielle had almost reached her room, the light grew dim. Only a few candles burned in the sconces; many had gone out, and the chairs and tables against the walls seemed to hover in the shadows. In her haste to leave the library, she had forgotten to bring a candlestick or lamp.

She was just approaching the door to Rajio's room when she heard muffled crying. What was wrong? Where was his nurse? Avielle hurried to the door, opened it, and shut it softly behind her.

The moonlight showed Rajio sitting up in bed, huddled, clutching his stuffed lamb, Dumpkins. He was sobbing. His fine dark hair hung in his eyes.

"It is all right, Rajio," she said. "I am here."

"Avi!" he cried. "I am scared!"

She wound her way around his toy boats scattered across the floor. Avielle put her book down on the bed and spread his coverlet over him.

"What are you scared of?" she asked.

"Those black cloakmen! That Edard told about. The

killing men. I can see one behind my old rocking horse. In the shadow. Don't you see him?"

Avielle looked. Behind his rocking horse hung a long drape drawn back from one side of the window. The cloth swelled out at the top, was gathered in at the middle by a cord, and then flared out again at the bottom. It did look like a figure in a long belted black robe stalking against the moonlight outlined in the window.

"It is only the curtain," she said. Yet, she felt a moment's chill when the drape swayed in the wind. Ridiculous, she told herself. She walked toward the window and reached up to touch the drape—to show Rajio there was nothing to fear. Then an image from the *Legend of King Padrad* rushed into her mind, and suddenly the drape hovered over Rajio and her like a giant monster-man.

It would not harm Rajio. *It would not.* She would not allow it. And then Avielle wanted light—a candle, a lantern, a fire, the sun! True burning golden light. A strange pressure built inside her head, then an ache behind her eyes.

And then, and then, came the light.

"Avielle!" cried Rajio. "Your belt!" Avielle looked down. The firefly pattern she had woven in her belt was shining.

"Oh," she whispered, "oh." Then, as she breathed, as her hands came up, the golden fireflies beamed onto the drape and flittered and fluttered as the drape rippled in the breeze. Their light illuminated the drape, revealing it for what it was—dark blue cloth.

"See, Rajio," she whispered, "the monster was all in your mind."

But now Rajio was on his knees, pointing and laughing. "They are flying, Avielle. Flying and flying!"

The golden fireflies danced, unabashed by darkness or demons or fear. Then, as Avielle's legs gave out and she fell onto her knees, the fireflies faded from the drape, the light faded from her belt, and the night was dark once more.

She pressed one hand against her chest, trying to calm her breathing. What had happened? What had just happened? But she knew. It was magic, it had to be magic; and it had come from her. *From her.*

Avielle stood, turned away from the drape, took off the belt, and threw it across the room.

She looked at Rajio, and when she spoke in the darkness her voice was hoarse. "You must not tell anyone about this. You must not tell anyone at all."

WIND WEAVER
CHAPTER SIX

Grig Durdin, the servant who oversaw the conveyances for the High Hall, was all agog when Avielle ordered an unmarked brougham to be brought out the next morning.

"But, Your Highness," he protested, "all the royal carriages are ready, and the footmen and drivers, too. You can go all in comfort and style. Befitting your rank." He scratched his bald head. "The people can cheer you as you go."

Avielle looked at him steadily. Was the man a fool?

"The people will not cheer me," she said, and regretted the words the instant they were out of her mouth. She should have simply ordered him to obey her.

A light seemed to dawn in Durdin's brain, and he looked sideways.

Avielle tapped her foot. "Only one footman and no royal livery for him or the coachman. Now please do as I tell you."

"Yes, Princess," he said, his voice sullen.

A half hour later Avielle was riding inside the brougham; it smelled of leather from the seats. She wore a sapphire blue hat that concealed her ears and her hair, which she had pinned up. A white veil falling in folds from the brim concealed her face, and white gloves covered her hands. She knew it was highly unlikely that anyone would recognize her, but she was taking no chances.

And no one, if she could help it, would ever know that she had Dredonian magical power—if, indeed, she did. Avielle was not certain about what had happened last night with the fireflies; she hoped there was another explanation, hoped Gamalda had something to do with it. She was on her way to find out.

"But if I do have magic powers," she whispered. "If I do . . ." Avielle had always clung to the idea that she was different from Dolvoka because she did not have any magic power—and thus could never do any great evil. It had brought her comfort. But now that comfort was threatened.

Avielle had burned the belt. But what if Rajio told someone? What if that person told everyone else? How then would she bear the hostile stares, the sneers, the whispers? It did not seem possible that people could revile her even more, shun her more, mistrust her more.

As the horses clip-clopped on the cobblestones, Avielle looked out the open window and saw soldiers in green and white uniforms riding past. She saw a lady in a yellow dress bedecked with ribbons and flounces—her maid, laden with packages, trailing behind. She saw delivery wagons, one heaped with coal, one with casks of wine, another with pigs—she covered her nose at their stink. The brougham slowed at a crossing, and Avielle saw the sign for a jeweler's shop. When she saw the gleam of a diamond in the window, she cringed, thinking of her interview with her mother—and for a few minutes her father—that morning.

"What in the world possessed you to smash Prince Graedig's gift?" her mother had asked. She was sitting on a green velvet chair in the morning room. Avielle's father, his back to the room, was leaning against the fireplace, its hearth cold and empty. "I realize the gift was a subtle insult," her mother added, "but I thought you would have had more forbearance. Why did you resort to a tantrum?"

Avielle stared at the diamond pendant hanging from a filigreed gold chain around her mother's neck. What should she tell her? Not the truth. Avielle had learned long ago that Edard would inflict more torment upon her if she exposed his cruelties.

"I dropped it," she said. Which was not entirely untrue.

"It was in a box, Avielle, for goodness' sake. If you had dropped it, it might have broken in half. But it was shattered."

"I . . . I had taken it out of the box." Also not entirely untrue.

"In the hall? Why? Oh, never mind. This is fruitless." She waved her hand, heavy with rings—all emeralds. "I would probably have smashed the wretched thing myself." Her mother sighed. "Do you realize the trouble this has caused with the Imsethian delegation? This marriage would have secured our relationship with Imsethia, who we desperately need as an ally now that Dredonia is threatening the kingdom. I know it was not an ideal match for you, but . . ."

"Not an ideal match?" Avielle interrupted. "You know he only wanted my dowry."

Her mother sipped a glass of water with rose petals drowned in the bottom, then set it down with a slight clink on the table. "Have you ever considered what will happen to you after your father and I die?" she asked.

"You mean when Edard is king?"

Her father turned from the fireplace and looked directly at Avielle. "You will be completely in his power."

Avielle felt a sharp pressure under her ribs, sharp and cold. She had thought of that many times.

"My daughter." Her mother touched her arm. "We see more than you think."

Then why haven't you stopped it? Avielle wanted to scream. Why haven't you done something? Why couldn't you have protected me more, loved me more?

There was a long silence. Avielle looked at her father. Something softened in his gray eyes.

"We must send you away, Avielle," he said, "whether you like it or not. To some man, a husband. There is nothing else to be done."

"But what if the place you send me to, or the man you send me to, is worse than Edard?" Avielle asked.

Her father started to speak, then stopped and turned to her mother. "Take care of this, Merrieta. I must see the Minister of Finance." And he left the room.

Avielle's mother was brisk and busy again. "We have to face facts, Avielle. You must marry in order to get away from Edard, yet you may be unmarriageable. You understand why, of course?"

Of course. Avielle closed her eyes. Everything always came back to that. She was unmarriageable because of the shadow of Dolvoka. Avielle wondered what her mother would say if she knew about the fireflies. What would happen if Rajio told? She had frightened him into keeping the secret by telling him that if he did not, she might have to leave him forever. He had thrown his arms around her neck. "I swear," he had cried, "I swear on the heart of Dumpkins that I will not tell."

"Avielle!" her mother said. You are not attending!"

"I'm sorry, Mother. You were saying?"

"I was saying that you may have to take whomever you can get. I will try to arrange something else."

"I will not marry a man I do not love. One who only wants me for my money."

"Nonsense! You have known since you were five years old that princesses do not marry for love but for expediency." She hesitated. "And I do not mean to be unkind, but I have watched you since you were born. You are reclusive, secretive, and guarded. You take no interest in others. I must say, Avielle, that I doubt you are capable of a deep and abiding love."

With a creaking of springs, the brougham stopped. Avielle found that her head was in her hands and there were tears upon her cheeks. *Incapable of love.* Was it any wonder she was reclusive, secretive, and guarded? Would her mother not be like that also if she had spent her life under Dolvoka's shadow?

Avielle heard the footman at the door and straightened, her back rigid. The door opened, and the footman lowered the steps.

"We've arrived at *Wind Weaver*, Your Highness," he said, then helped her down onto the street, his face properly impassive.

"Please wait for me here," she said.

He bowed.

She glanced up at the wooden sign suspended above the door. *Wind Weaver* was written in simple letters without furbelows, white letters on a blue background. Two swathes of cloth cascaded behind the big front window—one a plaid of green and red, the other a blue silk with a pattern of twining roses. Avielle took a deep breath and opened the door.

She stepped into a world of color. The colors of flowers, forests, and pearls; of rain; of light on water, shimmering and shifting; of snow; of jewels in sunlight; of autumn, winter, spring, and summer. The colors came from hangings on the walls, and from bolts of cloth wound on rolls—stacked horizontally in racks one on top of the other. Each bolt had its cloth pulled down a foot or so to show its beauty.

Looking from left to right, Avielle took a step forward, and then another, quiet steps as though she were walking in an enchanted room that might vanish if she disturbed it. Through a door to the left, she glimpsed looms.

Near the counter at the back of the shop stood a woman in an effervescence of lavender skirts leaning on a furled parasol as though she were a house propped up by a stick. On the other side of the counter, Gamalda was wrapping up a large package with a blue ribbon.

"The ribbon's a waste," said the woman. "Why don't you use string?"

"Oh, but ribbon is such a joy to the eye and hand, don't you think?" Gamalda said. "And you can make so many things with it. A bookmark, a hair ribbon, a string for a kitten to play with."

The woman just sniffed.

Gamalda looked at Avielle, not recognizing her through the veil, of course. "Welcome to *Wind Weaver,* my lady. I'll be with you in a moment."

Avielle nodded.

Gamalda tied a blue bow in the middle of the package and gave it to the woman.

"Send the bill to number seventy-two Orris Street," the lady said. Then, parasol in hand, she sailed out of the shop on a cloud of lavender scent—with the faintest suggestion of putrefaction.

Gamalda, wearing a blue dress, walked around the counter and up to Avielle. Today Gamalda's hair tumbled down her left shoulder like a river of gold, tied with a black velvet ribbon that set off her ebony skin. She opened her arms wide. "Good day to you, my lady. How may I help you?"

Avielle, not knowing how to ask the urgent question she had come to ask, held up a soft, white shawl hanging on a rack; it was made of nubby silk with swirling silver, almost feathery threads running through it. It was exquisite. She stood dumbly.

"If I may, my lady?" Gamalda took the shawl and draped it over Avielle's shoulders.

Avielle smelled the scent of cinnamon.

"Of course," Gamalda said, "I can't see if it really suits you because you're veiled."

"I have heard," Avielle said at last, "I have heard that you use magic in your weaving."

Gamalda hesitated, her fingers playing with the chain around her neck that held her spectacles. "I do."

"Everything here is . . . " Avielle groped for the right word, "is stunning. But I see no evidence of magic."

"The magic is in the quality of my work. My woolens never shrink. My linens never yellow or wrinkle. My patterns are always true. And when I am working on my looms, my threads never tangle—and let me tell you, my lady, only a weaver can appreciate what a gift that is."

"I see." Avielle could not keep the disappointment out of her voice.

Gamalda smiled. She drew a length of silver thread from her pocket and ran it over and over through her fingers. "What were you expecting?" she asked.

Avielle looked at her through the veil. What had she been expecting? For the cloth to speak? Roll off the bolts, streak out the door, scoop up passersby, then become magic carpets and fly away with them?

As Avielle looked around the shop again, her flippancy faded. The beauty of the place crept inside her, and suddenly she allowed herself to wonder. If weaving were a magical gift, what would it look like?

Half in a dream she pointed to a roll of cloth. "There, on that one I expected the pattern of rosebuds to bloom." She turned. "And on that one for the leaves to change from green to gold to red. And up there on the wall the mountains should be pink in the sunrise and white beneath the moonlight. I want to see weavings with patterns of sorrow and joy, or courage, mercy, and goodness." She stopped, feeling heat come into her face. Where had those words come from?

Gamalda took a step toward her and held out her hands. "Oh, yes. Yes. In the name of the Goddess, who are you?"

With some reluctance, Avielle lifted her veil and drew it back behind her head.

"Princess!" Gamalda stared, then bent one knee in a deep curtsey. "Your Highness."

When Gamalda rose, she said, "The shawl suits you well—the silver threads and white silk with your silverskin. I can see it trailing out in the wind behind you, catching the light. How lovely it looks! Please accept it as my gift to you. Let me tell you how honored I am that you've come to visit my shop." She pressed her hands together, the sliver thread she had been running through her fingers still in her hand. "Would you care for tea?"

Avielle stared at her. Tea? How could she talk about tea at a time like this? When so much was at stake?

"There is something, something important, I need to know," Avielle said. "Yesterday, when you held the belt I made, did you do anything to it?"

"Do anything to it?"

"Yes," Avielle said, leaning forward. "You put some kind of spell on it, and I want to know why."

"Why would I . . . ?" Gamalda looked puzzled. "I cast no spell on your belt."

"Please. Think hard. Maybe you did not realize. You held it so long. Maybe simply by touching it you . . ." Tears came into her eyes.

"Your Highness—if I may ask—what has happened?"

Avielle fiddled with the shawl's knot, not knowing whether she could trust this woman with her secret. But who else was there? Avielle looked at Gamalda's face:

patient, concerned, warm. Anyone who could make such beautiful things, who could curtsey so, who could look so, must have something bright and shining in her very heart.

Avielle told.

Gamalda listened.

There was silence.

"Tell me you did it," Avielle pleaded. "Tell me you did."

"You're afraid," Gamalda said, drawing the silver thread through her fingers. "And I think I know why. But I tell you, you can't deny this without denying yourself. Princess, you have a magical gift."

Avielle felt darkness closing around her.

"No," she cried. And she ran out of the shop.

THE PORTRAIT
CHAPTER SEVEN

Avielle rushed into the street and wrenched open the door of the brougham before the startled footman could help her. A moment later they were clattering down the cobblestones. Avielle wrapped her arms around herself and hunched forward. It was only then she realized she was still wearing the white and silver shawl Gamalda had given her. *You can't deny this without denying yourself. Princess, you have a magical gift.*

In the next block she heard a troubadour singing on the street corner. He sang the *Lament of the Lady Lamontelle,* which Avielle had heard many times before. It was a ballad about a woman who had risked her life for love.

You are not capable of a deep and abiding love.

Avielle clapped her hands over her ears. After three more blocks, they came to the edge of a square where people had gathered to watch dancers perform. But these were not just any dancers; they wore bird costumes and moved about, strutting, hopping, jumping, imitating different kinds of birds in elaborate dances. A heron dancer stood with one knee high, the gray felt feathers on her costume bunched around her neck. Strutting and scuttling, a pigeon dancer circled the others.

Birds, or rather reminders of them, were everywhere; Avielle could not escape them, could not escape the immense loss and longing, the immense heartache at the soul and heart of Rhia.

You have a magical gift.

Avielle swore to herself she would never use it, never risk the chance that Dolvoka's evil might rise in her. She would bury her power so deep that it would be lost forever in the forgotten realms in her mind.

The High Hall at last came in sight.

Avielle had almost reached Rajio's room. She had to warn him again not to tell anyone about the fireflies. As Avielle walked, she had the sensation of something whirling after her, something hunting her through the halls, with their arching stone ribs and frescoes. She opened the door to Rajio's room and saw—Edard.

He and Rajio were on the floor playing with Rajio's blocks—colored red, yellow, and blue—which they had built up into an elaborate castle. Neither of them saw her come in. Avielle could see Edard's profile, and, to her amazement, he looked happy, truly happy. Then Rajio looked up and saw her.

"Avi! Avi!" he cried. "My silver Avi!" He stood up, ran across the room, and hugged her.

Edard's face grew hard. He left a blue block perched precariously on one of the castle towers and said, "Come back, Rajio. We have not finished the castle."

"Now Avi is here, she can help us."

"She will not help." Edard looked up at Avielle. "Leave."

"No! No!" Rajio cried. "Let her stay. She can make fireflies dance on the curtain! Show him, Avi!"

Avielle froze.

Edard looked at her. "What does he mean?"

"Nothing," Avielle said with a little laugh and wave of her hand. "Nothing, just a game we played. Hush now, Rajio."

"Oh!" cried Rajio. "I wasn't to tell about Avi's magic! I forgot! Do not take Avi away, Edard."

"Magic?" Edard stood up slowly, staring at Avielle. She took a sudden, heavy step back, and the impact must have vibrated through the floor since the precariously placed blue block in the tower teetered, then tipped; and the whole castle came crashing down.

Rajio cried out, but Edard took no notice. A little smile formed on his lips, then grew larger and larger. He tugged on his golden turban, pulling it more snuggly over his ears.

"So," he said. "My dear little sister has a magic gift, has she? How fabulous. Tell me all about it, Rajio, and I promise I will not take Avi away."

"No." Rajio folded his arms over his chest. "I will not

tell one thing more." And tears started falling down his face.

"Come with me," Edard said to Avielle.

"But he is upset . . ." Her voice shook.

Edard grabbed her wrist and pulled her out of the room.

"So you are becoming more like the Cursed One every day. All this makes the little surprise I have prepared for you even more delightful. Now come with me."

"Leave me alone," Avielle said, wrenching free of his grasp.

"Now why should I do that? When have I ever done that? You are one of the great amusements of my life. Why would I ever leave you alone? Besides, if you do not want me to spill your little secret about your magic power, I suggest you do as I say."

Edard turned and began walking away.

Avielle followed him; she had no choice. She felt her shoulders shrink under the silver and white shawl Gamalda had given her. What would she do now? If she kept her magic a secret, Edard would use his knowledge of it as a way to gain power over her. That would be dangerous. The only way to gain relief from that was to tell everyone about her magic, and that would be dangerous, too.

Avielle felt a great pressure building inside her, filling her with fear and rage until she felt as though she might explode.

She walked after Edard down the hall, down another hall, and up the staircase in the north wing. They reached the second floor, the third floor, then the fourth floor. After that the staircase narrowed as it led up to the floor with the servants' rooms. They passed a startled maid coming down with a stack of linen in her arms. Beyond that was an even smaller staircase with room for only one person at a time. At the top was one of the many doors in the High Hall that led to the attic. Edard opened it.

Inside, rows of tiny dormer windows let in squeaks of light. Avielle smelled dust, cedar from the roof, and old couches and chairs where mice now reigned instead of kings and queens of old.

"This way," said Edard. She followed him past chest after chest; past a pile of broken toys; past a basket of black candles, many broken; past stacks of paintings leaning one against the other, their gilt frames gray with dust; past old books in sagging bookshelves; past a panel of a stained glass window showing a hand holding a silver bowl; past a pile of rocks with torn gold stars stuck among them; and past a trunk full of skeins of yarn—moth-eaten. Pinned on one sloping wall was a chart showing the constellations that revolved around Alamaria, the earth itself.

Edard stopped before one of the dormer windows. An easel stood beside it with a painting turned backwards.

"Here we are." He looked at her with a malicious smile. "I found this yesterday, when I was rooting around in an old stack of paintings up here. I cannot tell you what a singular pleasure it is for me to share this moment with you, indeed, perhaps the greatest moment of your life." He picked up the painting, flipped it around, and set it back on the easel.

Avielle stared in shock. It was a painting of her, but the artist had not got it quite right, probably because she had not sat for it. She looked five or six years older, and her blue eyes were a trifle too dark. She was not wearing the thin circlet of silver that she wore for high occasions, but a silver crown etched with wings on each side, and a ruby in the middle. She bit her lip. The wings were doubtless a little jab from Edard. But why had he gone to such trouble to have a portrait painted of her? And why had he hidden it away in the attic? She looked at him, perplexed.

"I see that you do not understand," Edard said. "Allow me to enlighten you, dearest sister. Direct your attention to the tiny bronze plaque on the bottom of the frame."

Avielle bent down and read the engraved words on the plaque: Queen Dolvoka Coroll of Rhia. Her eyes blurred. The darkness that had been hunting her encircled her like a shroud. She could not breathe.

"It doesn't prove anything," she whispered. "You could have had the portrait painted and the plaque made."

Edard drummed his fingers against his cheek. "I seem to remember a few months ago you were scampering around like a fool studying the paintings of Master Kalioram. If you look closely, I am sure a diligent student such as you will recognize his style."

Avielle saw the quick short brushstrokes, the thick

application of paint, the use of light that illuminated the face and left the background dark. And the colors of the gown—luminescent jewel colors. The crown gleamed silver. And his trademark, the left hand closed as though cupping a secret. It was indeed the work of Master Kalioram. And, she recalled, he had lived during the same years Dolvoka had.

Avielle could not speak.

Edard laughed, delighted. "It would appear that you *are* the Cursed One reborn. Everyone knows that all portraits of Dolvoka were destroyed. This one must have been missed. I assume you know what will happen to you if anyone sees this? I think this would be too much even for our dear parents."

Avielle lunged toward the painting. Edard flung himself in her way and clasped his hands around her throat.

"Oh no you don't! From now on, if you want me to keep your secret, you will do whatever I tell you. And the first and most important thing is that you will stop seeing Rajio. And you will come and go as *I* please. You will eat or starve at my whim. And when I am king, I will banish you to the most remote tower in the kingdom, where you will spend your life in captivity. *You will never see Rajio again.*" His hands tightened. "If you do not please me, I will show the world this painting, and the people will stone you in the street."

He forced her head around to look at the portrait. "Look well, Cursed One. Dredonian filth. This is who you are."

"No!" Avielle screamed. "Let me go!"

"Beg me."

"No!" She stretched her arms over her head and clawed at his turban.

"Stop it!" He grabbed her arms. "Do as I say or I will take the painting to the women in the weaving room this instant. Now beg me."

"Please let me go. I . . . I beg you."

He shoved her away.

She fell.

"Get out of my sight, filth."

She got to her hands and knees. She stood. She fled.

THE BLACK CROWN
CHAPTER EIGHT

Avielle ran down the attic stairs, down the servants' stairs, down and down and down until it seemed as though the stairs were part of a nightmare that would never end. The face in the painting chased her. Avielle sobbed. She would see that face until the day she died, see it every time she looked in the mirror, every time she closed her eyes to sleep.

When she reached the first floor, she ran past startled maids and footmen, past portraits of her ancestors who seemed to pull away in abhorrence, past arched windows framing the dusk, past corridors and draughts of wind and mice scurrying in walls.

At the end of the north wing she finally stopped and seized a candle burning in a sconce on the wall. Avielle glanced over her shoulder to check that the hall was empty. Then she opened a door into a small room with a chipped stone lion sitting on the counter. At the end of the room, behind a nook in the wall, a narrow stairway led downward, one that even the servants rarely used because it was far from the service rooms under the south wing.

Her steps stealthy now, Avielle crept down the stairs to the door that led to the first level beneath the High Hall; it contained the kitchen, sculleries, laundry, servants' hall, housekeepers' and butlers' rooms, and all the other myriad rooms necessary for serving those who lived above. But there was also a second door. Avielle opened it. Here was another staircase—hung with cobwebs and thick with dust—which she followed down to the deeper warrens: the maze of wine cellars and storage rooms that ran beneath the entire length and breadth of the High Hall. The servants accessed this place by larger stairways elsewhere.

Avielle wound through the maze, her candle shedding only a smudge of light on the chests stacked in the darkness. One was marked "CORONATION DRESSES," another "SILVER NEEDING REPLATING." There was an old cradle with a pillow whose lace edging had long turned yellow. Past this was a golden harp, its strings still intact. Avielle was always tempted to pluck it, but she never did for fear of someone hearing.

At last she reached a chest marked "COSTUMES FROM THE TALE OF THE LONELY DUCK." That tale was one of the many nursery stories about birds, such as "The Swan's Tale," "The Finicky Finch," and "The Tale of the Seven Troublesome Geese." These were tales that Avielle's nurses and governesses had pointedly avoided telling her.

Behind the chest, in the floor, was a trapdoor. Avielle

grasped the iron ring and pulled open the door, hearing a creak as the ladder attached to the door unfolded. With the candle in one hand, she climbed down the ladder. At the bottom was a narrow hall with three doors; two, she knew from past explorations, led to empty rooms. She opened the third door and at last stepped into the Chamber of Wings. She shut the door, leaned back against it, and felt her breath rushing in and out. *Curse you, Edard,* she thought. *May all the days of your life be cursed.*

She walked to the swan, held up her candle, and let her gaze trace each feather, each curve of the sinuous white neck. Here she was safe.

"Fresar," she said to the swan. She went to the heron. "Rastart." Then to the eagle. "Melilee. I will never hurt you, any of you." And on around the chamber she walked, urgently speaking names, looking at her friends. But comfort eluded her.

"Save me!" Avielle cried to them, stopping beside the chest on the floor. "Take me away to some far place where I can live in peace. Where nobody knows who I am. Away from Edard. Where I can do my weaving during long quiet days of sunshine or rain. Where I can forget who I am. Where Rajio can come with me. That's all I want."

There was no answer. There was never any answer.

She began to kick the locked chest over and over, dashing it with her toe and her heel, with her left foot and then her right. The stout oak did not give, though the brittle leather straps cracked and broke. Avielle gave one particularly fierce jab at the lock, and it fell to the floor with a clank.

She stared, breathing fast, eyes blinking. Then she knelt beside the chest and opened the lid. It was stuck. She tried again, putting all her muscle into it, and slowly the lid raised, the hinges screaming.

For a moment, for the merest second, a breeze seemed to shoot out of the chest, wind around her, whisk behind the tapestry of Fresar, and escape into the room. But it was so sudden Avielle thought she might have imagined it. The smell hit her next: mint, roses, sun shining on grass. There was another scent, too, rather musty, that she had smelled before but could not name.

Inside, folded carefully, was a length of red velvet with golden fringe; she ran one finger over it and found it as soft as goose down. She lifted it up and placed it on the floor. Beneath it lay a carnival mask with a contorted face that was a cross between a dragon and a lion. In contrast to this grotesquerie, the coloring was fair: pale white with a brush of pink on the cheeks, like the face of a fair Rhian maiden.

Avielle put the mask down on the red velvet and reached into the chest again. Lying in the center of a square of black satin was an oval ruby half the size of her palm. She picked it up; it sparkled blood red in the candlelight. It was worth a fortune. What was it doing buried away down here? Avielle laid it beside the mask on the red velvet. She lifted out the square of black satin. Below it, a pile of bird feathers filled the chest—which would account for the musty smell.

Avielle had seen very few bird feathers: only those on the cloaks her parents wore for high occasions, those on pictures made of feathers, and those on her mother's caged meadowlark. There were many kinds of feathers in the chest from many kinds of birds—she recognized them from illustrations she had seen in books. There were sparrow feathers and eagle feathers; loon, robin, lark, and osprey feathers; and others she did not recognize. She plunged her hands into them, feeling their odd combination of softness and stiffness.

As she worked her hands deeper into the feathers she felt something hard, grasped it and pulled it up, the bird feathers falling away.

It was a black crown. Avielle held it directly in the light of the candle. No, it was not black, only tarnished. She lifted her skirt and, trying not to think of what Salulla would say, used her petticoat to rub the surface. It was . . . silver. She turned it and saw the etching of wings on the side. And then, as though in a dream, Avielle picked up the ruby and found it fitted perfectly into the slot in the center of the crown.

The painting in the attic flashed in Avielle's mind. The crown in the portrait, the crown that sat above a face very like her own, was the same as the one she held in her hands. It was the crown of the Cursed One.

Slowly Avielle stood up, still holding the crown, as though horror had glued it to her hands. She looked wildly around the room and suddenly everything snapped together in her mind: the weavings of the birds, the peculiar objects on the table, the hidden chamber, the feathers, the crown. This was where Dolvoka had practiced her evil magic. This was where she had devised the terrible spell that had killed all the birds in Rhia.

Avielle flung the crown away and rushed out of the chamber.

Outside, the sky had turned dark, though a full moon lit the way well enough as Avielle, her thoughts blank, walked down the street away from the High Hall. Above her, hanging on poles, the street lamps had been lit and they provided some light, too. Light also poured out of the shop windows; most of the shops were still open. But Avielle did not see the light. She did not run. She did not hurry. She placed each foot carefully, one after the other, as though with each step she were pressing something down.

After Avielle had rushed from the Chamber of Wings and made her way through the maze and back onto the main floor, she had simply opened the first door that led outside and stepped into the night. And now here she was. Unveiled. Alone in the city, alone in the dark. She clutched the knot of the silver and white shawl that Gamalda had tied around her.

There were still people in the streets, though not nearly so many as earlier in the day, when she had ridden through the city in the brougham. It seemed to her as though the world and the people drew away from her, as though she somehow offended them, as though they knew that she had found comfort and refuge at the very heart of Dolvoka's evil.

As she walked, Avielle found that placing her feet required all her concentration. There was nothing in the world more important. Except . . .

Sun rays woven on a white linen dress.

Avielle took one step, then another. She pressed her foot down, rolling through it from heel to toe. When she crossed a street, she saw neither carriages nor horses nor cobbles, only . . .

A river of golden hair.

She took another step, pressed it down firmly. A small rock in her shoe lodged near the arch of her left foot, causing sharp little bursts of pain. She turned a corner and thought of . . .

The smell of cinnamon.

With each slow step, Avielle pressed her feet down harder and harder. She began to pant with the effort. At last she grasped a shop door, opened it, and went inside.

Color surrounded her, shining in the light of many candles. Gamalda turned, her blue skirt whirling.

"Princess Avielle," she said, startled. "What brings you here so late?"

Avielle could not speak.

"Your Highness—my dear—I can see that something is terribly wrong. What is it? What has happened?"

Avielle cried out.

A howl of wind shook the building. All of the candles wavered. Then she heard a deafening boom.

THE WHIRLWIND
CHAPTER NINE

The earth shook and knocked Avielle to the ground; Gamalda fell to her knees beside her. Another boom thundered through the air. The floor careened back and forth. Avielle clutched at the carpet. The wind punched like a fist through the window; shattered glass rang against the floor. A mouse skittered by. The world seemed to be ending.

"Here!" Gamalda shouted. "Come over to the cutting table! It will shelter us!"

Avielle could barely hear her over the wailing wind. Inch by inch—the ground was still shaking as boom after boom wracked the earth—Avielle crawled over to the big oak table Gamalda used to lay out and cut cloth.

"No! Not under it! Beside it." Gamalda pulled Avielle beside her.

The wind shrieked like a monster. Above them, wood creaked and groaned. One of the oak beams on the ceiling crashed down and crushed one end of the table. In the void, the beam made a space between the table and the floor where Avielle and Gamalda lay unhurt. Something struck Avielle's eye.

At last the booms stopped. The shaking stopped.

"Fire!" Gamalda cried. One of the candles that had fallen to the floor had not been extinguished by the wind. Flames curled up a roll of cloth that had also fallen to the floor. Gamalda worked her way out from the pocket beneath the timber. Avielle followed. Holding her skirts high, Gamalda stamped on the blaze. "Grab that length of cloth," she shouted, "and beat it against the flames."

Minutes later, the fire was out.

Smoke and dust filled the room. Bolts and rolls of cloth lay on the floor, crisscrossed one over the other, a few torn by the flying glass. The door had been blown off its hinges and lay flat.

"What was that?" Avielle cried. "What happened?"

"I don't know," Gamalda said, stepping gingerly over the broken glass. "A whirlwind, I think. But those booms! That doesn't explain those terrible booms that made the earth shake. Oh! Your eye—there's a big purple lump under it. Let me see, let me see. Good. No blood. Does it pain you?"

"Some," Avielle said. "But there are scratches on your hand. They are bleeding."

"It is slight." Gamalda pulled out a handkerchief and wrapped it around her hand. "Now come quickly, quickly! I must check on my neighbors."

Outside, visible in the dimmed moonlight, little cyclones of wind scurrying down the street whipped up grit and dust, filling Avielle's mouth, ears, and eyes. The air was so thick that she could see only ghostly figures milling about as people left the shops and crowded into Postern Street. Voices called, screamed, and shouted.

"Help! Help!" a girl in a pea-colored dress cried; her petticoat flashed white above her black boots as she ran down the street.

"What's happening, Penatta?" Gamalda called, but the girl did not hear her.

A smaller girl in a fur hat shaped like a barrel shot past, shouting, "Auggie! Auggie!"

"Tinty!" Gamalda cried. This girl, however, did not stop either.

Two soldiers raced by carrying a bleeding boy in their crossed arms. "Can you tell us what's happened?" Gamalda asked them. But they, too, hurried on.

A horse with no rider plunged down the street.

"Gamalda! Look out!" Avielle cried, pulling her back against a building.

A boy emerged from the cloud of dust in front of them. His skin, his hair, even his eyebrows were covered with dust. He looked like a terrified ghost. His green cap tipped to the right. On the left side of his head, blond hair stuck out like the tufts of straw on an old broom. A bloody scrape crossed his neck.

"Are you all right, Mistress Calima?" he asked Gamalda, panting.

"Just a few bumps and bruises. But Darien, what's happened? Do you know? Tell us! Tell us!"

"I can hardly bear to, Mistress," Darien said. "I can hardly bear to." Tears ran down his face, making rivers in the dust. "A whirlwind hit the High Hall! It ripped up all the stones and tossed them about like toy blocks. And there were explosions, too. Huge explosions!"

Avielle gasped and stood frozen. Her family!

A man ran by screaming, "Where is the baby? The baby?"

"But this is terrible!" Gamalda cried. "Are you sure?"

"I saw it all," Darien said. "The Dredonians must of done it. They must of. Those foul Brethren of the Black Cloaks."

"Why do you say that?" Gamalda asked. "Maybe this whirlwind—maybe it just happened to strike the High Hall."

A carriage dashed down the street, harnesses jingling, the driver lashing the horses.

Darien glared at Avielle as he shook his head. "The whirlwind was black as old Mr. Nickel's filly, and had strange lights in it. All green-colored—and purple ones, too. Not only that, but demon faces were spitting out of the funnels. Faces horrid as in a nightmare I never want to have. It was the Brethren all right. I'd swear on it."

"We will unleash death and destruction upon you," Avielle whispered, remembering the warning in the Brethren's letter.

"I don't have another second to spare," said Darien. "I have to get to Master Keenum and see if he's safe."

"And I have to find my family at the High Hall!" Avielle cried, poised to run. But Gamalda grabbed her arm.

"You'll find none left alive there," Darien said as he was turning away. "I'd stake my name on it. Everyone's been crushed or trapped beneath tons of stone."

"No!" Avielle shouted. And she began to run. Gamalda followed her.

They had to be alive—Rajio, Ismine, Cerine, Mildon, her mother, and father. They could not be dead. She did not believe it. It could not be true! She remembered her last cool words with her mother over the betrothal. Surely those could not be the last words they would ever speak together. She thought of the red hat she had promised to trim for Ismine. She had not finished it yet and she had promised. And surely she would hold Rajio in her arms again. *Surely* . . . she sobbed. She could not breathe.

As they got closer to the High Hall, the damage grew worse. The whirlwind had ripped off entire roofs and walls of houses and shops. Overturned wagons and carriages lay twisted in the street. In front of one house, a bed had been blown through the wall; the lacy pillows lay perfectly in place. Shards of wood and glass had struck people and horses who lay dead or dying in the streets.

But Avielle refused to hear their cries. She did not pause to help. She thought only of her family. Oh, Goddess, she prayed, let them be safe. Oh, please let them be safe! Her heart squeezed beneath her ribs.

The smell of smoke filled the air. Soon Avielle, with Gamalda still behind her, reached the massive boulders that formed the outer rim of the debris; there, they jostled their way through crowds of people. The smoke grew thicker and thicker, since the High Hall had been made not only of stone but of wood, too, and the wood was burning. Yet the fires were green, not red. Avielle staggered on, desperate, holding her arms out in front of her.

"Rajio!" she screamed, "Mother! Father! Ismine!" But so many other people were screaming so many other names that her screams could not be heard.

Gamalda put both hands on Avielle's shoulders and shouted in her ear. "We must go back! The evil fires are part of the magic spell; they will kill us if they can. And the smoke and dust are too thick. We can't find anyone in this."

"But my brothers and sisters!" Avielle cried. "My mother and father!"

"We can't fight this evil now," Gamalda said. "Come away! Princess—Avielle—your family would want you to be safe."

A green whirlwind surged toward them, filled with leering, twisted faces of death that shrieked and hissed. A whip of flame flicked out. It wrapped around a man's leg and dragged him screaming into the whirlwind. Avielle fell to her knees, flinging up her hands as she inched backwards.

Then a whip of flame lashed toward her.

Gamalda yanked her up. "Run! As fast as you can, Princess! Run!"

Later that night Avielle lay awake in a small room behind the kitchen in Gamalda's shop. The room was intact, as was part of Gamalda's room on the second floor. The shop also had a third floor that Gamalda had not invited Avielle to see. Except for broken windows, it, too, had somehow survived the whirlwind.

Avielle thought of the attic in the High Hall with the painting of Dolvoka, destroyed now. She thought of Edard, dead now. She had no grief for him, nor felt any guilt that she had none. Indeed, she would have him alive, and have the painting shown to everyone in the kingdom, too, if only she could have her Rajio with her.

"Rajio," she whispered. Where did he lie this night? Were stones tumbled upon him? Was he hurt? Cold? Frightened? Dead? And what about the rest of her family? Her throat burned as though she had swallowed hot sand.

A cat jumped on the bed, crawled onto Avielle's chest, and began to purr. She put one hand on the cat's soft fur. Slowly, she fell into a restless sleep.

"No," Avielle said the next morning, staring down at the corn muffin on the plate Gamalda had set before her. "Not yet."

"But why not?" Gamalda asked, sitting on the other side of the kitchen table and pinning up a strand of runaway golden hair into one of her numerous combs. "You're quite possibly the only member of the royal family left alive. You've got to come forward and let it be known you're alive."

"No. It is best I hide who I am for now. Others in my family may yet be found in the rubble. Or in the Healing Houses where Darien said the wounded have been taken." Avielle did not mention the real reason why she did not wish to reveal herself. Fear.

Darien had come in a few minutes earlier to give them news of the Healing Houses, and, incidentally, to eat the three corn muffins Gamalda had urged upon him. He had looked at Avielle almost sullenly, she thought, opened his mouth once or twice, pulled on a tuft of his hair, then gone away without asking the question that was obviously on the tip of his tongue.

"We'll check the Healing Houses as soon as you've eaten that muffin," Gamalda said. "But if you're going to hide who you are, we've got to figure out some reason why you're here." She rubbed her fingers against the rim of her plate, against her teacup, then against the chain holding her spectacles. "Darien's not the only one who's going to be curious, let me tell you. And he knows you come from the High Hall—remember he heard you say last night that you wanted to find your family there? Besides, your manner of speech and bearing gives away your high birth instantly. I've got some ideas—"

"Excuse me," Avielle interrupted, "but can't we please discuss this later? I cannot wait any longer. I must go to the Healing Houses."

"Of course. For now we'll just hope for the best—that there's so much turmoil from the whirlwind that none of my neighbors will ask about you. They're good-hearted, but nosey. We'll leave as soon as you eat that muffin. You've got to keep up your strength."

When they left the shop a few minutes later, Avielle saw that the heavy cloud from the explosion had settled, but grit and smoke still made a haze in the air. She could taste its bitterness on her tongue, feel its sting in her eyes. When they reached Peora Street, she and Gamalda entered the first Healing House. The room was crammed with people who had lost arms, legs, and eyes. "Mercy, mercy," Avielle whispered over and over.

Healers, as well as damadas from the Temples, moved among the injured. The smell of unwashed bodies, urine, and blood filled the air, which was stifling in the heat. Although Avielle went from person to person looking at every face in the room, she found no one in her family nor anyone she knew from the High Hall.

She searched for Gamalda and found her holding a damp cloth against the face of a young, brown-haired boy. Bandages were wound around both his arms. "There now,"

Gamalda soothed, "there." She stood up when she saw Avielle waiting and said in a quiet voice, "The dead are out back. Do you want to look?"

Avielle put out one hand, teetering as though she walked on a tightrope. If she fell one way she might never know her family's fate; if she fell the other way she might have to see them cold and dead with faces that would haunt her forever.

"I can't bear . . . ," she said at last. "I can't bear to, I don't know . . ."

Gamalda waited.

"No," Avielle said, looking down.

"Then I'll look for you. I know the faces of the queen and Ismine at least." And she went out the door into the back.

They visited three more Healing Houses but found no one in Avielle's family. Last of all, they went to the site of the High Hall. The destruction was cataclysmic. Avielle had not been prepared for the amount of rubble, for the utter ruin. Chunks of stone as big as houses lay tumbled upon yet bigger chunks. Ten teams of horses hitched together would not be able to pull them away. Yet, they looked as if someone had tossed them about like Rajio's toy blocks. Smaller blocks of stone, but still huge, were scattered everywhere. She saw square and jagged stones, dull and shiny stones, in black and green and pale gold; they glittered in the sunlight, casting angular blue shadows across the rubble.

This was all that was left of her home.

Avielle bent toward a pile of rubble. She began lifting smaller pieces of stone; she threw them over her shoulder, one after the other, again and again.

"Rajio! Rajio!" she cried. "I must get you out!"

"Come away, my dear," said Gamalda softly.

Avielle fell to her knees and, using all her strength, moved a large rock a few inches. She scraped her hands and arms; they began to bleed.

"Stop," Gamalda said. "You're injuring yourself. You can do no good here." She put her arm around Avielle's shoulders, helping her stand.

Avielle leaned into her and stumbled away.

VIANNA
CHAPTER TEN

For three days Avielle stayed in bed. Nightmares came to her, moans, screams, and then lapses into oblivion. Occasionally Gamalda brought her some vegetable broth, which she managed to sit up and drink. The spoon seemed so swollen she could not hold it; the bowl so tiny it seemed miles away.

Other times she sobbed until the sobs drenched her pillow. Gamalda did not try to comfort or talk to her, but came often and sat with her in silence. A few times, the darkest times, Gamalda held her, also silently. The cat, which Avielle could see now in the daylight, was orange-striped with a white bib. He came running up whenever she cried, jumped onto the bed, and bumped his head against her. He purred until she stopped crying, then curled up under her arm and went to sleep.

On the fourth day, a kind of calm rose inside her, and rational thoughts occasionally drifted through her mind. One in particular. The Chamber of Wings was destroyed now, too. How could she have found refuge and comfort in the very heart of Dolvoka's evil? *But I did not know,* she told herself over and over.

In the afternoon of that fourth day, Avielle sat up and looked around the room. She saw a heavy chest of drawers made of walnut. On a table shrouded in a red cloth sat a ponderous brown ewer and basin. To the left stood a brass candlestick, the tallow candle burned down to a mere gob of buff-colored wax with no wick in sight.

A sudden breeze rippled the white curtains covering the window, and let in a slip of light that fell in a band against a brilliant blue dress laid out on a chair.

Avielle stood up, clutching Gamalda's voluminous white nightgown around her, and walked to the table, her legs a bit shaky from being in bed for so long. She poured a silver stream of water from the ewer into the basin.

Her linen underwear, shift, and petticoat, all washed and ironed, lay beside the blue dress. The dress had laces that crisscrossed the front of the bodice. Around the neck a collar of soft white linen draped in a gentle curve. The dress was simple, but lovely—too lovely. She wanted to wear a rag, a black rag.

After Avielle dressed, she stood looking at the door. How could she step through it? Stepping through it meant stepping into a life without her family, meant admitting she could go on and have a life without them. It seemed like a betrayal.

Avielle put her hand on the latch—so smooth, so cold—the coldest thing she had ever had to touch.

She went out.

"You need a real meal," Gamalda said when Avielle found her in the room she used for dyeing thread. Some of the jars of dye had fallen during the whirlwind and had stained the wooden floor with a kaleidoscope of color—reds, greens, blues, teals, yellows, and more—in whirls, patches, and streaks. Striated through them all ran rivulets of black. Gamalda had lost several bolts of cloth to the whirlwind, and many of the dyes, but all of the looms still worked.

"Where is my own dress?" Avielle asked her.

"Well, I thought," Gamalda said, "since you're trying to hide that you're a princess—that your dress was too fine. Would call attention to you."

"Yes, of course." Avielle hesitated. "I do not mean to be ungrateful for this dress, but I need a black one. I must observe the six months of mourning."

"That blue one is the only thing I've got that will fit you," Gamalda said. "I've got a black skirt and blouse—it won't fit well. I'm so much bigger. But we can alter it today. Will that do for now?"

"Yes. Thank you."

"Now about that meal. You're thin as a stick. You haven't eaten properly for several days."

Avielle followed Gamalda back through the front room,

still strewn with large chunks of plaster and boards from where the ceiling had collapsed. The beam was a dagger thrust into the floor. A warm wind blew through the window—the glass had not yet been replaced—and the cloth hanging on the walls swayed back and forth. Gamalda had sponged off all the bolts of cloth that she could salvage and put them back on their racks. Someone had hung the door back on its hinges.

In the kitchen, Gamalda put a plate of cheddar cheese, brown bread, and apples before Avielle, then poured her a glass of milk.

Avielle looked at it all. Eating seemed like too much effort.

"Start with the cheese," Gamalda advised, "one bite of cheese. Master Riskin, the cheesemaker in the next block, made it. He's big and round and ruddy, and his cheese is as strong as he is."

Avielle bit into the cheese. Sharp, and slightly smoky, it was as good as anything she had ever eaten at the High Hall. She took a sip of milk, another bite of cheese, then before long found herself eating the bread and apples.

She was hungry. She was alive. Alive when so many were dead. The empty plate covered with crumbs seemed to reprimand her.

"Now for some tea while we talk," Gamalda said. "I've created a new blend—plum, vanilla, and cream. Let's hope it will be good."

As Gamalda made the tea, Avielle watched her. Today Gamalda wore ruby-colored linen, and Avielle thought of the red tablecloth she had been making for Ismine. Ismine with her laughter; Ismine with her hats and her ribbons and her lace; Ismine with stones piled on top of her. Avielle turned her head sharply toward the wall. There, backed up against the counter, were six oddly shaped teapots—though it was a stretch to even call them that. Some had sagging spouts, others had bowls that were half collapsed, still others had twisted tops. All were plain earthenware.

Gamalda saw her looking at them.

"Do you like my teapots?" she asked.

Avielle did not know what to say.

Gamalda laughed her big, rollicking laugh. "That's all right! They're a sad lot, I know. Made by a friend of mine. I keep them because they remind me of potential, of trying, and of the courage to begin even if I haven't got a clue where something might lead. Even if the results aren't perfect. And they also remind me of the danger of stopping too soon."

Gamalda set teacups on the table and poured the tea, which did have the faint scent of vanilla and plum.

Avielle curled her fingers around the cup, feeling its warmth, but her fingers felt so cold she wondered if they could ever be warmed. As she sipped the tea, her eyebrows rose.

"It is excellent," she said.

Gamalda tasted. "A tad heavy on the plum, but a success, I'd say." Then she put three teaspoons of sugar into her cup.

They both drank for a few minutes.

Gamalda spoke at last. "I know you're still in a severe state of shock and grief. But we've got to talk about your future."

Avielle stared at the apple core on her plate.

"Your Highness," Gamalda said. "Princess."

Avielle looked up at her then.

"I haven't forgotten," Gamalda said. "Nor should you. You're all we've got left. The Brethren of the Black Cloaks are still demanding the tribute of slaves. And the mines. They warn that they'll continue terrorizing us until we give in. Our wizards believe that the Brethren spent most of their power making the whirlwind, and much of their power is now spent. I tell you I pray to the Goddess that they're right!" She flung out her beautiful bare arms as though they were the branches of a great tree. The bracelets of gold and silver she wore tinkled together. "So," she continued, "we don't have another cataclysm to fear, at least until the Brethren gather their power again."

"So how will they continue to terrorize us?" Avielle asked.

Gamalda closed her eyes. "Each of the past four nights, specters in black cloaks have stalked through the city. They murder someone each night—no one knows where or whom they will strike. Or whatever other horror they might inflict upon us next."

Avielle grew rigid. She wanted to crawl away into some dark tunnel lined with soft dry leaves where she could sleep and be safe.

"Before the whirlwind," Gamalda added, "I believed that we shouldn't send the slaves—but now, I tell you, I just don't know. Someone has got to help us decide what to do. You've got to come forward to head the High Council, Princess. And lead your people in this time of great need."

The corners of Avielle's mouth and eyes felt dragged down by leaden weights. "The people will never accept me," she said. "All my life they have shunned me, hated me. You cannot begin to imagine it. The derision. The prejudice."

"But surely now—"

"And I have another reason for not coming forward. The Brethren of the Black Cloaks deliberately killed my family. If they learn that I live they will certainly try to kill me, too."

Gamalda leaned her elbows against the table. "There's some truth to that. But you could serve as a rallying cry. A reason for the people to come together in this time of turmoil and darkness. Oh, I can envision all kinds of good things that would happen from that."

Avielle drank her tea, slowly, deliberately. Then she said, "Why should I risk my life for people who have always shunned and hated me? Besides, if my parents with all their wisdom and resources could not prevail against such evil, how could I? Let the High Council rule. Let them decide what is to be done."

Gamalda leaned forward. "What of the crime the Brethren committed against your family? They murdered them. Are you going to simply walk away from that?"

And then it came. Avielle wanted to rip the copper pots off the walls and throw them to the floor; she wanted to sweep the misshapen teapots off the counter; she wanted to smash the teacups against the window. And she found herself on her feet, shouting curses and profanities at the Brethren of the Black Cloaks.

Gamalda let her shout.

Avielle finished. She was hoarse. Exhausted. She sank down into her chair.

There was a silence.

Gamalda covered Avielle's silver hand with her own strong black one. "You're angry. Distraught. You've suffered a terrible loss—I can't begin to imagine it. You need time to recover. I've brought all this up too soon. Much too soon."

Avielle wiped her tears with her napkin.

"If you're not going to come forward," Gamalda said, "what will you do now?"

"Now? I had not . . . thought. I have not had time to think."

Gamalda was silent for a moment, absently tapping her spoon against the side of her teacup. At last she spoke. "What if you stayed here? Stayed and became my apprentice? At least until you decide what to do about being a princess. I'd love it if you would. What do you think?"

Avielle stayed perfectly still for a second. She thought how lucky she had been to find this woman, who from the instant Avielle had met her, had seemed worthy of trust. *Trust.* Avielle tried to think whom else she had ever really trusted, and the list was very short.

"Yes," she said, "I would like that very much. I thank you for your kindness."

"Then we've got to concoct a history for you. Darien already knows you went to search for your family in the High Hall." Gamalda twisted up a lock of golden hair that had strayed into her eyes. "We've got to think of a reason why you'd been living there. And why you're a weaver."

Gamalda fell silent. She sat straight in her chair, both feet planted on the ground, her hands fingering a length of blue thread.

Avielle tried to imagine another story for her life, but found it difficult.

"I've got it!" Gamalda exclaimed. "We'll say you were the daughter of one of the queen's weavers. And you've got no other family to go to. Yes, that will do nicely. But we'll have to change your name. Hmm . . . How about Vianna? Pretty enough and not so different. Will that do?"

Avielle nodded. She would be completely anonymous. Wasn't that what she had always wanted? And now she had it. No one—except Gamalda—would know who she was.

TINTY
CHAPTER ELEVEN

The printer's sign—*Pea Printers, Perfection our Promise*—creaked in the wind as Avielle passed it on her way down Postern Street the next day. Every step was an effort, as though she were pushing a wheelbarrow full of bricks. She wanted to hide away in bed, but Gamalda had insisted that she go out for some air and sunshine.

"Augum Aslee's shop is across the street," Gamalda had said, pointing out the window, "at the west end of the block. Not far. I promised him this length of green wool for a shirt. Poor man, he suffers from cold in all seasons. It would be a great help if you'd deliver it for me. Besides, you'll get to meet Tinty."

"Tinty?"

Gamalda smiled. "You'll see. No words can describe her, let me tell you."

Avielle felt wary, walking down the street without a veil. She had wanted to wear one all the time, fearing that someone who had seen her at the High Hall might recognize her.

She knew the chance was slim because she had kept so much to herself; and also because everyone would think her dead with the rest of her family. Besides, she was only one silverskin among many. Even so, she did not want to take any risks. Gamalda, however, had said that she would draw attention to herself if she went veiled everywhere on the block. People would wonder why. In the end the two of them had decided Avielle would go veiled only if she left Postern Street.

Avielle heard a loud, high voice shouting inside of Pea Printing; she had heard it before coming through the walls of Gamalda's shop, which abutted it on the west. Gamalda had told her Mistress Pea was a loud woman. Avielle walked by the shop and went on. She looked at the people passing her, some on foot, some on horseback, some riding in wagons and carriages. Everything seemed normal. As though—in spite of the damaged buildings—nothing terrible had happened. As though hundreds had not been murdered. As though the Brethren of the Black Cloaks were not a continuing menace that might strike anytime, anywhere. How could people go on with their ordinary lives in the face of such fear?

Next to Pea Printing was the chandler's shop; its name, *Candle Magic*, announced that the proprietor had a magic gift and was a Dredonian Rhian. In the window stood a circle of unlit white candles with a tall white taper burning in the center.

On the doorstep, the orange and white tiger cat who had visited Avielle washed its face in a sunbeam. Gamalda had told Avielle he was named Underfoot, and that he belonged to everyone and to no one on Postern Street. Everyone loved him, fed him, and took care of him; and he visited whomever he pleased, whenever he pleased.

"Thank you for looking after me," Avielle told him, patting his head. "You be careful crossing the street."

Avielle crossed the street herself, dodging a hansom cab, her black skirt nipping at her heels. She stopped in front of a shop as tall and narrow as a zucchini. The sun gleamed on the yellow door. There was no sign out front; instead, gold letters outlined in red—replete with scrolls and flourishes—covered nearly every inch of the window. They said:

AUGUM ASLEE

PURVEYOR OF LOVE POTIONS

AND

MAGICAL SOCKS

SATISFACTION GUARANTEED

Augum Aslee must be a Dredonian Rhian, too. She wondered how his glass window had survived the whirlwind.

A sign on the door said, PLEASE KNOCK TWICE. Avielle did. A minute later a girl answered. She wore a mustard-colored dress with a triple row of purple buttons all up the front. Two of the buttons were missing.

"Do you have an appointment?" she drawled. "Or don't you? If you don't will you pay me gold to get you one?"

"No and no," Avielle said, staring at her. One side of her dark brown hair was curled. Little flurries of light corkscrewed through it. The other side of her hair was straight. Her neck was at least twice as long as anybody else's and the rest of her at least twice as small.

"I'm Tinitia Bottledown," the girl said. "But anybody calls me that will have my fist to reckon with. Go by Tinty."

"Your hair . . ."

Tinty giggled. "You should've seen me yesterday. It all stuck straight out from my head like a porcupine. I guess my gift isn't being a hairdresser. Just as well. Rich women and their snotty ways."

"Mistress Calima from *Wind Weaver* down the street sent me with a package for Master Aslee," Avielle said.

"I see from your black you're in mourning. Sorry for your loss. You're not alone, that's the sorrier thing. Cursed Black Cloaks. Get my hands on them, I'd dunk them in boiling oil. Throw in some pepper, too." And Tinty led the way into the shop.

Avielle's first impression was that she was inside the vast ancient reaches of someone's cluttered mind; one stuffed with the thoughts, dreams, and memories of a lifetime. Running down the walls were shelves and shelves and more shelves, all filled with everything imaginable and some things that were not. There were frayed wicker baskets overflowing with yarn, with varying sizes of knitting needles poking out of them. There were dusty scrolls, books crammed in piles, and dirty bottles—blue, white, yellow, green, big and small, narrow and slender. There were piles of clothes with their sleeves dangling down the shelves. The place smelled of mothballs. And herbs. These were arranged haphazardly in white porcelain jars all over the room, some on the floor, some on the shelves, their labels written in a spidery hand. Many of the labels were peeling off.

"This way," Tinty said. "He's in the back."

"Did you have no damage from the whirlwind?" Avielle asked.

"Oh, some things fell off the shelves, some things jumped back on. Didn't make much difference. Kept all our glass though. Come on."

Avielle passed a table with a plate of brown fruit that might have once been pears. Beside it was a little pile of chicken bones and a mortar and pestle with dried green leaves scattered around it. And then there were the socks. They were everywhere. Rolls and rolls of them crammed into every nook and cranny.

She followed Tinty to the back of the shop, where a man Avielle assumed was Augum Aslee sat knitting a red sock, his needles clicking. Behind him, on a stand, was the one clean thing in the room—a blue egg encased in a glass dome, which did not have a single smear or a speck of dust on it. Avielle wondered if the egg, which had undoubtedly had its insides blown out, was real. Eggs, even more rare than feathers, were inordinately expensive.

"Tinty, my girl, who's come?" Augum Aslee said, looking up from his knitting.

"Don't know. Some girl."

"Well, what does she want? Bring her here. I haven't got all day." His needles clicked faster.

Avielle walked over to his chair. Augum Aslee had the shaggy pumpkin-colored hair of a court jester. On it he wore a tottering green hat, as though to keep any more of his thoughts from flying out and landing on a shelf or under a table. His two eyes, as black as drain holes, peered out from under his hat and considered Avielle.

"Is it socks you want? My socks never fail. You'll have toasty feet even when it's cold as a bone in the month of Januan. My customers wear them to bed. Keep their feet tucked up to their big behinds, and a glow runs through their whole body."

He clacked his knitting needles together. "Or is it a love potion you're after? Some fine young lad you've got your eye on? Heh, heh. Well, to begin I'll need three hairs from his head." Suddenly he wrinkled his nose so much his upper lip turned inside out. "Can you pay?"

"I have—," Avielle began.

"Never mind that," Augum Aslee interrupted, pointing one knitting needle at her. "You've got a look about you. Do you see it, Tinty? Look sharp and learn something, girl."

Tinty drifted over and looked.

"It's something in her eyes," Augum Aslee said. "They go down and down, but then there's a wall." He leaned toward Avielle and his voice grew deep. "And in the wall, behind creepers and thorns, a hidden door. But she doesn't want to find it. She doesn't want to go through it into the land beyond."

"I have a package from Mistress Calima," Avielle said hastily. "Some cloth for a shirt."

"Ah, Gamalda! Wonderful woman." Augum Aslee leaned back and took the package. Whatever had just possessed him disappeared. "Packages tied up in brown paper make a nice crinkly sound." He did not untie the blue ribbon but ripped open the paper to reveal the green cloth. "A fine color that, a fine color." He shot a glance at Avielle. "I suppose you want something for your trouble? Give the girl a candy, Tinty."

Tinty reached into her pocket and pulled out a piece of hard, golden candy with hair stuck to it.

Avielle took the sticky thing in her fingers and said in a faint voice, "Thank you very much. I will be going now."

"He liked you," Tinty said at the door.

"How do you know?" Avielle asked.

"'Cause he didn't bellow at you."

"What do you do as his apprentice? Are you learning to . . . knit?"

"Nah. Tried that. Big failure—my magic ran in lumps and made little whiffling sounds. I got magic in my blood all right—comes from mum's side—she could calm a horse with the touch of her hand. But me, I can't find my gift. I will though. Or my name's not Tinty." And she glowered at Avielle as though daring her to call her Tinitia. Then she turned her back and shut the door.

PREJUDICE
CHAPTER TWELVE

"I'm sorry, Mistress Calima, but it's too much for me to fix," Darien said the next afternoon, looking at the beam that had fallen from the ceiling into the middle of the shop. "It'll take three men to move it, and four more to put another back in place."

Avielle watched him scratch his neck. Again, he wore his cap tipped so far to the right it was in danger of falling off. But this one was gray.

"Do you know any men who'll do the job?" Gamalda asked.

"Sure. Plenty of men have come in from parts of the city that weren't struck, looking for work. I know some steady fellows. But at least I can board up the window for you. So many people want glass there's not a sheet to be had. And," he said, scratching his neck again, "I can chop up some of the bigger pieces of wood and carry them out back."

"Why out back?"

"There's not a wagon to be had either. Every single one's being used to cart away rubble. I can start now."

"Wonderful," Gamalda said. "But first, are you hungry?"

Darien took off his cap and tossed it from hand to hand. "Well, I could never lie to you, Mistress Calima, not for fear of my immortal soul. Truth is I'm always hungry for your cooking. The messes I cook up for me and Master Keenum don't much count."

Gamalda smiled. "Why don't you two get further acquainted while I whip up some jamcakes? Strawberry ones." She walked away into the kitchen.

Without his hat on, Avielle noticed, Darian's tufts of blond hair stuck out all over his head.

"Who is Master Keenum?" Avielle asked.

Darien looked at the ceiling. "Old blind man I live with. Gives me room and board in exchange for looking after him."

"That seems like a sensible arrangement."

"Does it?" Darien stuck his tongue on the inside of his mouth so his left cheek bulged out.

"How do you come to be working for Mistress Calima?" Avielle asked.

He put his hat back on his head, adjusted it to its usual precarious tilt, and then shrugged his shoulders. "I do odd jobs here and there," he said at last. "Like this one. I get to keep my wages. I'm saving up."

Avielle wondered what was the matter with him. Now that Gamalda was gone, his demeanor had changed completely. All his cheer and forthrightness were gone.

She tried again. "How did you meet Mistress Calima?"

"Found me one day when I was living on the street," Darien muttered. "She fixed it all up between me and the master."

"She does have a tendency to take in strays," Avielle said. "As she so kindly did me."

Darien said nothing. He put his weight on one foot and tapped his other. He looked down at the floor.

Avielle could not decide whether he was being rude or was merely shy. She was about to break the silence when Darien spoke.

"Cursed Dredonians blowing up the High Hall." And he raised his eyes, stared directly at her, then said slowly and distinctly, "Cursed Dredonians with their ugly silverskins."

Avielle stood speechless, as she had stood speechless so many times in the past—swallowing the poison, feeling the blackness swim before her eyes—because it was the only thing she knew how to do.

Darien walked through the doorway into the kitchen.

Avielle did not follow. It had never occurred to her that some Rhians might hate Rhians with Dredonian blood because Dredonians had destroyed the High Hall.

A minute later she realized Darien and Gamalda were talking.

"Have you been over to the Temple since the whirlwind?" Darien was asking.

"Yes," said Gamalda.

"Thought you might. Your believing in the Goddess so much."

"There were lots of people there. More than I've seen in years. I guess everyone is praying for hope in this time. Hope and guidance."

"I hear folks are going for another reason. They think the Goddess brought the whirlwind because she's angry at us for forgetting to worship her."

"Nonsense," Gamalda said. "The Goddess doesn't bring evil upon us. Never! I tell you that men and women bring about evil by turning toward it in their hearts. But it's true that we've forgotten her. I pray that some day Rhians will worship the Goddess with full glory again."

"I went to the Temple myself yesterday. Prayed to be safe. Understand?"

"Yes, I certainly do."

So did Avielle. Indeed, each day she had been growing more afraid of what terrible thing the Brethren might do next.

"I hope people are bringing offerings to the Temple," Gamalda added. "The damadas' robes are no better than rags."

Avielle held very still. Damadas. *Esilia*. In all her agony and grief she had not even thought about Esilia. Esilia who was probably dead, too.

* * *

"Here she is!" cried a voice. "Here's Gamalda's new apprentice!" Two days had passed. Avielle, weaving a blue placemat on a small loom in the shop, looked up. She saw a stout, ruddy-cheeked girl in a ghastly greenish-yellow dress with darker green dots. Her nose was as pointed as the cones of paper that held a tiras' worth of candy.

Another girl in an identical dress, with an identical nose, in an identical face, stood beside her. Both wore white aprons with bibs tied over their dresses. They looked about sixteen years old.

Avielle blinked, wondering if she were seeing double.

"I'm Renatta Pea," said the first girl.

"And I'm Penatta Pea," said the second girl.

Avielle knew she must have looked astonished because both girls giggled. "Oh, we've befuddled another one," said Renatta. "It's always such fun. What a darling she is."

"We're the Pea twins from the Pea Printing shop next door," Penatta said, "that's why we're wearing—"

"—these hideous pea-colored dresses," Renatta finished.

"Our ma says—"

"—it helps business. Makes our printing shop special."

"I see," said Avielle, looking from one to the other.

"We're going to switch places now," said Penatta.

"And whirl about—"

"—and see if you can tell us apart."

The girls danced around each other, their skirts billowing out, until Avielle grew dizzy watching them. Finally they stopped.

"All right," they said together. "GUESS."

Avielle pointed. "You're Penatta. And you're Renatta."

The girls looked crestfallen.

"How did you know?" Renatta asked.

Avielle stared. Could they really be so dense? But she went along with their game because politeness had been ingrained in her from the moment she could speak.

"I knew because you are holding a piece of paper, Renatta," Avielle said. "And your sister is not."

"Drat!" Penatta jabbed her sister. "You gave it all away!"

"Never you mind," said Renatta. "We'll fool her next time. She's such a pet." She handed Avielle the sheet of paper, which was covered top to bottom with black printed words. "We brought you a broadsheet full of the latest news—"

"—A welcoming present. Printing broadsheets is the main part of our business," Penatta explained. "Everybody—lord to scullery maid—has got to know the news. Ma says, and nobody dare contradict her, that knowledge is meat and drink to the mind—"

"—and a slap in the face of ignorance, " Renatta finished with a triumphant nod of her head.

Avielle scanned the broadsheet. The titles of the stories screamed out in large, bold type.

WILL THE HIGH COUNCIL CONCEDE TO DREDONIA'S DEMANDS? COLLEGE OF WIZARDS MUM ABOUT TIRION'S DEFENSES. SOPRANO SHRIEKS THROUGH CONCERT. BLACK CLOAKS KILL VIOLIN-MAKER. EAGLE SPOTTED ON WESTERN BORDER—WILL IT STAY? QUEEN'S MEADOWLARK FOUND UNHARMED IN ITS GOLDEN CAGE IN THE RUBBLE. PEPPERMINT CANDY DRIVES MAN MAD. PREJUDICE RISING AGAINST DREDONIAN RHIANS.

The print blurred before Avielle's eyes. So she had suspected correctly: Darien's rancor was not an isolated case, but indicative of widespread feeling. Now Avielle had something more to fear—the prejudice of Rhians against the Dredonian Rhians who lived in their midst. And her mother's meadowlark—Avielle could see her mother feeding it seeds, running one hand through her pearls, laughing. How in the name of the Goddess had it survived?

"Vianna?" Renatta asked. "What's wrong, sweetling? Your cheeks are red. I've seen tomatoes paler."

"I thank you for your concern," Avielle said, "you are very kind. But I am fine."

"Talk kind of high, don't you?" Penatta observed. "Tinty was telling us how you were raised in the High Hall."

"What was it like?" Renatta asked, leaning forward. "What did you do there? Were there balls every night?"

"Silk dresses?"

"Jewels?"

"Handsome princes?"

Avielle rolled up the broadsheet, hearing it crackle, feeling it slide against her fingertips. Yes, there were princes: one from a foreign land who was so repelled by her that he did not want to touch her; and another who had made her life so miserable that she was glad, fiercely glad, that he was dead.

"I was a weaver," Avielle said. "I worked with Her Royal Highness Princess Avielle." She watched their faces, waiting for them to exclaim. However, to her surprise, they did not exclaim. All the animation, all the gaiety, mischief, and laughter left their faces.

"Her?" Penatta whispered. "You saw her? Her that they hid away?"

That they hid away? Avielle had always thought that she had hidden herself away. Then she remembered how her parents had never given her a Presentation Ball, and thought Penatta might be right.

"What was she like?" Renatta asked.

Penatta hugged herself and spoke before Avielle could answer. "How horrible! Being near her! Was it as everyone feared? Was she growing as evil as the Cursed One? Could you see it in her?"

Avielle felt cold creep over limb, tongue, and heart. The common people were no different from those in the High

Hall; they all thought the same of her. Despised her. It would never be any different. Never.

"Bowldy-hoot!" exclaimed Renatta. "I never believed a word of all that. Fool stuff for fool minds. Why should the princess be like the Cursed One just because they were both silverskins?"

"You calling me a fool?" asked Penatta.

Renatta ignored this. "We look like Ma. But that doesn't mean we got her bad temper. And thank the Goddess for it."

"But the princess had royal blood," Penatta argued. "Everybody knows that's stronger than common blood. And what about the Creed of Ancestors? Everyone's got some trait passed down from their ancestors. The only good thing about all this evil come upon us is that the princess is dead and gone. You'd of seen. Sooner or later the bad magic would have burst out in her. Who knows what would have happened then?"

"Pish," said Renatta. "She had no magic."

But she did, Avielle wanted to say. She does. And she must maintain constant vigilance to see that it never turned "bad." And the only way for her to do that was to never use it. Not once.

"Nobody thought of her as you do," Penatta said. "An innocent. Bah."

"There's some," said Renatta. "More than you think."

The twins were glaring at each other now. Avielle felt herself looking at Renatta like a hopeful dog. Could what she said be true? Could there be some among the common people who had believed she was not predestined to commit evil?

If only she could believe it herself.

IN THE TEMPLE
CHAPTER THIRTEEN

Avielle spent the next two days weaving, seeking solace in the old familiar rhythms, but solace eluded her. She was still struggling to adapt to her new life. So much had changed so fast that she scarcely knew where she was, who she was, or what she was supposed to be doing. And, too, Avielle was still struggling with the onslaught of feelings that filled her heart.

On the third morning, as her hands wove, she kept thinking about the story in the new broadsheet that Renatta had brought over earlier. She stopped weaving and plucked it off the table beside her. The smell of ink filled her nose. High Councilman Herector, head of the High Council, whom Avielle had known back in her life in the High Hall, had written the story. In it he wrote:

Our good King and Queen Coroll refused to bow to the evil Brethren of the Black Cloaks and send our good citizens to be slaves or to surrender the mines

> *that are the source of our prosperity. But this was before they knew what power the Brethren of the Black Cloaks could wield. The High Council will now decide what is to be done. Our wizards are doing everything in their power to protect us. But so far, they have not been able to defeat the Black-Cloaked Specters who strike each night.*

Finally, High Councilman Herector urged the people of Tirion not to be frightened or downhearted.

> *We who live in Tirion must show the rest of the people of Rhia that we are strong and courageous. We will not despair, nor be filled with grief, nor be defeated by evil. We will go on with our lives—working, gathering with family, walking beneath the sun. We must march bravely on so the Brethren will not defeat our spirits.*

Avielle crumpled the broadsheet into a ball. March bravely on, indeed. What about those who were not courageous? What about those who were racked by grief? What about those who did feel despair? Surely there were hundreds like her, too afraid to speak for fear of ridicule, for fear of being called disloyal to the realm.

She threw the balled-up broadsheet across the room.

Who spoke for them?

* * *

The next morning, the sun rose as pink as a baby's hand, outstretched to catch the pale moon. Avielle stepped outside to perform the morning ritual with the birdseed. As she filled her hands with seeds from the feeder by the door, ready to fling them into the wind, a town crier ran by.

"Girl found alive in the rubble!" he cried. "Girl found alive in the rubble! Name of Esilia Mireva! Alive in the rubble!"

"Esilia," Avielle whispered, the birdseed slipping through her fingers.

"I'm sorry," a damada with a flashing gold tooth said at the door to the damadas' cloister behind the Temple that afternoon. "But Damada Esilia is far too weak to see anyone." She squinted so hard her face looked like a raisin.

For the first time since the whirlwind, Avielle wished she could lift her veil, reveal who she was, and order this woman to step aside.

"Will she live, Damada?"

"The healers don't know. She suffered terribly from thirst. But she's eager to start working with the books."

"The books?" Avielle asked.

"Damada Esilia has been assigned to work in the Temple library. The thought of all those books is probably keeping her alive. Now I suggest, young woman, that you go into the Temple and pray for Damada Esilia's swift recovery. And praise the Goddess for returning her to us."

"I will, Damada," said Avielle.

"Who shall I say called?"

"Av—" Avielle stopped just in time. "Vianna," she said at last, though she knew that would be meaningless to Esilia.

White stones crunched under Avielle's shoes as she walked down the path in the garden courtyard between the damadas' cloister and the Temple. The roses—red, gold, white—were past their peak now that it was late in the month of Akim. A round fountain with a statue of a fish spurting water from its mouth stood in the center of the garden.

When Avielle reached the front of the Temple, she stood outside looking up at it. Made of wheat-colored sandstone, the high dome in the middle curved against the sky. Six arches swept across the front, supported by white marble pillars engraved with gold. But there were cracks in the pillars and chips in the gold. The sweeping staircase leading to the rows of doors had chunks missing. The Temple showed years of neglect.

Avielle stood, torn, uncertain whether she wanted to go in. She still had not forgiven the Goddess for letting her family die or for letting the Brethren of the Black Cloaks terrorize Rhia. But Esilia had lived. Avielle wanted to give thanks for that. And she still clung to the hope that someone in her family might be found alive, too.

When she entered the Temple, the sharp, clove-like smell of incense filled the air. The dome soared upward, painted with scenes of planting and harvesting, but no one had cleaned them in many years, and they were dim with smoke. All across the far wall, a stained glass window rose three stories high. In brilliant jewel colors it showed the Goddess caught in a moment of dance; her silver dress—patterned with flowers, fish, and spirals—swirled around her. On her golden hair sat a crown of golden flowers. Light rayed out from each one, spreading in a halo around her head. A white swan soared up from her left hand: the Quasana, the Messenger of the Goddess.

After Avielle found a place to kneel—the Temple was crowded—she noticed that cracks zigzagged through many of the pieces of stained glass; an especially bad one ran through the Goddess' mouth. The Temple was far from the High Hall and so had avoided the damage of the whirlwind. The cracked glass, like the Temple's exterior, was due to a shortage of funds for repairs.

A door opened and shut. Wearing a ragged brown robe, a damada walked in slowly, strewing corn across the room. The corn spattered onto the altar, which held a blunt stone carving of the Goddess with rounded breasts and a pregnant belly. Corn struck the loaf of bread in front of her. Corn fell into the jug of milk that stood on her left, and into the cup of wine that stood on her right. Corn spattered across the pumpkins, then rolled across apples, grapes, and other offerings of food before finally falling to the earthen floor. Avielle wished she had brought an offering.

She prayed to the Goddess: *I praise you one thousand times for saving Esilia. Make her well. Let my family be found. Keep me safe, protect me. Why did you let the High Hall fall? Why did you let my family die? Send a plague upon the Dredonians. Keep the evil of Dolvoka from rising in my blood.*

After Avielle had prayed for perhaps half an hour, a line of damadas filed in and began to chant, swaying in their brown patched veils.

The High Damada, who wore a gold necklace with a sunburst hanging on the end, stood before the altar and the Cadella, the Service to the Goddess, began. First, the High Damada recited the Scripture of Creation.

"In the Beginning Time," she said, "before Alamaria was made, the Goddess slept in an egg that floated in the darkness. There the Goddess dreamed of love, and a great light filled the shell, a light so bright the egg could not contain it. Cracks formed along the shell, until at last the pieces flew out in a burst of light. And the fragments of the shell became the stars shining in the darkness.

"Thus the Goddess was born. With the eye in the center of her forehead, she made Alamaria. She shaped two white swans to sit at her right hand and at her left. She named them the Quasana and the Malaquasana, to be her Messengers. And then the people she made, and loved them, the great and the small, the courageous and the meek, the joyful and the despairing. And then she made the animals and flowers; then mountains she made, the forests green, and the smallest flakes of snow. The rivers she made, and chose one for her raiment. And she loved all that she had made.

"Thus the universe was born, and thus the Goddess chose Alamaria as her home in the center of all things, the place from which she would rule the heavens. And thus it came to pass that all things, sun, moon, planets, and stars revolve around Alamaria. And the Lady of Light is at the center of the universe and in the center of her heart is love."

Three bells rang.

"So it was," Avielle chanted with the others. "So it shall ever be."

"Great powers the Goddess gave her Messengers. But soon dark thoughts grew in the mind of the Malaquasana. He grew jealous of the Goddess and began to lust to have power over the people. He flew across the sky, sipped the darkness between the stars, and his evil turned him black. As he flew, the shadow of his wing drew evil across Alamaria. Long did the Goddess struggle with him, and at last she cast him out to the darkest depths of the universe. But evil had already taken root in the hearts of men and women, fighting with the good of the Goddess."

Three bells rang.

"So it was," Avielle chanted with the others. "So it shall ever be."

Then the High Damada faced the altar, took a silver bowl in her hands, and raised it high over her head to perform the Sacrament of Love.

"Oh, Goddess most high," she said, "accept our offering of love, light, and peace. And we beseech you, fill us with your love, light, and peace." The candlelight reflected off the silver bowl.

Avielle repeated the Goddess' words along with everyone else in the Temple.

Then the damadas passed baskets holding egg-shaped cookies among the worshippers for them to eat as part of the ritual. When everyone had eaten, the High Damada stepped forward and spoke.

"Though you have forgotten the Goddess until these dark days have come upon us, she has not forgotten you. She will aid us in this time of trouble. Some have asked whether the goddess is evil for letting this evil come upon you. We must remember the Three Precepts. The First Precept: The Goddess is love, and is to be loved, and all are her children. The Second Precept: The Malaquasana brought the capacity for evil into the world. The Third Precept: Men and women have the choice whether to do good or evil.

"Let us now pray and submit to the Goddess' wisdom."

Let my family be found, Avielle prayed silently, *let them be found. If it be your will. It must be your will! It must be!*

The next day, someone in the royal family was found. The searchers uncovered Rajio's body in the rubble. He was dead.

RAJIO
CHAPTER FOURTEEN

"We'll go with Master Alubra," Gamalda said late the next afternoon. "He's Mistress Alubra's husband—she runs the silver shop across the street. He's as big as they come, and he'll help us keep a place at the front of the crowd. Are you sure you want to do this, Avielle?"

Avielle nodded—just barely. Twenty minutes later, they started down Axillian Street, which wound through the city from the High Hall—or what remained of it—through the Eastern Gate. Then the road began to snake through two low hills sparsely covered with salal bushes. There were no houses here, for this was the Road to the Tombs.

"I can go no further," Avielle said as they reached the first of the ancient holly trees that marked the last quarter mile to the catacombs. "No closer to the tombs." Somewhere down that road, deep inside the catacombs, lay Dolvoka's body. Indeed, her evil spirit seemed to exude from the bowels of the hill and roll down the road like a foul breath. Avielle knew that the evil was not only waiting for her, was not only drawing her toward it, but was also seeking her, and dread came over her. Never in her life had she set foot in the tombs, and never would she. "No closer," she whispered to Gamalda.

"Then we'll wait here for the funeral procession to pass by," Gamalda said. Avielle clutched a handful of her skirt. She put her other hand on Gamalda's arm, trying to draw strength from her.

It was well that Master Alubra had consented to accompany them, for the crowds that lined the entire road from the gates of the city to the catacombs were huge, and he managed to keep others from stealing their places in the front. Many wore black.

A breeze made her veil flutter, and Avielle hoped rather than believed it might blow away some of the sadness in her heart. All night she had thought and dreamed of Rajio. Rajio making castles out of his blocks; Rajio bouncing so fast on his rocking horse he almost flew off; Rajio sitting on her lap with his arms around her shoulders saying, "Avi! Avi! My silver Avi!" In her dreams, his fleet of toy boats had sailed over the sea into darkness. And she had lunged after him screaming, "No! No!" Trying to hold him, trying uselessly to hold him as he slipped away.

At last Avielle heard the vanguard—silver trumpets ringing upon the air. The burial procession neared. Then, as the vanguard—soldiers on horseback—walked up the road, Avielle saw the trumpets shining like white flames in the sun. The soldiers wore green uniforms and had swords at their sides; their horses' hoofs drummed against the dirt road. After them came the High Council, including High Councilman Herector and Lord General Maldreck, on horseback, too.

Avielle shrank back and turned her head, fearing to be recognized in spite of her veil. Next, riding white horses, came the honor guard dressed all in white; they too, wore swords at their sides, but their scabbards were studded with jewels. Their flag bearer held high the flag of Rhia—wrought with a white lark on a green ground—which whipped in the wind. At last, its wheels creaking, rolled a simple cart pulled by one golden bay. The cart was draped with white velvet; on the velvet, surrounded by white chrysanthemums, lay Rajio. On each side of the cart rode one of the honor guard. No one followed behind the cart, and Avielle looked at the empty space with a kind of horror. There were no mourners. No family walking behind him. For all his family were dead.

Except me, Avielle thought, except me. And she wanted to scream, and for a moment thought she was screaming; but it was the people around her who were screaming, and throwing bouquets of flowers, too. Then their screams grew distant to her as the white-draped cart rolled closer and closer. She had to get nearer, seeing only the profile of Rajio's dear little face so far away was not enough. Her heart thundered in her ears. She began to move forward.

"What are you doing?" Gamalda exclaimed, pulling her back.

"I cannot let him be buried alone!" she cried. "With no one to mourn him."

"Are you ready to expose who you are?" Gamalda asked in a whisper. "Have you thought this through? Is this really the right moment? You're acting upon your emotions."

Avielle stood, the two forces struggling inside her, screaming yes, screaming no, until she feared she would be torn in two.

The procession passed by. Avielle's shoulders slumped.

"She was a good friend of Prince Rajio's when she worked at the High Hall," Avielle heard Gamalda explain to Master Alubra. But he only looked at Avielle sideways and grunted.

"How could the Goddess let such evil happen!" Avielle exclaimed. "All the evil that has happened! She is evil herself!"

"No," Gamalda said. "We are the ones who cause evil, when we turn toward the Malaquasana in our hearts. The Goddess is all powerful and wise. We must keep praying to her."

A week later, as Avielle was carrying a roll of white damask cloth to a rack in the front room, she took pleasure in the beauty of the cloth. Then she felt guilty for feeling any kind of happiness after what had happened to Rajio and the others in her family, and indeed to all the other victims of the Black Cloaks. The day after the funeral Avielle had stayed in bed, curled around Underfoot. Gamalda had told the ever-curious inhabitants of Postern Street that Avielle had been overwhelmed by the crush of the crowd at the funeral procession. Over the next few days, she grew stronger and better, and now here she was admiring a roll of damask cloth. But the ache was there still, and would to some extent, she guessed, be there forever.

She heard shrieks coming from the Peas' print shop next door. "Stop her! Stop her!" Avielle had heard Mistress Pea shout before—she had a voice like a trombone—but this time she sounded truly alarmed. Avielle set the roll of cloth in the rack and hurried to see what the commotion was all about.

Inside the printer's shop, Avielle saw Tinty whirling and jumping, crashing into tables and shelves, sweeping paper, lead type, and jars of ink across the floor.

"I won't have this!" shouted Mistress Pea. "Stop this instant, you wicked girl."

"Oh! Oh! Oh!" cried Master Pea, cowering behind a black printing press in the midst of the pandemonium.

However, as Avielle watched Tinty, it appeared that she could not stop. Big blocks of wooden type flew into the air over her head and danced with little spurtings and fountains of pale green light. They formed one word after another:

SHREW!

GOSSIPS!

CHEAPSKATES!

All words, Avielle knew, which unfortunately described the Peas in their most unflattering light.

"Vianna!" Tinty wailed as she spun. "A bucket of water!"

"Stop her!" Penatta cried, swishing her pea-green skirt from side to side.

"Stop her now!" Renatta ducked a flying inkpot.

DUMBER THAN TWO PEAS IN A POD! the woodblocks spelled.

"I'll have your head for this, Tinitia!" roared Mistress Pea.

TINTY! FISHWIFE!

"Oh dear! Oh my! Oh dear!" whimpered Master Pea as another shelf tumbled down.

SNIVELING WRETCH!

Avielle dashed into the kitchen behind the shop, pumped a pail of water, and ran back. She heaved the water onto Tinty's feet.

The blocks of wooden type fell and clattered on the floor. The spurtings and fountains of green light faded. Slowly, Tinty stopped dancing and stood in a puddle of water, dripping.

"Wasn't that something!" she exclaimed.

"Augum Aslee will pay for this, you wicked girl," Mistress Pea said. "I am a woman to be reckoned with, and I swear I'll have his egg for this!" She turned to her husband. "Well, say something, man. Don't stand there gaping like an idiot."

Master Pea knelt on the floor and started gathering the wooden blocks of type in his arms. "My darlings," he crooned to them. "It was a spell. I know you didn't mean to say such terrible things about us. I'll clean you off lickety-split, and you'll be good as new."

Avielle and Tinty offered to help clean up the shop, but Mistress Pea said she'd had enough of wretched, useless girls and shouted at them to get out of her sight or she would pelt them with boots. So Avielle half dragged Tinty back to Gamalda's shop to restore her with a cup of tea. Gamalda, who had come down from the third floor—where Avielle still had not been invited to go—heard the whole story and tried to disguise a smile quivering at the corners of her mouth. Then the bell rang, and Gamalda went into the front room to wait on a customer.

Tinty blew on her tea, then smashed her nose against the teacup. "Auggie'll be furious," she said, her voice slightly muffled by the cup. "I may have to cut and run."

"Surely it is not so bad as that," Avielle said.

"You don't know nothing. Mistress Pea's been after his egg for ages. Thieving old scow."

"But what were you trying to do, Tinty?"

"Thought my magic gift might be printing. What a crock." She paused. "He'll make me look for something, that's what he'll do. To punish me. Done it before."

"I do not understand."

"You've seen the shop. Like a warren of pack rats it is.

He'll tell me to find one particular thing. Get it? One particular thing in all that mess. Take me weeks. Maybe months." Tinty took the cup away from her nose, blew bubbles in her tea, swirled it with her finger, then drank the tea all at once. She eyed Avielle. "So what's the matter with you? Red eyes, weaker than a string bean. And that cat"—she turned to Underfoot who was sleeping on the mat in front of the stove—"that cat hangs around here all the time when he should get over to Augum Aslee's and catch a few mice." Underfoot opened one eye, then shut it again. "So what's up. You can tell old Tinty."

"You must know. Everyone gossips so around here. Prince Rajio's death—it struck me hard. You see, I knew . . . I knew him well from the High Hall. Very well. Almost like a little brother." Avielle's throat closed up.

"That's rough. I know. When my ma died I slept with her horse every night for a month. Never took a bath. Reeked like I don't know what. Finally my pa dragged me out and dunked me in a washtub."

"When was that?"

"Back three years now."

"What did you do after the bath?"

"What do you think? Went straight back to the barn. Nobody was going to take me out before I was ready. Let them try. I stayed there another month. Then I walked out."

"I do not know," Avielle said slowly. "I lost all my family when the High Hall was destroyed. And just now,

Prince Rajio. I do not think I will be over this in two months."

"Didn't say I was over it! It's always here—" Tinty chucked herself under the chin. "But you stop bleeding. You have to. 'Cause you start drowning in your own blood."

Tinty turned her empty teacup upside down and shook one drop out onto her finger. Then she licked it. "I know what would cheer you up. You been over to Waterbee's Bakery yet? They make the best crisscross cinnamon crisps in Tirion—probably in the kingdom. Chocolate-filled. Got any money?"

Avielle nodded. Gamalda had given her money.

"Then let's go!"

GAMALDA'S WEAVINGS
CHAPTER FIFTEEN

The next afternoon Avielle walked to the grocer's shop on Hickory Street three blocks away to purchase flour. Gamalda still had ten pounds in her bin, but they had heard that there were shortages of food because vendors and delivery men, not knowing where or how the Brethren of the Black Cloaks might strike next, feared to come to Tirion.

The afternoon was gray and trundling with clouds. Leaves twirled in the fierce wind. It was the third day of the month of Septess, considered the first month of fall, although it would not be official until the equinox on the twenty-first. In the distance, Avielle could see the White Tower of Cialaya rising like a bright promise on the hill flanking the southern side of the city.

A sudden gust of wind blew Avielle's veil off her head. She lunged for it, but the veil skipped into the street, danced around carriages, carts, and horses, until it landed on the other side, where a child caught it and ran away. Avielle hesitated, touching her bare cheek, but the grocer's store was only a few doors down, so she went on.

"Out of the way there," said a man with a drooping mustache when she reached the grocer's. He was staggering out the door with a fifty-pound bag of flour slung over his shoulder.

"Sorry, miss," said the grocer, when she asked for twenty pounds of flour. His stomach sagged over the leather apron tied around his waist. "That was the last of the flour just going out the door. People have been buying food like there's no tomorrow. And maybe there isn't. It's a sad time we've come to, a sad time. Lost my wife in the whirlwind."

"I am so terribly sorry," Avielle said.

The shelves in the store were almost empty. Only a few pickles floated forlornly in the bottom of the pickle barrel. Three peppermints stuck to the side of the candy jar.

"What about that one?" Avielle pointed to a fifty-pound bag of flour leaning against the wall.

"Oh, sorry! That's not for sale." The grocer grabbed the bag and dragged it behind the counter. "That's for the family," he said, puffing a little. "You understand."

A red curtain over a doorway behind him twitched, and a girl about Avielle's own age peered out. Her eyes were set so close together that Avielle thought it a wonder there was room for her nose between them.

"When do you expect another delivery?" Avielle asked the grocer.

He scratched his bearded chin with a slate pencil and leaned over the counter. His breath smelled of boiled beef.

"Supposed to get a delivery on Tuesday. But, times being what they are, I can't say for certain. The miller may fear to come to the city, and I can't say as I blame him."

The girl burst out from behind the curtain. "Don't you bother coming back," she said. "We won't sell anything to you. Not so much as a rotten tomato. We don't sell to filthy silverskins."

Avielle felt heat rush into her cheeks.

"Now, Neska," the grocer said. "Hush. Don't say such things to a customer."

"Get out." Neska grabbed a broom and brandished it like a club. "It was those like you killed my mother. Get out now!"

Avielle turned and left. As she walked down the street, she pressed one hand against the pain that bit into her chest. She felt as though her silverskin shone out like a beacon. People passing did seem to look at her unkindly, but she might have been imagining it; after all, people had been looking at her unkindly all her life. She wanted to take a paintbrush and paint her skin white so she could be a true, pure Rhian. She wanted to feel safe.

Avielle walked on through the city until she reached the next grocer's shop. They had no flour there either. She heard the same story at each of the four grocers she checked. At last, she gave up.

On her way home, she decided to take a shortcut through an alley to avoid the stares, inimical or not, of passersby. However, when she had proceeded halfway down it, she approached a group of boys lounging around a back doorway. They stared at her as she approached. Avielle walked faster so she could pass them quickly.

"It's a silverskin," one of the boys muttered.

"It's a silverskin or my aunt don't have fleas," said another in an orange hat that looked like an oven mitt.

Avielle stopped ten feet away from them when they all began shouting at her.

"Silverskin!"

"Filthy silverskin!"

"Go back to Dredonia!"

"Spy! Spy!"

Avielle backed away. The tall boy wearing the orange oven mitt bent down, scooped up a handful of mud, and flung it at her. It struck her right shoulder. Then all the boys started scooping up handfuls of mud and rocks. Avielle turned and ran. Mud pelted her back. A rock struck her neck with a flash of pain. Footsteps pounded behind her, coming closer and closer. Avielle reached the street and darted into the crowd, weaving through the people until she had left the boys behind. Filthy and sobbing, she made her way back to the shop.

The door was locked; Gamalda must have gone out. Avielle unlocked the door with the key Gamalda had given her, went inside, and locked the door again behind her.

Avielle unfastened the clasp on her filthy cloak; it made a slight hissing sound as it slipped over her shoulders and dropped to the floor in the middle of the front room. She did not pick it up. A moment later she was in the kitchen pumping water into an old, stained wooden bowl. When it was full she carried it into Gamalda's dyeing room.

She found black dye and mixed it into the water, the wooden spoon thunking against the side of the bowl. Avielle reached up and drew out the hairpins in her hair, pinching the smooth, thin metal slips with her fingers, and then dropping them onto the table. When they were all out, she unbraided her hair, shook it free, and combed it out with her fingers; it fell to her waist.

She stood looking down at the liquid in the bowl, a black pool, a dark well without stars, without moon. Avielle gathered her hair straight up from the crown of her head, bent, and dunked her head in the bowl. She swirled her silver hair around and around in the black dye, her fingers scuttling like little spiders to work it in, until her hair and her hands turned black.

"Your hair may be black, your clothes black, but your skin is as silver as the moon. You'll never change that," said Gamalda later that afternoon when she came back from her errand and saw what Avielle had done. "Don't you see? Don't you know the moon's beautiful? Haven't you seen it shine as it slips against the stars? Doesn't it guide us in the darkness?" She put the package she had been carrying down on the table and her bracelets clinked. "Oh, Avielle, why did you do this?"

"Because I want to be safe! Hatred is growing against silverskins. People are blaming us for all the evil the Black Cloaks have done—and are still doing." She told Gamalda what had happened at the grocer's and in the alley.

Gamalda was silent for a long time, her fingers running over the package. At last, she sat down. "There are pigs in the world. Many pigs. And there's evil brought into the world by those who have turned toward the Malaquasana in their hearts. But there's only one way to truly be safe from them—from anything!"

"How?" Avielle asked.

"By the thoughts that you think in your head. Safety comes only from how you look at the world. It exists only in the mind. There is no safe way to look—the color of your hair doesn't matter—and there is no safe place to be." She paused, gazing at Avielle. "But there's something more to this act of dyeing your hair. Something deeper. You want to deny everything about yourself that's Dredonian."

Avielle said nothing.

"I know why," Gamalda continued. "Because there were fools—fools! Who thought that you might be like your Dredonian great-great grandmother Dolvoka. And they pounded it into you until you came to believe them."

Avielle sat on her black-stained hands. Her shoulders hunched.

"Then there's the question of the belt," Gamalda said. "The belt with the shimmering golden fireflies that shone upon the drape. Which we've never talked about."

"It was nothing. I was mistaken."

"Don't lie!" Gamalda's voice was stern. She rubbed one of the bracelets on her wrist, a silver one with a blue stone, and then looked at Avielle, who was still standing before her. "Don't lie about this. You have a magic gift for weaving, I tell you. Ignore it at your peril. For if you do, you'll continue to slip away from the truth of who you are. Just as you've done step-by-step throughout your life because of the way you've been treated." She leaned forward and slapped the table. "How could anyone have raised a child so. The brutes!"

"You think they did wrong?"

"Of course they did wrong!"

Avielle felt something snap and slip and slide inside her; it was as though she had been thrown a stick in the water to save her from drowning, but she did not know how to clasp it.

"And now you're doing wrong to yourself," Gamalda said. "Listen to me, Avielle. The magic that comes from your Dredonian blood could be a source of great strength to you."

"You don't understand!" Avielle held out her black hands. "I fear . . . to do harm. To do evil."

Gamalda stood up. She seemed to grow taller and taller, a tree stretching from root to crown.

"You are not her," she said. "Do you understand me? Listen well. *You are not her.* You are Avielle, an individual, a princess, in your own right. And I tell you that magic power by itself doesn't make a person good or evil. You choose whether to use it for good or evil."

Avielle scrubbed her black dress against her blackened hand, but the dye would not come off. "I wish I could believe you. I so wish it."

"I've waited too long for your grief to end," Gamalda said. "Come. I've got something to show you. Something that might help."

Avielle followed Gamalda up the stairs to the second floor where Gamalda had three rooms: a bedroom, a small sitting room, and a little room for keeping accounts. But Gamalda did not stop there. She opened another door, a door that led to a place Gamalda had told her she wished to keep private. Avielle had, of course, abided by her wishes.

They started up a second flight of stairs. Gamalda let her fingers brush lightly against the banister; both it and the stairs had been varnished to a golden color, making a soft glow against white walls that were neither scuffed nor stained. When Avielle put her weight on the seventh step, it creaked, but even the creak seemed mellifluous. Then the stairs stopped, and they stood on the third floor.

Avielle thought she had stepped into a room of pure

light—soft, suffused light that shone through the three tall windows at the front of the room, and through the two skylights on the ceiling. Then she saw weavings of all colors and sizes and shapes hanging on white walls.

"Oh!" Avielle exclaimed. "May I look?"

"Of course," Gamalda said. "That's why I've brought you here. I've got my best work hanging on these walls."

Avielle walked to the weaving straight in front of her. It showed a scene of quaking aspens, their trunks silver white with black circles, their leaves green coins. The craftsmanship was finer than anything Avielle had ever seen before, and she did not understand how many of the stitches had been made. As she looked, the leaves turned yellow and fell from the tree, some lifting and swirling as though a breeze blew them. Avielle's mouth opened. Then, leaves gone, the trees showed the bare filigreed branches of winter. A few moments later, the fresh, new leaves of spring uncurled.

"How can this be?" Avielle asked Gamalda. But Gamalda only pointed to the next weaving.

It was simpler but even more exquisite. It showed a waterfall cascading from a high cliff, tumbling and frothing over rocks, throwing up plumes of white spray until it finally fell in a silver sheet into a cirque below. But the waterfall was moving; the wind it whipped up made the ferns sway.

Avielle rushed from one weaving to the other, barely waiting to look at one before going to the next. A moon waxed and waned as it rolled through a starry sky. A meadow of wildflowers—red, gold, yellow—blew back and forth in the wind. A path bent and wound through a forest of trees. A tulip unfolded from bud to flower. A deer grew from fawn to stag—with a magnificent rack of antlers on its head. Finally, a sun rose in swathes of pink, purple, and gold, heralding the day to come.

It was magic, magic such as Avielle had never seen before in her life; magic of light, goodness, and beauty. There was no evil here. Indeed, whatever this was, surely it was powerful enough to stand against evil.

Avielle felt the light in the room wash over her, felt it cup her in its hand, felt what she could only describe as the brush of a wing on her cheek. She turned slowly back to Gamalda and raised her stained, black hands into a ray of sun.

"Teach me," she said.

THE LADY ON THE BLACK HORSE
CHAPTER SIXTEEN

"Your magic power, of course, comes from your Dredonian blood," Gamalda said. "It's the source of your weaving gift." She and Avielle sat together in the kitchen later than night. They had cleared away the supper dishes and were eating slices of apple torte—sweet with walnuts, cinnamon, and sugar forming a brown crust on the top. "Finding your magic won't be easy," Gamalda added, cutting the last piece of her torte. It was their final treat before they began to ration their food, for who knew when the vendors would start coming to the city again.

"What do you mean?" Avielle asked.

"To find it you must turn and embrace the Dredonian part of yourself—yes, I know you loathe and fear it. And you've defended against it for so long that the path to it will be well guarded. It'll be difficult to reach. Perhaps"—she tapped her fork against her plate— "perhaps even impossible. It's covered by the dark and has got to be brought into the light." She ate the last bite of apple torte, then went on.

"But I tell you, this is the only way you'll get rid of your great-great grandmother's shadow. And you've just got to get rid of it, Avielle! And this is the only way you'll find your own magic gift, and discover the truth of who you are."

Avielle sighed. "Where must I go?"

"Go?"

"To walk this path you speak of. To begin searching for my magic. Where in the kingdom do I begin?"

Gamalda smiled. "Right here. You will search for your magic by weaving on my loom on the third floor. I believe that your weaving will lead you to the magic power in your Dredonian blood." She paused, then added, "And, in turn, your magic power will lead you to be a weaver of great power."

Avielle considered. How was such a thing done? There were no roads, no landmarks, no maps.

"But I have woven many times before without anything magical happening," she said. "The fireflies on the belt were the only exception. So why should weaving on the loom on your third floor be any different?"

"Because I'll teach you a chant," Gamalda said. "A chant that will lead you into a dream trance as you weave. Take you down to a place were you can link with your magic. It's the same chant I use."

Avielle was silent for a moment. Then she asked, "why do you hide your magic weavings on the third floor?"

Gamalda pulled out a strand of blue yarn from her

pocket and began running it through her fingers. "Because they're my refuge. When I had them in the shop, people used to crowd in just to see them—what a madhouse! Let me tell you, it became impossible to do business. I never sell them. I occasionally give one away to the right person."

"How did you find out about your magic?" Avielle asked. "Did you always know? Or did you have to search for it, like Tinty?"

Gamalda made a loop out of the thread. "I came from a poor family in the mountains of Iorenna—oh, how those white cliffs loomed up! My parents discovered my gift. I went from teacher to teacher, to bigger and bigger towns until at last I came to a man called Pelanol. He had a moist red mouth like a crack in a tomato." Gamalda shuddered. "But he was the greatest weaver of magical power in Rhia. He took me in as his apprentice, not without a grudge, mind you. For he was a proud, greedy man who didn't want to surrender his secrets. I learned all I could, but after awhile . . . I knew the heart of my magic was missing.

"I began to travel across the land searching for I knew not what. Then one day as I was riding through a piney wood, I came upon a little white cottage. An old woman came out. I asked her if I might fill my water skin at her well."

"Yes, come," she said. Hobbling, she led me through the woods up along a brook. We came to the place where the brook bubbled out of the earth.

"Here is the door to what you desire," the old woman

said. "It leads to the source. Caught in the trees, caught in the wind, in the sound of water, in the creak of trees, in the glitter of snow, in the colors of the flowers—from these come the source of your magic. Yet, this is only the beginning.

"Take this stone lest you forget." And she left me alone. For three days I stayed at the source of the brook. And let me tell you, what I learned there is beyond words to say. But you may have noticed that all my magic weavings are of the natural world. The chant of the dream trance came to me there. I went back to the cottage to thank the old woman, but she was gone. I left her a length of fine blue wool and rode on."

"It sounds like a fairy tale," Avielle said.

"Yes!" Gamalda laughed. " But there's this." She slipped the silver bracelet with the blue stone off her wrist. "It's the stone she gave me. I had it made into this bracelet, and I wear it always."

Avielle picked up the bracelet. The stone was blue, the size of a thumbnail, with layers of crystals thrusting out from one end. Roses twined, engraved upon the silver.

"It's the same kind of stone that surrounded the brook," Gamalda said.

Avielle pulled her plate back and ate the rest of her apple torte. As she felt the crunch of walnuts between her teeth, and the tang of apple on her tongue, she weighed everything she knew about herself and her situation. She pressed down her fork, lifting every crumb on her plate, taking as long as possible. Finally the only thing left to do was to lick the plate, and, regrettably, she was still too much of a princess to do that.

"I am frightened," Avielle said. "But I will try to find my magic. I will take up the shuttle and weave on the third floor."

Avielle crept down a dark tunnel with obsidian walls as sharp and jagged as teeth. Water dripped in the distance—plopping, echoing—with pauses in between each drip. Somewhere in the back of her mind, Avielle knew she was weaving on the loom on the third floor, but Gamalda had used the chant to lead her deep into a trance, and her mind was ranging free of her hands. It was the morning after their conversation about magic.

When Avielle at last came out of the tunnel, she saw a round hall ringed with seven arched doorways. All the doorways were open except one. Before that doorway, a beast from a nightmare loomed eight feet above her. Its breath smelled of excrement. Its seven red eyes—all watching her—glowed above its snout. Black and purple scales covered its hind legs, which were shaped like a lion's. Oddly, it had human hands, huge, with nails like claws; its left hand was bleeding. Avielle was about to choose one of the other doorways, then changed her mind.

"Stand aside," she said, taking a step forward. "And let me pass." The beast merely swiped out its bloody hand, picked her up, and scooped her inside its slavering mouth.

Avielle screamed as its fangs bit through her flesh and crunched her bones. At last, it swallowed her. Down she slid, down and down, until she fell into burning black sand. She lay for a moment, her heart pounding, then sat up. Sand crusted her cheek and scratched her eyes; and when she looked up, sand stretched around her in a desert where an orange sun blazed overhead.

Avielle saw lines traced into the black sand as though someone had drawn them there with a stick. They sketched the shape of a crown. Thirst came over her, thirst as she had never known or imagined, thirst so great that she would surely die. Her tongue shriveled to a dry old rag.

Then she heard the sound of horse's hooves and, with a great effort, lifted her head and looked over her shoulder.

A black horse ridden by a woman in black galloped toward her. She rode sidesaddle, and her long skirt of black taffeta, velvet, and shining silk trailed behind her. As she grew near, she dropped to a trot. Over her face hung a whisper of a black veil, so sheer that Avielle could see the woman's face beneath it. Her skin was fair. Her lips were red. Her golden hair wound in a coronet upon her head. In her left hand was a silver goblet sloshing with water.

Avielle staggered up, raising her hands to grasp the goblet.

The woman, looking straight ahead, held out the goblet and, with a flick of her wrist, overturned it so the water splashed onto Avielle's head.

Avielle cried out, reaching toward the woman as she rode away. Avielle sank down into the burning sand. A single drop of water fell on her parched tongue.

She heard a voice from far away calling her name, "Avielle! Avielle!" It was Gamalda calling her back. Avielle floated up and up—it seemed an immense way that took endless years to travel—until at last she felt her hands weaving. She opened her eyes.

"Avielle?" Gamalda's voice sounded in her ear. Gamalda's hand gripped her shoulder.

Avielle stopped weaving and slumped forward over the beam on the loom.

"You're all right, Avielle," Gamalda said over and over. "You're here. You're safe."

Avielle's hands, however, were shaking.

"Look!" Gamalda exclaimed. "Look how much you wove in only two hours. Your hands moved so fast I couldn't follow them. It was magic, Avielle, magic."

Avielle straightened, looked down at the cloth she had woven—it was five feet long, most wound on the cloth storage beam—and then cried out. It was black, but in the middle was a lump of dark purple and blue, like a horrible bruise. Then she leaned closer. In the very center, fine as a hair on a baby's cheek, a thread of silver ran and rippled like water.

DARIEN AND MASTER KEENUM
CHAPTER SEVENTEEN

"Answer the door, Darien, lad," Avielle heard a man say after she had knocked on the door of Master Keenum's rooms; they were above *Candle Magic*, Mistress Rocat's shop on the corner.

A week had passed, during which Avielle had woven twice more on the third floor; both times, however, she had only wandered weeping through dark empty corridors. The cloth she wove was solid gray, and the only thing magical about it was the speed with which she had woven it, and the way the white thread initially upon the loom had changed color. She felt she was getting nowhere, but Gamalda counseled patience. Gamalda had sent her to Master Keenum's to pick up some thread, for he was a spinner. Avielle was not looking forward to seeing Darien.

The door opened, and Darien looked out.

"Oh," he said. "You." He blocked the doorway. He was as tall as she was, though he was a year younger. His tufts of straw-colored hair stuck out like guards, and even his ears—protruding from his head like cabbages cut in half—seemed to obstruct her way.

Avielle had seen Darien a few more times since the incident in Gamalda's shop when he had revealed his hatred for silverskins—and her. Except for one quick startled glance when he had seen her black hair, he had avoided her—and she him.

"Gamalda sent me to pick up some thread from Master Keenum," Avielle said. "May I come in?"

Darien did not move.

"Don't go forgetting your manners, lad," said Master Keenum. "Come in Miss Vianna, dearie."

Darien stepped aside at last, and Avielle went in. She found herself in a large tidy room with a bed in one corner piled a foot high with colorful quilts; they hung down the side of the bed one over the other in stair steps of color. Put a body beneath that pile of quilts, Avielle thought, and you could generate enough heat to boil a kettle on top. To the left of the bed stood a long rickety table with dust snared in its curving legs. On it was a battered book; a bottle of ink; a piece of brown wrapping paper covered with letters that looked smeared and blotted; and a pen. At the back of the room, behind a blue looped-back curtain, Avielle could see a small kitchen with a cot. Probably Darien's bed.

But the oddest thing about the room was the stones. Stones were lined up on the mantle over the fireplace, stones sat on a little table near the door, and stones lay in circles on the tops of overturned flower pots, all with precision, all with intent. Round oblong, square, rectangular—other stones had no particular shape at all. They were smooth and jagged, shot with crystals, pocked with holes.

"Come, let me see you, Miss Vianna," said Master Keenum, who sat before a spinning wheel. "I've heard snippets and snaps about you from the good folk here on Postern Street. Ears can hear even if eyes can't see."

Avielle walked over and stood in front of him. She could see at once that he was blind, because his eyes were a cloudy opaque blue, and his head tipped to the left with that intent listening look that blind people sometimes had.

"I am pleased to make your acquaintance, Master Keenum," Avielle said.

"Your voice," he said, "the sound of it—I think, yes. Bring me Lidel, Darien, lad." Darien walked over to one of the overturned flower pots, selected a rough black rock that had bands of white crystals bursting out from one side, and put it into Master Keenum's hand.

As Avielle watched Master Keenum rub it with his thumb, she wondered if all the rocks had names.

"Umm," he mused. "The contrast here. The dark rough stone with the smooth white crystals inside. And the pull between them. Umm. Take it if you will, Vianna, take it, my dearie, and rub it in your hand."

Avielle did.

"Now, if you please, let me have the rock back and give me your hand."

Avielle gave him her hand, suddenly glad that most of the black dye had worn off, even though he would not have been able to see it. Master Keenum felt her fingers, pulling them gently and twisting them. His own hands were neither rough nor smooth, but had blue veins thick as old roots. He pressed his thumb against her palm. He tested how her hand and fingers flexed, then ran his own fingers over her knuckles. After various other tests, he seemed satisfied and released her hand.

"Well now, well," he said. "Lidel tells me snippets and snaps about a person," he said. "I wanted to see what she'd tell me about you."

"You have a magic gift," Avielle said, startled. "You are a Dredonian Rhian, though you do not look it."

"Ha!" He laughed. "You'd never guess my ears are pointed under all this thicket of gray hair, would you? But they are, pointed as the sickle moon. But never mind that, never mind, my sweet dearie. Let me tell you what Lidel tells me. She says you have many friends."

"I am afraid I have few friends," Avielle said. Darien would be pleased to hear that.

"Nonsense! Stone doesn't lie. Perhaps you have few friends now, but one day you'll have plenty. And that's not all, no, not by a long shot. There's still a feast to be had from Lidel. She says your friends will save you. Imagine that! From what, though, that's the question. Ah, she's cryptic, my little Lidel is. But that's her nature and there's no gainsaying it.

"But enough of that." He dropped Lidel in his lap and folded his hands. "You seem a fine enough girl. Tinty likes you, too. I hear tell you've already experienced some of her wayward magic."

"Yes, sir, I have." Avielle tried to keep her voice steady, though her mind was wildly chasing after what he had said.

"Once Tinty came here to try her hand at magical spinning. She spun all right, but the spindle kept turning into a sheep's head and baaing. Isn't that right, Darien?"

"Yes, sir."

"Well, well," Master Keenum said. "But you've come for Gamalda's thread. There's the package ready on the table."

Startled to hear that so many people on Postern Street were talking about her, Avielle went to the table. Beside the package lay the battered book and the piece of blotted, smeared paper she had noticed earlier. She bent forward and saw that someone had been practicing writing the alphabet. There was a long row of *S*'s, all sadly mangled.

"Is this your writing, Darien?" she asked.

"It's nothing," he mumbled.

"Nothing!" Master Keenum exclaimed. "Why the lad's

trying to get him some learning. Can't afford the schools yet, though he's saving all he can."

"You're trying to learn to read and write all by yourself?" Avielle asked.

Darien shrugged. He pulled on the shoulder of his sleeve and let it sink back.

Avielle picked up the book. It was a primer, the corners dog-eared, the pages dirty, torn, and swollen, as though the book had been left out in the rain. As she leafed through it something tightened in her chest. She'd had the finest education money could buy and a library full of the best books in the kingdom. Never had she thought there might be children struggling to learn with almost nothing to help them. Avielle had always assumed they would all go to school. That some could not afford school had never occurred to her.

Why? Because she had never left the High Hall. Because, in her lifelong struggle against Dolvoka, she had thought only of how the people hated her, never about the state of their lives. There had been no room in her mind for that. Avielle looked at Darien, who was staring back at her.

Teach him to read, said a voice inside her. She dropped the book as though it had burned her hands. Why should she help him? Because . . . because she could. She could offer to, anyway, even if he refused. Offering seemed to be the essential thing.

"The weight of ten thousand stones hangs in the silence of this room," said Master Keenum. "What's wrong, dearies?"

"If you would like, Darien," Avielle said at last, "it would be a great honor for me to teach you to read and write."

A light dawned in Darien's face. Then he picked up a jagged gray stone and hefted it in his hands. Avielle wondered if he were going to throw it at her.

"I don't think so," he said.

"Why not?"

"Because you're a silverskin."

Avielle hunched her shoulders. In the past, she would have left or used her humor to draw a protective ring around herself. But this time she did not run. This time she drew no ring.

"What's all this nonsense, Darien?" Master Keenum asked. "Can you hear the color of skin? Tell me lad, just what does it sound like?"

Darien said nothing.

"Silence speaks, too, lad. You're a boy. Avielle here's a girl. You're both Rhians. Both kind and good, with pretty good voices, too—these old ears haven't failed me yet. What more is there?"

Again, Darien did not speak.

"Take a chance when it comes your way, lad," Master Keenum urged. "Remember those dreams knocking around in your head? Don't let fool notions about the color of someone's skin stop you."

Avielle, watching different emotions struggle over Darien's face, wondered what his dreams were.

"All right," he said, though still defiant.

"Shall we begin with *S*?" she asked.

PEARLS
CHAPTER EIGHTEEN

"A Black Cloak murdered them in their beds," said Mistress Pea, her voice like a trumpet played by an angry child. It was early the next afternoon. "The whole family. Leatherworkers, they were. Door thrown down. Screams. Shouts. Beyond imagining, the neighbors said. I have it all on the best authority. I know Master Bundy who knows Mistress Etimorra who knew the family next door. He knows I'm a woman to be reckoned with and would never dare tell me a lie."

There was too much relish in Mistress Pea's voice, Avielle thought, looking at her with distaste. They stood with some of the other occupants of Postern Street. They had gathered outside Master Lughgor's stained glass window shop, *Windows Refulgent,* which was across the street from Gamalda's shop and Master Steorra's shop—he was an astrologer—and on the opposite end of the block from Augum Aslee's.

The Black Cloak had struck only four blocks away. Avielle drew the silver and white shawl Gamalda had given her tighter, her fingers combing the fringe over and over, but she could not pull it tight enough, close enough. If only she had a cloak to wrap around herself, a cloak with voluminous folds that would protect her. Instead, she draped the shawl like a scarf over her head, pinching it beneath her chin with her thumb and forefinger.

The Black Cloaks could have struck here on Postern Street. But they did not, she told herself over and over, they did not. Yet, how could she be glad of that when it meant someone else had died? And somewhere someone was dying each night. She closed her eyes.

"The High Council must put a stop to this!" exclaimed Mistress Alubra, the silversmith. She was wearing a hat with a light gray veil drawn over her face. "They must submit to Dredonia's demands. Send the slaves and surrender the mines. How much more must we suffer before we can be safe again?"

"It's the five thousand slaves who'll suffer," said Master Lughgor. He had a nose like a pillow with a dent in it. "And it won't stop with that yearly tribute. The Brethren will want more. You'll see. A piece at a time, sure enough. You've got to see it. The king and queen did, may they rest in the arms of the Goddess."

"He's right!" Darien said. "We can't give in."

Saracinda cleared her throat. Saracinda, Avielle knew, was one of Master Lughgor's apprentices. Also in the crowd were Mistress Rocat, the candlemaker, and a few other apprentices. Several shop owners on this block on Postern Street—Master Steorra, whose shop was called *Celestial Confabulations*, and Master Cavenda of *Cavenda Books: Books of Now, Then, and Yet to Be*—had not come out. Neither had Augum Aslee, Master Keenum, or Gamalda. Tinty, however, kept wandering in and out of the crowd, looking for coins in the street.

"It's really," Saracinda said, "well I don't know. But it could be quite true. But then it might not be so." Her words came out as softly as petals rubbing in a breeze. "The queen might know what to do, were she still alive. What do you think, Vianna?"

Avielle stood dumb. From a place inside her came a shameful thought that she had hidden away ever since the whirlwind hit. However, now that the Black Cloaks had struck so close, so very close, the thought rushed forward, and she could not hide from it any longer.

"The High Council must send the slaves," she said. "So the terror will stop." Her cheeks grew hot. Her words lay there for all to see. But it was the truth; it was what had to be done.

"Our wizards will find a way," said Mistress Rocat in her breathy voice. "They'll never waver. They'll defeat the Black Cloaks."

"Dead in your bed, or slave in a mine," said Tinty, spinning a tiras coin in the air. "Some choice. I'd rather take a bath in a thorn thicket."

"They struck so close," Avielle said. "Should we set a watch? Gather weapons?"

"Don't you know anything?" Darien glared at Avielle. "They're specters. Magical constructs. Arrows go right through them."

"Then how will we be safe?" Avielle asked. "What shall we do?"

"Eat breakfast," Tinty advised. "Who's making jam-cakes?"

"Gamalda!" Avielle cried, rushing into the shop later that afternoon. She had just picked up the latest broadsheet from the Peas'. Gamalda was not in the front room. "Gamalda!" Avielle cried again.

Gamalda came running out from the weaving room. "What is it? What's wrong?"

"Read this!" Avielle threw the broadsheet down on the counter, and as Gamalda read it, Avielle—still unbelieving—read it again herself.

PRINCESS AVIELLE MAY STILL BE ALIVE!

According to Grig Durdin, former head coachman at the High Hall, who survived the whirlwind, Her Royal Highness Princess Avielle may still be alive. He claims he saw the princess leave the High Hall shortly before the whirlwind hit. When Durdin was

asked, "Was the princess running away to save herself, as though she knew the whirlwind was about to hit? Do you think she was—considering she had Dolvoka's evil blood—in league with the Dredonians' plan?"

Avielle let out a strangled cry. Gamalda put one hand on her arm.

"Well, that's the odd thing," Durdin said. "She wasn't running. She was walking real slow-like, like someone in a dream. It was dark, but I'd swear it was her. I thought she just stepped out for air 'cause she didn't have no cloak on, only a shawl that trailed behind her all white and sparkly like. And she weren't carrying no luggage like a person might if they was going to flee."

When asked why he waited so long to convey this information to the High Council, Durdin said, "I took a brick to my head during the whirlwind. I've only just now got all my wits back to me."

If Princess Avielle is alive, why hasn't she come forward? Was she, too, wounded during the whirlwind and lies somewhere out of her wits? Or has she fled the city in fear of the Black Cloaks? The High Council is offering a sizable reward for information leading to her whereabouts. But, to quote Lord General

Maldreck, "Even if the princess were found, I doubt the people would accept one so polluted to be their queen. We are better off rid of her. Let a new dynasty begin." However, High Councilman Herector says, "The princess is the last of the royal family, the last of the House of Coroll that has ruled our kingdom for seven hundred years. If she is alive, we should at least consider the possibility that she should be our queen." It is the opinion of this writer, however, that most of the populace would agree with Lord General Maldreck.

If Princess Avielle is not found, the High Council will wait through six months of mourning the royal family before they select a new dynasty to rule Rhia.

She should be our queen. The words turned into little black sticks and circles before Avielle's eyes. She had thought that, in the unlikely chance she decided to reveal who she was, she would come forward as a princess. But this, she saw now, was wrong. If she came forward now, she would come forward as the *Queen of Rhia*. Nothing in her life had prepared her for that eventuality. It was as far beyond her as a cedar tree was above a blade of grass. It was a role she did not want, a role the people did not want her in . . . *would the people ever except one so polluted for their queen?* A queen, unless she was a tyrant, had to care about the good of the people. Avielle did not think she could ever care about those who thought so ill of her.

Avielle put her head in her hands. "Now the Black

Cloaks will hunt me, and the people will hunt me, too, for the reward. I am not safe here anymore. I may even bring danger to you. I do not know what to do."

"There are many silverskins in the city," Gamalda said. "And, mind you, they don't even know for certain whether you're alive. But you best go veiled now whenever you leave the shop. We'll simply tell our kind neighbors that you want to keep your complexion fair. Let them think you are vain."

With steps as slow, measured, and stately as those of a princess following a bier, Avielle walked through a huge chamber, its ceiling and walls lost in a black cloud that hovered overhead. She knew she was weaving on Gamalda's loom on the third floor late that same afternoon, but her mind was ranging free in a dream trance. Her long, heavy skirt rustled; it was all black—taffeta, silk, possibly velvet—but she was not certain because she wore black leather gloves that kept her from feeling the cloth. As she walked, she made no sound for she trod on dead, dank leaves that smelled of rot. She took off her hat and veil so that she could see better, let them trail after her for a while, then let them drop away. After what seemed like years, she saw a row of short sticks stretching away in endless rows on either side of her.

She stopped to look at them. They were candles, black ones, whose wicks looked as though they had never been burned. She reached down to touch one, thinking maybe she could find a way to light it and brighten this gloomy place, but then she sucked in her breath and drew back her hand. For the candle was the skeleton of a finger, the bones as black as though they had been charred in a fire. All of the candlesticks were black skeletal fingers; they pushed out of the ground with wicks springing from the bone tips. The shadows they cast were shaped like black crowns.

Avielle hurried away down the center aisle, her heart beating fast. She must get away.

A man in an old brown hat stepped in front of her.

Avielle stopped. The man picked up her right hand and pulled off her glove. Then he pulled off her left glove, too. He held out a pearl, which shone, faintly luminous, and placed it in her left hand. Then he vanished. Avielle rushed on. A girl in a pink dress stepped in front of Avielle and gave her another pearl. She, too, vanished.

And so it went. Avielle would run a few steps through the dead candles, and then someone would appear and put a pearl in her cupped hands. When both her hands were full of pearls, she came to a door made of black oak. Although Avielle leaned against it, it did not budge. There was neither knob nor latch. And she could not have opened it anyway because her hands were full of pearls.

Avielle felt a menace growing behind her; she glanced over her shoulder and saw the dead candles marching toward her. She turned back to the door, lifted her cupped palms, and threw the pearls against the black oak. Without a sound, the door opened; she ran through, and heard it slam shut behind her.

Avielle came out of the dream trance. Her hands had stopped weaving, though she still clutched the shuttle. Gamalda put her hand on Avielle's shoulder.

"Look, Avielle," she said.

With a great effort, Avielle straightened and looked down at the loom. The weaving was black, dotted here and there with dots of white shiny thread—like pearls.

"I do not understand what it means," Avielle said to Gamalda later when she tried to explain what had happened in the vision. They were in the kitchen washing dishes. Gamalda, who was drying them, put one away in the cupboard; it clinked against the others in the stack.

"You don't need to understand, not precisely, anyway," Gamalda said. "Such visions come from a place in our minds that is full of images. Kind of like a painting. Something that we can only understand intuitively." Today she wore blue, a sapphire blue, and Avielle thought she was like the sky: big, free, and vast.

"Sometimes grasping after meaning too hard makes it slip away," Gamalda added. "Don't work too hard at all this, Avielle. Don't spend too much time weaving on the third floor or thinking about the visions you have there. Not to the exclusion of everything else. That could be harmful. I tell you, magic can't be rushed. It'll bloom in its own time. Meanwhile, you should get out more. Go see Tinty. Go meet everybody on Postern Street. You're too much alone, Avielle, I think."

"But I like being alone. I feel uncomfortable with other people."

"Exactly my point. You've retreated, just as you did in the High Hall. And there's no reason to anymore. What you feared and retreated from—people thinking you were like Dolvoka—doesn't exist here. Nobody knows who you are."

"It exists in my mind," Avielle said. She had never told Gamalda about the portrait; indeed, it was a secret she would bear to her tomb, even into the afterlife, if there was one.

"I know," Gamalda said. "That's one of the reasons why you're seeking your magic. But you can also learn about the people here, get to know them. My neighbors are wonderful! You may be surprised at what learning about other people teaches you about yourself. And they can learn about you, too."

Avielle plunged the last dish into the soapy water and scrubbed hard. Who would want to know her and why? For her vivacious personality? Her radiant beauty? Or, more possibly, her sparkling conversation? Perhaps she should tell them she looked like Dolvoka. That would certainly provide an interesting opening for conversation. She sighed. Whatever she did, most likely they would all eject her from their shops with boots placed on her body in various embarrassing places.

NOW, THEN, AND YET TO BE
CHAPTER NINETEEN

The front of Mistress Rocat's shop, *Candle Magic,* as the sign said in golden scrolling letters, was made of slightly crumbling bricks. Avielle touched one, and little crumbs of mortar came away in her fingers. It was Wednesday, and two days had passed since her vision of the Hall of the Dead Candles. It was the first day of fall, the twenty-first day of Septess, and the weather had turned cool. The sign, caught by a gust of wind, creaked over her head as she opened the door to the shop. Gamalda had given her money to buy candles.

Avielle's first sensation was a wave of warmth; next, a pleasant wave of smells—lavender, mint, musk, beeswax; then, and this superceded all the other sensations: light. All of these came from the candles. However, the curious thing, Avielle thought as she walked toward the counter, was the way Mistress Rocat had displayed her candles. Many were simply hung on hooks on the walls, but others stood—unlit—in concentric circles on the tables. However, in the center of each circle, one candle burned like a flaming heart.

"Miss Vianna," said a soft voice. "What is your wish this day?"

But Avielle, transfixed by the burning candles in the centers of the circles, did not answer. The burning candles were all different sizes and shapes, some tall and slender, others mere stubs. She had the distinct impression that she had entered a temple to some unknown, but exalted and esoteric, god.

"Did Gamalda send you on an errand?" Mistress Rocat asked, clearing her throat.

"Oh, yes." Avielle looked up. "Forgive me, Mistress Rocat. I was just admiring your unique arrangement of candles."

"I myself think it rather beautiful," Mistress Rocat said. She spoke in a whispery voice, as though afraid of blowing out her candles. When she walked out from behind the counter, Avielle noticed something extremely peculiar about her. She was wearing her clothes inside out. Did she wish to draw attention to their quality by showing the beauty of their stitching? What a remarkable idea. But no, Avielle saw upon looking closer. The stitching was actually coming loose in places, as evidenced by straggling threads here and there. Though Mistress Rocat was thin and willowy, her clothes were tight.

"You see," said Mistress Rocat, walking through the room and gesturing with her rather large hands, "all the red candles are in one circle, the blues in another, and so on. And where the circles intersect—what surprises of color then! My flames never waver. That is my magical gift." She smiled. "I myself think it rather wonderful—if you'll excuse my saying so."

And indeed, Avielle saw, Mistress Rocat had pointed ears that tapered like one of the flames on her candles.

"I'm so very sorry to hear about your family," Mistress Rocat said.

Somewhat startled, Avielle looked at her. Did everyone on Postern Street know everything about her?

"Thank you for your kindness," Avielle said.

At that moment the door burst open, and a man whose skin was as black as a dark closet rushed in and slammed the door behind him. He had a pen stuck behind each ear.

"Almost out of candles—work will come to a screeching halt," he said. "As usual then?"

"Certainly, Master Steorra," Mistress Rocat answered, stepping back a little before his vehemence.

Master Steorra, who, Avielle recalled, owned *Celestial Confabulations* on the east side of Gamalda's shop, ran around blowing out the candles in the centers of the circles. He plucked them out, tall ones and stubs alike, and bundled them in his arms.

"Send the bill—as usual?" he asked. "Can't stop now—just on the verge of a breakthrough—fabulous stuff, but that dreadful Mistress Zinan's coming for another astrological reading. Wants to know if her husband will make a fortune. Ha! Bottle-nosed beetle. Blasted nuisance."

"I'll send the bill as usual, Master Steorra," Mistress Rocat said. "Good-bye."

The man rushed out of the shop.

"My," said Avielle. She had seen Master Steorra once or twice striding past Gamalda's shop, but had never spoken to him. He always seemed to be leaning forward as though he wanted to be six paces ahead of himself. Gamalda had told her he was eccentric. He was an astrologer and interpreted the positions of the stars and planets to read people's fortunes. But he was also some kind of poor scientist. "Why did he take only the candles in the centers of the circles?" Avielle asked. "And why purchase stubs?"

Mistress Rocat shrugged. "Who knows about that man? They say he has a strange contraption in the little courtyard behind his shop. Uses it to look at distant stars. I myself think we have no business with such things. If the Goddess meant us to see them, she'd have put them in sight of our very own eyes."

She winked her little eyes several times very fast. "What we really need to see is what's going on in the High Council. Every one of them will be scheming to be pronounced the new king or queen when the country comes out of mourning. I myself think Lord General Maldreck will win."

Lord General Maldreck! Avielle's throat tightened. That man with no neck take her father's place? Impossible. And Mistress Maldreck as queen? She had the face of a lizard and sniffed all her food.

"Well, we shall see, won't we, dear?" Mistress Rocat said.

"Yes," Avielle said. "We shall see." She bought four dozen white candles for Gamalda, thanked Mistress Rocat, and left.

Late that night, Avielle took seven of Mistress Rocat's candles to her little room off the kitchen. She lit one. Then she held the end of another candle in the flame until it softened. She pressed it down on top of the old dresser and slowly let go. The candle stood straight up. Avielle repeated this until six candles stood in a circle. She placed another candle in the center. Then, after lighting a match, she lit one of the candles in the circle and said, "Mother." She lit a second and said, "Father." On and on she went lighting candles and saying names until she had also lit candles for Ismine, Cerine, Mildon, and Rajio. She stepped back, looking at the circle of flame. The candle in the center, however, she did not light. It stood there, its wick drooping, bereft, in darkness.

As she lay in bed thinking of Lord Maldreck becoming king, she felt a rushing in her blood as though all her Rhian ancestors were speaking to her, pleading with her not to let the House of Coroll fall. And then a voice, quite clear, did speak.

Avielle! Light-Bringer! You are the last of our kind. You are our only hope for Rhia. You must not fail us!

Avielle sat straight up in bed, looking, listening. But the room was empty.

* * *

The next morning Avielle stood on Postern Street looking up at the sign above the bookseller's door. *Cavenda Books: Books of Now, Then, and Yet to Be.* The shop, painted brown, had paint flaking off here and there. The two big windows had no blinds or drapes, and they stared, looking out at the world, unblinking as an owl.

Avielle put her hand on the brass doorknob. She had come partly because of Gamalda's suggestion that she meet the people on Postern Street, and partly because she missed the Royal Library at the High Hall. Gamalda had a few books, mostly on weaving and art, but Avielle longed to see a place filled with polished oak shelves and with row upon row of books: books with golden titles printed on their spines; books with gilt edges; books with leather bindings in brown, red, blue, and white. She longed to be able to put out her hand and pluck the reflections and fancies of another mind from the thousands of possibilities hovering in the air. So she had come here.

When she entered the shop, the smell hit her first—the familiar old smell comprised of leather, paper, glue, and dust, though there was far more dust in the air here than there had been in the Royal Library, where Esilia had wielded her duster. Avielle had tried again to see Esilia, but again the raisin-faced damada had refused.

As Avielle looked around the shop, she saw that there

were indeed shelves and rows of books, just as she had hoped, but the shelves were rough pine boards dotted with nails like silver pimples. The shelves reached far up the wall into the dim reaches of the ceiling. Avielle eyed the rickety things with trepidation, certain they would come crashing down if even one book were extracted. On the floor, crates bulging with books were stacked three deep, blocking the books on the shelves behind them. Avielle expected the room to burst from the pressure of all the books inside. She smiled.

The lord of all this bookish splendor lolled in an overstuffed golden chair with a plethora of cushions. He was so relaxed that his body—overstuffed too—seemed part of the chair. Avielle thought someone might mistake him for the chair and sit on him by mistake. But his preoccupation with his book would probably prevent him from noticing.

"Good day to you, sir," said Avielle. "If it is convenient, may I browse among your books?"

The man, who was perhaps in his late forties, did not look up. "Browse." He waved one hand. "Circumnavigate. Engage. Enlarge." He licked his forefinger and turned a page. His face was as red as a sliced tomato, with little brown moles scattered here and there like seeds.

Avielle looked at the rows of books and hesitated, not knowing where to plunge in, not knowing where the different categories of books were located. Then she realized she liked not knowing where to plunge in—in fact she adored not knowing. She chose one aisle and began walking down it, holding out both hands and letting her fingers bump against the spines. Many of them were not stamped with gold, but with plain black ink; and many did not have leather covers, but cloth covers. These were books for the common people.

She stopped halfway down the row and looked up at a sign that said, *NUTS AND BOLTS*. Whatever did that mean? Carriages had nuts and bolts, as did mills and other mechanical devices. Avielle pulled out a book, then glanced at the shelf above with some apprehension; fortunately it stayed erect. She read the title of the book: *Physiology*. With some difficulty, she forced it back between its neighbors. Then, tilting her head, she scanned the nearby spines. *Istotle's Treatise on the Geocentric System. Optics. The Music of the Spheres*. All the books under *NUTS AND BOLTS* were texts on science. Master Steorra would browse here, Avielle thought.

Halfway down another row, Avielle stopped at a sign that said, *WAY BACK THEN*. Again she studied the titles on the spines: history. She found books of stories and poetry under *FLIGHTS OF THE IMAGINATION*; books on art and artists under *THE EXQUISITE*; books on philosophy under *WORKS OF THE BRAIN*. And so on. After half an hour, Avielle decided there were perhaps three possibilities to describe Master Cavenda's character. First, he was deranged. Second, he had an odd sense of humor, which he enjoyed inflicting on his customers. And third, and this pleased her most, he looked at the world sideways. Whatever he was, she liked him enormously.

By the back door of the shop, she found an oak barrel filled with cast-off books in terrible condition: torn pages; chipped covers; broken spines; one red book had half its pages missing; and other books had no covers at all. All seemed forlorn. She wondered what journeys they had taken, what abuses they had suffered, whose minds they had enlightened, and whose hands they had passed through to finally bring them here. The sign over the barrel said *WORDS ARE WORDS—TWENTY TIRAS EACH*. Why, she would have thought nothing of ordering a book worth ten times that much, and she often had. How blind she had been, how ignorant. Avielle wondered if Darien had bought his battered primer here. She wished she could have bought him a few more lesson books.

She and Darien had been making extraordinary progress with his lessons. His reading was progressing faster than his writing, which was still tortuous and plagued with blotches. The tails on the capital letters *R* and *Q* especially troubled him. Sometimes, when he sounded out a new word, he would be so pleased with himself that he would forget to be sullen toward her. Indeed, they even laughed together. Master Keenum, spinning thread, joined in the merriment, one of his beloved stones on his lap. However, when the lesson was finished, Darien always remembered his grudge against her and grew sullen again.

After perhaps an hour of browsing through the bookstore, filled with regret that she had no money to purchase those volumes that had caught her eye—one by the poet Rutaska Olea in particular—Avielle returned to the front of the shop. Master Cavenda still lounged with his book in his golden throne and did not appear to have moved an inch, though perhaps he had collected a bit more of the dust spiraling in its slow ballet through the air.

"I have two questions, Master Cavenda," Avielle said, stopping before him. "If you please, sir."

He grunted but did not look up. She wondered how he was ever able to sell anything.

"First," Avielle continued, "I have found the books of *Then* and the books of *Now*. But I cannot find the books of the *Yet to Be*. Are they the prophecies?"

He snapped the book shut. "No, they are not the prophecies! Blathering of idle men who should have found something more useful to do."

"Well, then, can you direct me to the books of *Yet to Be*?"

"Yes, I can." He looked up at her; his eyes were almost gold. "I direct you to yourself."

Avielle stared. "I do not understand."

"No one does. No one *thinks*. The books of *Yet to Be* are the pages of your life, aren't they? The ones you have yet to write. And where do you think you'll find the source of them? Here, of course." He fluttered one hand at the books. "One place anyway. Part of it. See? In all this vastness. In all this wealth. Wisdom of the ages. Words swim into the ears. Don't they whirl inside the head? Don't they?"

"Well—"

"And there, if you're no dolt, they stick to your brain. They inform your life and become part of the *Yet to Be*." He fumbled in a pocket on his shirt, pulled out a pair of gold-rimmed glasses, and put them on. Then he seemed to see her for the first time. Avielle realized that he was near-sighted, probably from reading all those books. "Are you a dolt?" he asked.

"I . . . I think not. But I suppose—wouldn't a dolt think he was not a dolt? So how can one know, really, unless someone else tells them?"

"That tells me you are a dolt," Master Cavenda said.

"Why?"

"Because you need someone else to tell you who you are. Away with you! Scat! Do you think I have time for clever dolts?" And he picked up his book.

"You haven't answered my second question," Avielle said, undaunted.

He sighed. "This book you are keeping me from reading is *A Past and Present History of Dredonia*. Don't you understand? There is nothing more important anyone should be doing at this moment. How else are we to know what to do now? In this crisis? I ask you? If we don't know everything about the Dredonians?"

"Know about them?" Avielle clamped her hands on her hips. "Know about them?" And the words shot out like a fist. "They are murderers! We need no further enlightenment.

We should kill them. Break their backs and their necks and throw them into a snake pit. Let every single one of them die in terrible pain. We should kill them all before they kill us."

Master Cavenda licked his forefinger absently, as though he was turning a page.

"You have a mind the size of a teacup," he said. "Yet you grew up with books, didn't you? Highly educated. I can tell by the way you speak, diction, vocabulary, syntax, all that. You would have bought a book, maybe lots of books, if you had the money. Genteel family, I'd say. Fallen on hard times? Am I right?"

Avielle turned her head sharply, embarrassed to have been caught in such a moment of rage.

Master Cavenda leaned forward, for the first time separating himself from his golden throne. "I'll make a bargain with you. I'll give you a book—yours to keep, you don't have to pay—my choice. All you have to do is promise to read it."

Avielle's eye caught a flicker of movement. She saw Underfoot sitting in one of the crates of books in a corner. He looked up from washing his white bib and stared at her. Then he returned to his bath with meticulous care. Avielle's hands slid down from her hips. Her shoulders relaxed. Her thoughts were blank, a white circle, as though the anger had washed them all away. Into that circle rose the image of a book. He had offered her one. She wanted one—badly.

"Very well," she said. "I agree." She hoped he would go to *Flights of Fancy*, for though she knew the chances of him picking the book by Rutaska Olea were slim, she would be grateful to have any volume of poetry. Or better yet, perhaps he would go to the lesson books and pick out something she could use to teach Darien. However, to her surprise, he did not even get up.

"This one," he said. And he held out the book on the history of Dredonia.

Avielle flinched. "No."

"What?" he said. "You promised, remember? Afraid of getting out of that teacup? Of stretching your mind to, say, the size of a bowl?"

She was afraid. But princesses did not break their word. She hesitated. She *could* break her word; she could, because she had chosen not to be a princess anymore. But she found herself holding out her hand. She found herself taking the book.

PINI AND OGALL
CHAPTER TWENTY

Two days later, with a burlap bag slung over her shoulder, Avielle wandered up a canyon between two hills anointed with pine trees whose scent brought her mind both clarity and calm. She thought of Master Cavenda's book still lying unopened on her bedside table, then she put it from her mind. She wanted to enjoy the day, forget about Dredonians, grief, despair, and the Black Cloaks who were still killing each night. Gamalda had sent her to the canyon to gather glorionna sun daisies for a brilliant golden dye. "You've got to go high up in the canyon to find them," Gamalda had told her.

Clouds like the puffs of wool on Master Keenum's spindle splotched the blue sky. The round leaves on the aspens chattered of their recent change from green to gold. Because it was late in Septess, the wild rose bushes were beaded with rose hips instead of blossoms. Only the greetings of the wind through the pines, the hum of an insect, and the occasional rustle of a squirrel or some other small creature, broke the silence.

Avielle wondered what it would be like to have the branches full of birds, to have the woods full of their song, and to see them flying back and forth across the sky. For the first time in weeks she seemed to see what was around her, to feel the blessing of the Goddess. For who could be angry with her here?

The canyon curved up to the east, and Avielle climbed until she reached a meadow with massive granite boulders—some pointed, some blunt—scattered about like the teeth of a giant. Avielle amused herself by wondering what had happened to his tongue. Then she glimpsed the first flash of gold, the glorionna sun daisies, and stood, spellbound.

Vast sweeps of them stippled the meadow and the western hill with gold. Their hearts were amber, their leaves pale green, their petals as yellow as corn. If she were queen, Avielle decided, she would take the glorionna as her sigil. How could she pick even one? Strip Alamaria of such glory? Gamalda was counting on her, however, so Avielle roamed among the giant's teeth, picking the blooms and dropping them into the burlap bag. She thought how they were like the sun that circled Alamaria, Alamaria that was the center of the entire universe.

When the bag was nearly full, Avielle's head snapped up as a new sound debuted in the meadow: a sweet high piping, with notes trilling and sailing and whisking, then notes long, smooth, steady, and serene. It could not be a bird, surely it could not be a bird. As though in a dream, Avielle began walking toward the sound, which, because it echoed off the giant's teeth, proved difficult to find. At last she walked around a particularly large fang-shaped boulder and saw two boys.

The tallest, standing, was playing a pipe that shone silver in the sunlight. The smaller boy sat crouched on a rock, his knees drawn up to his chest and his arms clasped around them as though he were afraid of losing some essential part of himself. Both were Dredonian Rhians with the full set of Dredonian features—silverskin and hair, the scalloped crown at the top of the forehead, the pointed ears.

As Avielle walked toward them, she thought that the oldest could not be more than twelve, the youngest eight or nine. Perhaps their parents were nearby, and they had come out for a picnic. The elder boy saw her and stopped piping. The little boy dropped his head on his knees and moaned.

"Good day," Avielle said. "Your music is lovely and so appropriate for this beautiful place. Have you come to spend a day out of the city? It is indeed refreshing out here, isn't it?"

The boys said nothing. The littlest one continued to moan. The older one slid his hands down along the flute until both fists grasped the bottom, as though he were preparing to wield it like a club.

Whatever was wrong with them? Perhaps they were merely shy. She tried again. "My name is Avi . . . that is, Vianna." Then she noticed their clothes. The older boy wore a red-orange tunic cut straight across the neck from shoulder to shoulder, so that his collar bones—thin and straight—showed. A blue cord wrapped twice around his waist, then the tunic belled out in stiff, quilted panels to his knees. The puffed sleeves were gathered at the elbow and tied with more blue cords. Below the tunic, the boy wore tight blue leggings. On his feet were brown leather shoes with furled tips.

The little boy wore a similar outfit, but all in a gray so dark it was almost black. Streaks and smudges of dirt covered both boys' clothes.

Avielle frowned; she had never seen anyone dressed like them. Then she knew. *She knew.* And rage shot like a flaming arrow inside her.

"You are Dredonians!" she exclaimed. "Dredonians! You murdered my family!"

"No," said the boy, in heavily accented Rhian. "We killed no one."

"Your people destroyed the High Hall!"

"Not our people. Evil Brethren of the Black Cloaks who rule us. Who make war."

"You hate us all. You are wicked, cruel."

"No. Not people of Dredonia. Not us. I, Ogall." He pointed to himself, then to the crouching boy. "My brother, Pini. It was Brethren who did this evil. We hate them, too."

Avielle looked at him, her chest rising and falling. She wanted to seize his flute. She wanted to smash him and hit him. "If it is true you hate them so much, then why don't you stop them?"

"They too much powerful. Magic too much strong."

"You do not belong in Rhia," she said. "Get out! Go! Go now!"

"We not can. We hide from the Brethren. Pini has much magic power. The Brethren take him to evil school. Make him to learn evil magic. I stole him. We flee. We wandered to here. Dredonia never safe for us no more. The Brethren never find us so far away here. Pini wishes to use his magic for good, not evil."

Avielle looked at Pini, now rocking back and forth. "Why is he moaning?"

"He fear you, fear all Rhians. Many stories told of your evil."

"Our evil!" Avielle said, outraged. "We are not evil. You are the ones who are evil." She could feel the hard kernel of hate inside her, and the hand of fear that she had flung up like a ward.

"Where are your parents?" she asked. "Are they a curse upon my land, too?" And she whirled about, looking.

"Dead." Ogall's voice trembled. "Murdered. Tried to keep Brethren from taking Pini. So Brethren kill them."

Pini kept moaning. Ogall put his arm around him.

Avielle stood still. So there were those among the Dredonians who also lived in fear. Fear from their own kind. Her mind could not grasp this; it was too sudden, too foreign. Pini never looked up from under that crouch, and locked behind that fear was the gift of good magic. But what if Ogall lied?

A blackness swimming before her eyes, Avielle spun around and started to walk away.

"Wait," said Ogall in a hoarse voice. "We hunger."

She stopped, but did not turn toward them. They are children, she thought, only children. But they were Dredonian children.

"Fish swim in stream," Ogall said. "We catch some. We know roots and plants to eat. But each night colder. Can you help? Pini is so small."

Avielle half turned toward them. She looked at Pini, still crouched, and for a moment she hesitated.

"We can pay with good Dredonian magic. Do you need good magic, Vianna?"

I need nothing from Dredonians, Avielle thought, and left them. At least, she told herself, closing her eyes, I did not try to hurt them.

As Avielle walked back through the giant's teeth, the sack of glorionna daisies clutched in her hand, she heard Ogall's flute. The sweet notes were soon lost in the cold, heavy air.

THE VANDAL
CHAPTER TWENTY-ONE

Early the next morning, Avielle and Gamalda were just finishing their toast, porridge, and tea, when a knock came at the front door. The door was locked; they had not yet opened for business.

"I'll go," said Avielle. She walked through the shop yawning, for she had slept poorly, unable to put her meeting with Ogall and Pini out of her mind. She had not told Gamalda about them because she knew Gamalda would have wanted to help. Twice during the night Avielle had risen and lit the candle beside her bed, thinking to read the book Master Cavenda had given her, but when she saw the gold words *A Past and Present History of Dredonia* stamped on the cover, she had blown the candle out.

Someone rapped on the door again just as she opened it, and a man half fell into the room.

"Why, Master Steorra," Avielle said, surprised.

"Oh! Miss Vianna. I seem to have lost my footing." He straightened and began tugging on his sleeves, then his collar, then his waistcoat. Avielle had a chance to observe him more closely than she ever had before. He was a young man, tall and thin, with a face as long and black as a piece of licorice. Indeed, Avielle thought, his entire body had a rubbery quality, as though his arms and legs could be bent or rolled without snapping off. His brown eyes were luminous and quick, alight with some kind of inner fire.

"I would not presume to bother you so early," he said, when he had his clothes arranged again. "Barely had your porridge I'm sure, moon still out—fabulous thing the moon, not flat you know—but I was passing by. I had to stop, though I'm really quite in a hurry, but as one neighbor to another—"

"Master Steorra," said Gamalda, coming up behind them. "I thought I heard your voice. Nice to see you. Have you had your tea?"

"Had last night's—like it bitter. But I really must tell you. You must know."

"What must we know?" Gamalda asked.

He glanced at Avielle. "Your window has been besmirched. Dreadful. Vandals. Hideous creatures ought to be hanged."

Avielle looked at the window. The new glass had been installed last week. Lengths of cloth displayed in front of it covered most of the window, but beyond them, she thought she saw red on the panes.

"Come outside, Mistress," said Master Steorra, "and see."

Avielle followed them through the door. When she saw the window she stopped. Sound stopped. Everything stopped. A red painted skull leered on the glass. Beneath the skull someone had written in red letters:

FILTHY SILVERSKIN GO BACK TO DREDONIA OR DIE

Avielle felt as though she were being sucked into the sky. Then she seemed to be floating, looking down on herself from high above, looking down on the horrid words.

"This is dreadful!" Gamalda exclaimed. "Who would do such a thing!"

The sound came back. Avielle heard the creak of the milk cart rolling past, the clip-clop of the horse's hooves on the cobblestones, the jingle of the harness. Was it Darien, she wondered? Had Darien done it? No. Their lesson times were growing easier every day. Then whom?

"Black at the center of their hearts," said Master Steorra. "Probably someone with the sun sign of the Arrow—with the planet Demord the Demon rising. A worm! A fiend!"

"Such hate," Gamalda said. She put one arm around Avielle. "I'll get a pail of water and wash it clean. Come away, my dear. Come away."

"Jump up, Underfoot," said Avielle, who was sitting up in bed later that night. "The night is cold, and I would welcome your warmth and comfort if you are inclined to give it." The orange-striped cat considered her for a moment, then licked his white bib and arranged his white whiskers, as though he did not wish to seem too eager to accept her overtures of friendship. At last, with a sudden spring, he leaped onto the bed and stretched himself out languidly, with his head on her lap and his feet down by her ankles.

"You are a very long cat," Avielle said, scratching his chin. "And good and noble, too. I would give you a knighthood if I had one to bestow." Underfoot did not condescend to open an eye, for he was already knight, lord, prince, and king.

Avielle picked up the book that Master Cavenda had given her and stared at the gold words on the black cover. *A Past and Present History of Dredonia.* Was her mind a teacup? Was she afraid to stretch it into a bowl? A bowl was a useful thing, after all. One could wash one's hands or face in it. Drink from it. Mix a cake in it. Fill it with stones or flowers. And perhaps best of all, use it for a hat when the rain pelted down. A teacup might shelter your nose at best. Indeed, she saw now, a bowl was decidedly more useful than a teacup.

Reluctantly, Avielle opened the book and flipped through it. It was six hundred pages long, written by Lorian Gutan, a Dredonian Rhian. Avielle began reading the introduction.

The Dredonian religion worships the First One, who is the creator of all things. This religion is based on the creed of goodness, tolerance, love, and forgiveness.

Avielle's eyes opened wide. How could that be when the Dredonians were evil? She thought of Ogall and Pini, who had not seemed evil at all. She read on.

These teachings are based on stories in the scriptures written by men and women who were sages and wise wizard-priests of ancient times. For hundreds of years (excepting the War of the Mines one hundred years ago, which Rhia won, and when Princess Dolvoka was sent as assurance to the peace treaty—most unfortunately as history has proven), Dredonia was a kind and good neighbor to the countries surrounding her. The Dredonians produced magnificent art, literature, music, and were great healers and philosophers. They used their magic powers to bring good to their people and to all their neighbors.

But approximately seventy years ago a sect of wizard-priests called the First Foundationalists came into power in Dredonia, and they remain in power to this day. They command that all Dredonians follow an old dark interpretation of the religion of the First One, which is based on an obscure text by Tittibet, whom they call divine.

The First Foundationalists believe their approach to religion is the only way to the First One, and that all who do not share in their beliefs should be slain or enslaved. Furthermore, they believe the wizard-priests of the First One should dominate all aspects of life: from the clothes people wear, to the words they are allowed to speak, to the thoughts they are allowed to think. The wizard-priests are called the Brethren of the Black Cloaks because such is their garb. Their magic grows more evil each year, and they use it to dominate and control the people of Dredonia, curtailing their freedom. Any who resist are tortured and slain. They brainwash Dredonian children into thinking Rhians are evil.

Avielle looked up. Again she thought of Ogall and Pini. Evidently what they had told her was true. She read on.

And thus the Brethren have created an army of fanatics who will eagerly give their lives, be it only to see one Rhian dead. They will be difficult to defeat. All of these events will be described in more detail in the following chapters.

Avielle closed the book. How could such evil be stopped? Then a thought whispered through her mind. If she revealed herself, claimed the throne of Rhia, and ordered the slaves to be sent, all the terror would stop; blood would stop flowing through the streets of Tirion. Everyone would be safe again.

However, as she petted Underfoot, she realized yet again that the people who had barely tolerated her as a princess would never accept her for their queen. If the High Council did decide to send the slaves, she would be the first person they would pick. *Filthy Silverskin Go Back To Dredonia*

Or Die. And the Black Cloaks, knowing who she really was, would probably kill her first.

She blew out the candle and sat shivering in the dark. And then came the voice: *Avielle! Light-Bringer! You are our only hope for Rhia. You must not fail us!*

The next morning Avielle wove on the third floor. As her mind wandered in the dream trance, she walked beside the ocean at twilight. Waves pounded the beach. She smelled seaweed and salt. Something bumped against her chest; she raised her hand and felt a linen bag stuffed with pearls hanging on a cord around her neck.

Soon she came upon an enormous soot-covered lantern standing half buried in the sand, like a sunken ship washed up on a beach. Avielle tore off one sleeve of her black taffeta, silk, and velvet dress and began to rub the glass. Over and over she polished it, trying to clean away a small patch of soot on the bowl of the lantern, which was as high as she could reach. She succeeded only in swiping the soot into a mess of gray swirls. Finally, she dropped the sleeve and began scratching at the glass with her fingernails.

When her fingernails were worn to the quick, a beam of light shone through the soot; the glass cracked, and out of the lantern flew a stream of bright bells—bronze, gold, silver—that pealed a song upon the air. Over Avielle's heart came a gladness and she knelt, exhausted, looking up. High up, perched crookedly over the glass cone at the top of the lantern, was a black crown.

The cloth showed fans of nearly every hue in a grand kaleidoscope that was a shout of color. Avielle had to hunt for the black crown, but it was there, tiny, crouching under a red fan.

INTO THE FIRE
CHAPTER TWENTY-TWO

The next afternoon, Avielle stood in the street looking at the silversmith's sign in the window. The words *Silver Dreams* had bold letters painted to look as if they had been engraved—a pattern of crosshatches ran down their lengths and around their curves. The last letter, the *S*, was missing a bit of its flourish. Red velvet drapes swagged deeply over the windows, then were pinched back at the sides and bound tightly with golden cords as though they might become unruly and had to be kept in their place.

The shop was wedged between Master Lughgor's stained glass window shop on the east and Master Cavenda's bookshop on the west. Augum Aslee's was one door down from Master Cavenda's. These four shops formed all the establishments on the block across the street from Gamalda's.

Gamalda had urged her to continue meeting the people of Postern Street, and Avielle, reluctantly, had agreed. She believed Gamalda was correct in thinking she needed some relief from the magic that was emerging when she did her weavings on the third floor.

A little bell fastened to the door jangled when she stepped inside the warm room. She thought of Ogall's flute, which had not jangled, but sung purely, truly. She thought of Pini curled up.

Hammering, slow and rhythmic, came from the other side of a partition swathed in black velvet at the back of the shop. All around her, silver objects flashed and shone from shelves, stands, and tables. But before Avielle could do more than receive an impression of beauty, Mistress Alubra scooted out from the back.

"Welcome, welcome!" she began, then stopped. "Oh. You're that Vianna, Gamalda's apprentice." And she appeared to lose all interest.

For a moment, Avielle did not answer. Mistress Alubra had been veiled the last time Avielle had seen her. Now she was not, and Avielle found herself staring at a bright red scar slashing Mistress Alubra's face from the outer edge of her eye to the corner of her mouth—the only blemish in a face otherwise smooth and fair. She was perhaps thirty years old. Avielle realized she was staring and recovered herself at once.

"Stare all you like," Mistress Alubra said. "Take a good look." She turned her face and stepped closer to Avielle. "Why should you be any different from the common herd?"

Avielle clasped her hands together. "I apologize for my

rudeness, Mistress Alubra. Please forgive my poor manners. They were unforgivable and unkind. I am so sorry."

Mistress Alubra raised her eyebrows, and the top of the scar lifted, too. "Well, I guess you are different from the common herd. In your apologies anyway. Now. Why has Gamalda sent you? Usually she would come herself to buy from me. If I were a less accommodating woman I might find myself tempted to be offended."

"Gamalda means no slight, I assure you," Avielle said quickly. "She sent me to look, if you please. Not to buy."

"Oh, she did, did she? Sent you to look? Well that's a fine state of affairs."

Mistress Alubra wore a red-and-blue-striped dress. A black lace-up belt pushed her breasts up so high they looked like soldiers standing at attention. When she took her corset off at night, Avielle suspected her bosom must sag some distance to be "at ease."

"What about The Chandelier?" Mistress Alubra asked. "Gamalda knows I have precious little time to work on it. Why should I waste time attending some apprentice who only wants to *look*? And who doesn't know anything except how to apologize prettily?"

"I can look by myself, if you please. You need not attend me."

"Need not attend you? Would you listen to the girl? Probably stick a serving spoon in your pocket the second I take my eyes off you."

"I am no thief," Avielle said. "And if I were going to steal something—if, I say, *if*—I would certainly choose something more worth the risk than a serving spoon. Perhaps that magnificent candlestick with the larks twined about the base."

Mistress Alubra almost smiled, but managed at the last moment to purse her lips instead.

"Well, I must say you don't have the look of a thief," she said. "Too puffed up with pride, I suspect. And Gamalda did buy a small silver tray from me last week, a nice heavy one, engraved with maple leaves. So I suppose you can look. But don't touch anything. Don't breathe on anything. Don't even stare at anything too long least you bore holes into it with those intense blue eyes of yours."

Mistress Alubra pulled out a silver hairpin that looked like a rapier, twisted a stray lock into the haystack of black hair poofing on top of her head, and jabbed the pin back in. Then she scooted away around the partition.

Avielle turned at once to the shelves, all lined with black velvet to better set off the gleaming silver. She saw silver pitchers, wine ewers, and picture frames. She saw silver goblets, boxes, and candlesticks—some engraved with flowers, others with birds. There were silver necklaces wrought with chains and pendants. There were silver tea services with pots, creamers, and sugar bowls. And the rings! Big ones, small ones, round, square, filigreed, and smooth.

Avielle saw a silver ring with a large oval disk. Sculpted

upon it was the sign of the Light-Bringer holding the sun and moon, with stars for hair trailing behind. Avielle bent over to examine it.

"I told you not to get too close!" Mistress Alubra exclaimed.

Avielle started. She had been so intent on the ring that she had not noticed that Mistress Alubra had come back into the room. "I am sorry. But . . . I mean to say, there's nothing in this room that is not exquisite."

The scar on Mistress Alubra's face faded from fiery red to pale pink. "Smooth one, aren't you?"

"If it is not too much trouble, may I see your workshop? I would love to see how such splendid things are made."

Mistress Alubra tugged at the laces on her black belt as though she could not quite breathe at this effrontery.

"It would be a great honor," Avielle added

"Oh, very well. But Gamalda had better buy another tray."

Avielle followed Mistress Alubra around the partition into a room much warmer than the showroom. The first thing she saw was a forge against the back wall with a fire burning inside it. On the wall, dozens of tools hung neatly on an enormous rack. Avielle recognized dividers, protractors, tweezers, templates, metal rulers, and hammers—indeed, she had never imagined that so many different sizes and shapes of hammers existed in the world. Tables with silver items in various stages of fabrication were pushed against the walls.

Beside the tables sat several stumps embedded with what looked like metal stakes with broad flat heads.

An apprentice boy—about eighteen with hams for forearms—sat in a chair hammering and shaping a dull gray disk against the flat head of one of the stakes. He hammered the center of the disk at the point where it met the flat head, turning the disk clockwise after every blow. When he had worked his way around in a complete circle, he began to hammer back around in the opposite direction.

"What is he doing?" Avielle asked. "Why is he hammering the metal?"

"It's raw silver," Mistress Alubra explained. "It slowly raises up from the disk under the force and direction of the hammer blows."

Raises up to what? Avielle wondered. "What are you making?" she asked the boy.

"A bowl for the Goddess," he said, without pausing in his work.

"For her Temple," Mistress Alubra added. "Don't exaggerate, Pegor."

"For her," Pegor insisted. "For the Sacrament of Love."

The Sacrament of Love, Avielle recalled, was the most sacred moment in the Cadella, the Service to the Goddess. The High Damada held up a plain, but beautifully wrought, silver bowl and prayed to the Goddess to fill the people with her love, light, and peace and offered the love, light, and peace of the people to her.

Pegor laid his hammer down on the table and adjusted it so that it lay perfectly in line with the other tools. Moving slowly—his back hunched, his hands grasping the disk as though if he dropped it all the world would shatter—he carried the disk to the forge. Then he clamped the disk in metal tongs and thrust it into the fire.

"What is he doing!" Avielle exclaimed.

"The silver can only be worked just so long before it must be annealed," Mistress Alubra explained.

"Annealed?" asked Avielle.

"Put into the fire to make it malleable again so it doesn't crack when hammered. So it can be worked some more.

"But enough of all this." She waved her hand. "You must come and see the work of my life." She led the way along the room, passing two other apprentices, both girls. One was fashioning what looked like a mold out of wax; the other was polishing a pendant. Mistress Alubra stopped at a huge table. "Here it is," she said. "The Chandelier."

Avielle bent closer to see. Curving rods with graceful curlicues and swashes, with cups on the ends to hold candles, rose up from the table like an ornate fancy from a fairy tale. There were four tiers. The bottom tier, the largest, was completely finished, as was the second. The third was only half finished, however, and the design of the curving rods changed halfway around. The top tier had only the central column in place.

"Brilliant, isn't it?" Mistress Alubra asked. She put her

hand to her face, her fingers fluttering over the scar. "If I were a less humble woman, I would wax poetic."

"Yes," said Avielle, for indeed, The Chandelier was brilliant, and she could imagine how when it was finished it would be the crowning glory of any ballroom. And yet it seemed a strange hodgepodge of ideas; ideas tried, half formed, then forgotten, and abandoned. "But," she said, trying to put her comment delicately, "the design is not . . . consistent."

"Well, aren't you perceptive? Of course the design is not consistent! Naturally. I thought of several new design elements last week—a vast overarching theme—and it works much better. But what would you, an apprentice weaver, know about such matters?"

Before Avielle could answer, Mistress Alubra went on.

"Now I will change the whole piece to match my new design. You can't rush your life's work. It has to be perfect."

"How long have you been working on it?"

"Twenty years."

"Twenty—years?" Avielle stared at her.

"I refuse to send something out into the world that might be flawed. A less exacting woman might not care about her reputation. But, now that I have found its shape at last, The Chandelier will surely be done next month."

Avielle, however, suspected this would never happen. Mistress Alubra would continue tinkering with The Chandelier until they laid her out in her tomb. Indeed, Avielle could imagine her pounding away with her hammer in the darkness, never satisfied, always certain that success lay just around the corner, eternally whispering, "brilliant, brilliant."

"But," Avielle said, "if you do not finish it, the world will never see the result of all your labor. The beauty of your work, the light of it."

"The world?" she scoffed. "What do I care for the world? The Chandelier is for me."

But Avielle thought it a great pity that The Chandelier would never be lit. As she listened to Mistress Alubra, she saw something sparkle from the corner of her eye; she turned and saw a silver piece displayed upon a stand. In spite of the heat in the room, she turned cold. And then a cord inside her pulled her toward the piece, and she would have noticed nothing or no one who stood in her way.

It was a circlet of silver perhaps an inch high, shining faintly pink in the reflection from the fire glowing in the forge. Sculpted in the silver, cherry blossoms were entwined with images of the full and crescent moon. In the center of the circlet—brilliant, winking, flashing with light—shone a diamond the size of a cherry.

"What is this?" Avielle asked, though she did not want an answer, though her heart was a stone of sorrow. She knew the circlet was something that only a princess would wear. She knew Mistress Alubra had made it for either Ismine or Cerine.

"That," said Mistress Alubra, "I made for her Royal Highness, Princess Avielle."

Avielle pressed her hands to her stomach. A hundred horses galloped over her, swift and hard, and she could not breathe. *For her?*

"And I was never paid for it either—the whirlwind struck and put an end to that. But they had sent me the diamond to set in it. The diamond's worth far more than the silver and labor I put into the crown. Or so I've been told by them that know. Which is why I keep it hidden back here." She traced one of the cherry blossoms with her finger. "It's the best work I've ever done—excepting The Chandelier, of course—so I decided to keep it as a safeguard for my old age."

"But—" Avielle knew even through the blur in her mind that she must speak carefully. "But the princess already had a circlet—I saw her wearing it when I lived at the High Hall. Why was another made? Who commissioned it?"

"The queen herself. Her way of saying good-bye, I guess."

"Good-bye? Why good-bye?"

"Where have you been hiding yourself? And you once living at the High Hall? Didn't you know that sooner or later the princess would be betrothed? Too bad she bungled it with Prince Graedig—shamed the whole country with that. Would have been a good thing to have the Imsethians on our side in the war."

Avielle looked at the circlet again. Her mother had made it as her blood price. Had it been a way for her mother to ease her conscience?

"Try it on," Mistress Alubra said. "I made it for a silverskin, but I've never seen how it would look on one."

"Oh—I could not."

"Of course you could."

"No." Avielle backed away.

"What nonsense is this? Do you know how many girls would give their firstborns to wear a crown like this just for a minute? Besides, I've just spent all this time away from The Chandelier showing you around. If I were a less forgiving woman, I'd think you ungrateful. It's the least you can do." She took the crown from its stand. "Let's go over to the mirror."

A creature caught in a cage, Avielle followed her.

"This will do." Mistress Alubra stopped before an oval, silver-edged mirror, raised the crown—much higher than she needed to—and lowered it onto Avielle's head.

"Perfect!" she exclaimed. "It looks just as I imagined. The silver is not too highly polished. So the contrast with the silverskin is not harsh. Of course, your black hair takes away some of the effect. Even so, if I were a less humble woman, I would say I'm a true artist. Here, step closer to the mirror, girl, so you can see." And she pushed Avielle toward the mirror.

Avielle saw her silver face framed by her black hair—silver-tipped at the roots because it had been two and a half weeks now since she had dyed it. She thought of the last time she had seen her face with a crown—Dolvoka's face in the portrait. That crown, painted so brilliantly, had been silver, too, but Avielle knew it was really black, black as she had found it in the chest in the Chamber of Wings, black with its blood red ruby, black as Dolvoka's heart. Now, in the mirror, Avielle saw the shadow of it upon her head, heard an evil voice chittering from the black wings engraved upon its sides. She could feel the crown like a vice around her head, like a knife against her skin. A horror came upon her, and her shoulders hunched.

With her slight movement, something sparkled in the mirror: the diamond in the silver cherry blossom circlet. As Avielle looked at it, so bright, so pure, the horror slowly faded, and she straightened. Her thoughts cleared. And for one moment she wondered how one would become a true queen of Rhia.

She heard Pegor's hammer strike the raw silver.

"Girl, girl!" exclaimed Mistress Alubra. "You're not listening."

"I am sorry," Avielle said. "What were you saying?"

"I was saying that Her Majesty spent hours with me—hours! Going over the design of this circlet. She wanted cherry blossoms because they're strong—blooming in the early spring when winter might still kill them. The princess was born first day of spring, you know. The queen wanted it to be perfect. She put a mother's love into the whole thing."

Again the hammer struck.

"Are you certain?" Avielle asked faintly.

"Oh, yes." Mistress Alubra nodded. "I have a mother's own heart. And I say the queen spent so much effort on the circlet because, despite having to marry the princess off, she wanted the princess to know she loved her."

Avielle felt something whispering around her heart. It swirled gently, until something, a current of air? A scent? A thought? A warmth settled upon her. It fell like a mantle over her shoulders, the merest slip of cloth, transparent around her. It hung from her shoulders so lightly that she barely knew it was there. She received it, whatever it was; it held her, and she held it, her heart aching.

Behind her, Pegor thrust the silver disc into the fire.

STARS
CHAPTER TWENTY-THREE

Again, Avielle's mind wandered freely as her hands wove on the loom on the third floor. She was walking up a steep hill in a fierce wind that blew her dress back against her. She still wore the black dress with the taffeta, silk, and velvet skirt, though she had lost the gloves, hat, and veil back inside the Hall of the Dead Candles, and one of the sleeves by the Shipwrecked Lantern. The linen bag stuffed with pearls still hung on a cord around her neck.

A river of stones began rolling toward her down the hill; the stones tumbled against each other, clunking and clacking, gathering speed, kicking up dust. They reached her, and those closest pounded her feet and ankles while the others swept past her. Among them, tossing and turning end over end, was a black crown.

Her feet bruised and battered, Avielle began to run uphill through the river of stones, hoping to reach the end of them. She began to sweat and unlaced the bodice of her dress, tore it off, and dropped it behind her. All she wore now was her white chemise and her long black skirt over her petticoat. Avielle ran faster and faster, but there was no end to the stones.

At last she bent down, grabbed one, and threw it as hard as she could into the oncoming stones. A note sang out. A light flashed. The stones changed into hundreds of little stars rolling down the hillside, making it tremble with light. Avielle knelt and let the stars flow over her hands and into her lap. They felt soft and whispery, as fairy wings might feel. They felt warm, as the coming of dawn after a cold, bitter night.

Avielle came out of the dream trance and looked down at the loom. The cloth was made of red, yellow, and orange starbursts, their rays overlapping, on a black ground.

"I'm about ready to give it all up," said Tinty with her mouth full. Three days had passed. She and Avielle were sitting at a little table in Waterbee's Bakery munching cinnamon crisps. All around them, people were eating pastries and drinking chocolate or tea at the dainty round tables covered with blue cloths. A long counter with a glass front ran the length of the room. Inside the counter were tarts, pies, pastries—the round, stacked Knights' Delight was Waterbee's specialty—cakes, cookies, and enough other desserts to fulfill the dreams of every child in Tirion.

"Give up what?" Avielle asked, breaking off a chunk of crisp.

"Searching for my magic gift."

"Oh, no! Tinty, you cannot."

"How come?"

"Because it is part of who you are. And besides, I admire you for trying to find it. For being so patient and persistent. You are very . . . courageous."

Tinty's hand, holding a rather large hunk of crisp, stopped halfway to her mouth.

"I am?" she asked. "Me?"

Avielle nodded.

"Well. That's something. I guess it is. Coming from you."

"Only, Tinty," Avielle said, pouring cream into her tea, "you might try to think a little about the things you attempt, before you rush into them."

"Oh, that's fine." Tinty waved her crisp. "That's grand. Give a compliment one second and take it away the next."

"You know what I mean. Maybe I could help you. We could talk over your magic before you try to do it."

Tinty smiled slyly. "I'll tell you what I know. I know your secret. Or my name's not Tinty Bottledown."

"What secret?" Avielle asked, considering whether to order a blueberry tart. "That I like tarts better than pastries?"

"No. Far more interesting, *Princess*."

Avielle dropped her teaspoon; it clattered on her plate and crumbs of cinnamon crisp went flying. She stared at Tinty. "How did you . . . how did you know?"

"Didn't. Till just now. Your face gave it all away. I put

two and two together. What it said in the paper—about the princess walking away before the whirlwind. How you showed up here living with Gamalda right after. No family. A weaver to the princess—everyone knowed the princess was a weaver. A silverskin. And your high talking ways. I just thought to myself, Tinty Bottledown, it has to be. And so it is."

"Tinty." Avielle leaned forward. "You must not tell anyone, do you understand? Not anyone."

"You're hiding because those nasty Black Cloaks might get you?"

Avielle nodded.

"But we're all in a muddle. The High Council, that puffed-up Lord General Maldreck. Imagine if the High Council chooses him to be king! I'd magic him into a toad, see if I wouldn't. Besides, you're sharp. Maybe you could help us figure it all out."

"But the people would not want me to because—"

"Oh, I know all about it. 'Cause of you're being a silverskin like that nasty old bird slayer. What bonk."

"They would not want me," Avielle repeated.

"I would." Tinty looked intently at her cinnamon crisp. "You're good to me," she mumbled. "I think you'd be a grand queen."

"Hush! If you tell, Tinty, I might *die*. Promise."

"Oh, you can count on old Tinty. But say, isn't it a hoot to wear a crown? Why I bet I could make one right now out of this cinnamon crisp." And she put it on her head and began waving her arms around. "Maybe my gift is baking, hadn't thought of that." She began to mutter nonsensical sounding words: Treotta, sugarina, creamamiram, marzipanta . . ."

"No, Tinty, don't!" Avielle cried. However, it was too late.

Stars flashed. The cinnamon crisp swelled bigger and bigger, then stretched around until it reached the back of Tinty's head. The pastry grew up and up and up until it was a foot high. Swirls of icing began to loop around it. Gumdrops poked out like jewels: the red ones like rubies, the green like emeralds, the blue like sapphires. A great diamond made of crystallized sugar appeared in the center. It was a concoction of a crown.

Suddenly Avielle felt something winding around her own forehead, and found that a pastry crown was growing from her head, too, as indeed one was growing on every head of every person in Waterbee's Bakery. Someone shrieked, someone shouted, someone laughed.

"Stop, Tinty!" Avielle exclaimed. "You must stop!" But Tinty had that dazed expression on her face that always appeared whenever she did magic.

Finally the crowns stopped growing; each was about a foot high, with eight points around the top; and each was a different, fabulous confection of pastry, whipped cream, icing, and spun sugar.

"Who did this?" roared Master Waterbee, his mustache quivering with outrage.

Tinty slunk under the table, but her crown still thrust up above it.

"You!" He grabbed her by the arm and pulled her up. "Tinitia Bottledown. I should have known."

"The name's Tinty!" Tinty shouted.

"How did you do it?"

"Magic. I thought maybe my gift was baking."

"Might be," said Master Waterbee, rubbing one side of his nose. "I've never seen the like."

Tinty's face lit up. "You mean, I've found my gift at last?"

Master Waterbee reached over, broke off a slab of her crown, and raised it to his mouth. All the customers in the room held their breath. He bit into the pastry and chewed. Then his face turned as purple and pinched as a prune, and he spit out the pastry into a gob on the floor.

"Bah!" he exclaimed. "Wretched! Tastes like pig fat. Get yourself and your stupid magic dross out of my shop."

THE FESTIVAL OF THE QUASANA
CHAPTER TWENTY-FOUR

The next day, carrying a small white paper bird in her hand, Avielle walked toward the Temple to attend the Festival of the Quasana, Messenger of the Goddess. Held each year in the huge white courtyard behind the Temple, it was the one festival of the Goddess that most people still attended. Gamalda, much to her disappointment, had stayed at home to nurse a head cold.

Avielle could not wait to meet Esilia, who she hoped would at last be well enough to see people again. The thin black veil over Avielle's hat hid her well, from Grig Durdin, Lord General Maldreck, or any others who might be searching for her to earn the High Council's reward. She would have to find a quiet moment and place to tell Esilia who she was. She was certain Esilia would keep her secret.

Avielle looked up. The day—the last day of Septess—was sunny with a cool, crisp note and not a cloud to be seen. She turned the corner around the back edge of the Temple and stopped, her breath catching in her throat. Tirion trees—from which Tirion had taken its name—stood intertwined in a ring around the edge of the courtyard. They were not tall, perhaps twice the size of an old apple tree, and their leaves had fallen and left their white branches etched like candelabras against the blue sky.

This, however, was not all. Thousands of folded white paper swans hung from the branches of the trees, fluttering, quivering, almost laughing with light. All honored the Quasana and encouraged the birds to come home.

The festival, held since ancient times, had originally honored the Quasana alone. It was only since Dolvoka's curse had killed all the birds, including the sacred swans, that the rites of the festival had been expanded. Now, integral to the festival was the hope that the birds, beloved by the Goddess because she had chosen one as her messenger, would return.

Avielle started forward with gladness in her heart. Her parents had brought her to the festival once when she was a little girl. The royal family attended each year, and, even now, Avielle could see the gilt chairs set up for them on a green carpet at the center of the courtyard. They had been brought out even though there was no one to preside in them this year. She imagined the outburst were she to go and sit in one; the shouts, the thrown tomatoes; why, even the Tirion trees would thrash in indignation.

After that one visit when Avielle was young, her parents had never brought her to the festival again. She suspected now that there must have been comments. She remembered how she had pleaded and cried the next year when she had learned she would be left behind. And how her nurse, despairing of her, had called in her mother. Her mother had admonished her, saying a princess must do what was best for the people, and it was better that the people did not see her.

Now, as Avielle walked through the courtyard, she saw people in black sprinkled throughout the crowd. Many had lost friends or family in the whirlwind or to the Black Cloaks' dreadful nightly attacks.

But the day was too bright for such gloomy thoughts, and Avielle began to search for Esilia. Damadas walked through the crowd in their ragged robes and veils. It was a crime against the Goddess, Avielle thought, that they were so shabbily dressed. She knew Gamalda made offerings of cloth to the Temple, but the offerings of one person did not go far. Avielle decided to ask Gamalda if she could weave something for the damadas as well, maybe something especially for Esilia.

All along the edges of the courtyard, people hung the white paper birds they had made onto the trees. Ladders leaned against the tree trunks to give access to the higher branches. One little boy in a blue hat sat on his father's shoulders to hang his bird. "A little higher, Father," he called. "I've spied the perfect branch."

"Aye, and you'll break your neck or my back before you'll get to it," his father said. He was laughing, however.

Avielle stopped to hang her own little white bird, so slender, so brave and hopeful, then walked on. Children ran everywhere, shrieking and laughing, darting through the crowd, their faces stained with raspberry jam from vendors' scones, their voices mixed with the music from musicians playing here and there. One man playing a lute had a yellow beard that sprawled over his chest like a sleeping child. Another sat on a stool playing a harp, his fingers rippling. Farther off, a woman with a purple scarf knotted around her neck trilled on a little pipe. Avielle thought of Ogall. She thought of him trying to catch a fish for Pini.

"Mistress?" said a voice.

Avielle looked down. A little girl about six years old in a patched red dress stood looking up at her.

"Show me how to fold my bird?" the girl asked. "I can't get it right."

"Certainly," Avielle said. She took the grimy, crumpled piece of paper and bent down on one knee. "You have most of it right," she said. "Simply turn this half back along this fold, using that fold for a guide. Do you see?"

The girl nodded.

"Then fold this section up for the neck and bend the tip for a head. And there! The Quasana!"

The girl looked at her in wonder. "Thank you, mistress," she said. And she ran back into the crowd.

Avielle walked on. At last, she heard a familiar voice.

"Let me wipe the last of that jam off your face," said a

damada to a boy in a blue coat. "There now, run along." Then the damada, leaning on a crutch, straightened up. Her veil, hanging over the back of her head, framed her face.

"Esilia!" Avielle cried.

Esilia turned. "Yes?" she asked. "Your voice is familiar but—"

"Will you come with me, please?"

Looking puzzled, Esilia followed Avielle along a stone path bordered by boxwood hedges. Although Esilia used the crutch, she walked quickly. They skirted beds of purple and white chrysanthemums until they reached a private portico under the back of the Temple, where Avielle thought they could talk privately.

"What is this about?" Esilia asked. Her fuzzy almond-colored hair slipped out around her veil. "The rites are about to begin. I haven't much time."

"Esilia, you must neither cry nor scream." And Avielle lifted her veil.

Esilia's face turned pale, and she took a step back. "You look like . . . but your hair is black though the roots are silver . . . but you, you're dead, you were crushed. I'm dreaming." Then she took a step forward, hands raised. "Is it true? It is true! You're alive! How?" And her face filled with joy as she started to curtsey.

Avielle grabbed her as though to embrace her and whispered in her ear. "You must not treat me like a princess. And call me Vianna." She pulled the veil back over her face.

"First," Avielle said, "tell me what happened to you, after the whirlwind hit the High Hall."

"It's a blur—thank the Goddess. I heard a boom. Then I fell—it seems like I fell forever. Things . . . struck me. Then it was as though I slept. When I woke, I saw light coming through a crack. The stone on top of me was propped up by other stones. I lay in a kind of . . . pocket." She twitched her veil. "My leg was broken. I sat up and felt a stab in my ribs—one of those was broken, too. I put my mouth to the crack and started shouting." Her head dropped. "No one came. No one heard."

Avielle wanted to put her arm around Esilia's shoulder, but clasped her hands behind her back instead. Esilia looked out at the white Tirion trees, at the children in white, and the white paper birds. "I thought I'd never see anything or anyone again. I prayed to the Goddess to accept me into the depths of her heart, for I knew I was going to die. I wandered in and out of consciousness. Once I saw the Quasana."

"You did?"

"I thought he was coming to bear me to the Goddess on his great white wings. The thirst was so terrible. At last I heard shouts. Though I was hoarse, I screamed. 'Are you there?' someone called. 'Help!' I cried. And they found me."

Esilia began to cry. "They found me, they found me, they found me."

Avielle stood stiffly, then pulled a handkerchief from her pocket and gave it to Esilia.

"The damadas tell me it's not bad to remember it," she said, " so long as I don't dwell on it and torture myself with it. But . . ."

"But?"

"I don't understand how the Goddess could let such a terrible thing happen! Such an evil thing. And not just what happened to me, I mean. But to everyone who was hurt and killed. And to people still being killed each night by the Black Cloaks."

"I have been thinking upon that, too," Avielle said. "I have no answer. She watched while my entire family was killed. While your mother was killed, too. I am so sorry."

"Yes, and I'm sorry about your family." She straightened a little and squared her shoulders. "But I've been talking too much. Tell me about you. Why are you hiding who you are from everyone?"

Avielle found herself telling Esilia everything that had happened to her. When she finished, Esilia took her hand.

"Oh, Princ—Vianna," Esilia said, "how much you've been through. I . . ." Suddenly Esilia shifted her gaze and looked over Avielle's shoulder. "There, in the sky! Southward, do you see that?" Esilia pointed.

Avielle turned and looked. She saw a gray smudge shaped in a V moving toward the city, moving far too fast to be a cloud. Other people in the courtyard had seen it, too.

"Look up!" they shouted.

"In the sky!" they cried. "There, in the sky!"

"Do you see it?"

The smudge grew nearer, and Avielle saw a sight she never dreamed she would see. She saw wings—wings rising and falling, wings sweeping and curving, wings soaring and swooping.

"Birds!" Esilia cried.

"Birds!" the crowd roared.

"How can it be?" Avielle whispered.

"Birds, birds, birds!" the crowd chanted. "The curse is over! The curse is lifted!"

"They're coming home!"

"At last!"

"The Quasana has carried our prayers to the Goddess! She answers!"

"Dolvoka is vanquished!

"See them fly!"

People pushed and bumped and shoved in the courtyard, all trying to get a better look. Parents who shouted, "See! Look!" hoisted their children up so they could see better. Avielle saw the little girl in the patched red dress standing on her father's shoulders.

As the birds drew near, Avielle could see that they were all black and all large. Condors? Black eagles? No, they were too big even for that. She frowned. They came closer and closer, filling the sky like a thundercloud. Their mouths opened, showing gleaming fangs. Scales covered their bodies, and blood dripped from their wings.

"Run!" Avielle screamed. She pulled Esilia deeper into the portico. She opened the back door to the Temple, pushed Esilia in, and slammed the door behind them. They rushed to a window.

People were screaming now, running in every direction, bumping and trampling each other in their haste to get away. The birds dropped down with their talons out. They dove into the crowd, tearing and rending, sweeping people up and then dropping them so they smashed upon the stones of the courtyard.

Avielle ran to the door and flung it open. "Here!" she called to the crowd. "This way!" But few heard her over the din. Those that did came running in with dazed looks on their faces. When Avielle looked out again, she saw a man throwing out beams of green fire from his hands into the flock of Black Birds.

"A wizard!" Esilia cried.

The wizard's fire struck the bird, and the bird screamed and fell. Again the wizard shot out green fire, and a second Black Bird fell. But soon, too many Black Birds surrounded the wizard, and they crushed him to the ground and started feasting upon him. Another group of people staggered to the Temple door, and Esilia let them in.

Avielle saw a flash of red as a cruel talon swept up the little girl in the patched red dress.

"No!" she cried. "No! I must help her. I must save her!"

"There's nothing you can do!" Esilia grabbed her. "Nothing any of us can do. They'd only kill you, too."

"Let me go!" Avielle sobbed. "Let me go!" She crumpled to her knees.

Esilia knelt beside her and prayed. "Oh Goddess, most holy, most high, I beseech you! Stop this evil!"

The Black Birds flew over to the Tirion trees. They began breaking off branches, destroying those fine old trees that had stood for three hundred years.

At last, when death and destruction filled the courtyard, the Black Birds screamed and flew into the sky. There they whirled and whirled, spiraling tighter and tighter, until they became a plume of smoke and vanished.

AVIELLE'S GIFT
CHAPTER TWENTY-FIVE

"They were a perversion!" Gamalda exclaimed when Avielle at last dragged herself back to the shop and told her what had happened. They sat hunched at the kitchen table. "A perversion of the longing for birds that has been in the hearts of Rhians for a hundred years," Gamalda added. "The Brethren knew this!" She slammed her hand down on the table. "Once more they struck at the heart of the people."

Avielle felt cold, a creeping, gnawing cold that seemed to paralyze her. "Soon we will all be dead!" she cried. "I cannot live with this dread, this doom. I cannot bear it."

"You've got to," Gamalda said. "I tell you any one of those people murdered just now by the Black Birds, or crushed in the rubble of the whirlwind, or killed by the Black Cloaks, would give anything to be alive. Even to be alive in desperate doubt, despair, and fear."

Avielle bowed her head. "We will never be safe again."

"I know it's hard, but we must try not to think that way. Think instead of the glorionna daisies blooming in the canyon.

Or of Darien's kindness toward Master Keenum. Or of Mistress Alubra always making sure Master Steorra remembers to eat. We've got to think of the good things happening in the world, Avielle. The evil would like us to forget the good and become twisted by despair. We do so at our peril."

"The wizard," Avielle said. Then she lapsed into silence.

"What about him?" Gamalda asked.

Avielle raised her head. "He gave his life to help the people. He must have known he could not defeat the evil birds. And he undoubtedly had the power to save himself. Yet there he was, out there, fighting, though he knew he would die. How does a person get to be like that?"

Gamalda reached out and took Avielle's hand. Gamalda's wrists were as thick as some people's ankles, and Avielle felt the strength of her grip.

"A person gets to be like that," she said, "by loving other people more than their own self."

Avielle wove on the third floor, and as she did she walked across a mountainside sprinkled with snowdrops, brave and delicate harbingers of spring. Patches of snow melted here and there, and the rivulets of water washing over the slope made it come alive with tremolos of light: light shimmering on water, on snowdrops, on stone.

Avielle heard a cry. She stopped. She heard it again and turned to her left. There, lying on a bed of snowdrops, was a naked baby, a girl not more than three months old.

Though her skin was silver, and she had all the Dredonian features, it was impossible to know whether she was Dredonian or a Dredonian Rhian. She whimpered softly, her wide blue eyes looking up at Avielle.

Avielle stepped across her and walked on. The baby cried again.

Avielle turned back. She unfastened the hooks on the waist of her skirt and slipped out of it, the black taffeta, silk, and velvet rustling. All she wore now was her white chemise, petticoat, black shoes, long black stockings, and the bag of pearls hanging from her neck. She was about to wrap the baby in the skirt when she saw her mother standing six feet away—her mother, and yet not her mother. Her red hair hung in tangled thickets, her skin was tight across her face, and on her head was a black crown.

"Give me the baby," she said. And she lunged toward Avielle.

Avielle dropped the black skirt, clutched the naked baby, and began to run across the mountainside, her shoes plunging first into snow, then into water, scattering snow-drop petals.

Her mother shouted, pursuing her.

Avielle ran faster. She came to the edge of a cliff. Below were clouds so bright they blinded the sun.

Her mother screamed. Her fingers grazed Avielle's back. Avielle slipped and fell onto one knee at the edge of the cliff. The baby howled.

"You will not have us," Avielle shouted. "We have come too far."

Avielle held the baby tight to her chest with one hand, clutched the bag of pearls with the other, and jumped into the light.

She came to herself, panting, bending over the loom. She rubbed her eyes, then straightened. The cloth was pure white with a pattern of interlocking red diamonds and swirls.

Late that same afternoon, Gamalda stood in the third floor workroom holding the red and white cloth in her arms.

"Oh, Avielle," she said. "I tell you this is stunning! Your art and craft are growing stronger."

"I feel lately," Avielle said, "that when I am weaving I see a far off glimmer. Like a coin cast into a well. And if I could only find my way down through all of the dark water, I could pick up the coin, and it would be bright and shining."

"That coin would be your magic, I think. And something more." Gamalda ran her fingers over the cloth. "I think this would make a wonderful shawl." She threw the cloth around her shoulders; it swirled, then settled around her.

Her face changed. Her back straightened, and her pale green eyes widened. She took a breath that seemed to fill her entire body.

"What is it?" Avielle asked. "What is wrong?"

Gamalda held up one hand, palm out, signaling her to wait. A minute passed.

"Extraordinary," Gamalda said at last, taking off the cloth. "Bring me the piece you wove where you turned the stones into stars."

Avielle went to the chest where she kept her work, reached down under the other weaving pieces she had made, many of which had not amounted to much, and drew out the cloth with red, yellow, and orange starbursts. As Gamalda had done with the white and red cloth, she draped it around her shoulders. Again, she stood with the still, listening look upon her face. Finally, she took off the cloth, laid it on the table, and sat down. Avielle sat down across from her.

"You've asked me when your weavings would begin to show pictures that move like mine," Gamalda said, looking down at the cloth. "I thought this would happen as you began to find your magic power. But I was wrong. How wrong!"

Avielle tried to hide her disappointment. "But what about the first time?" she asked. "With the belt? The time with Rajio when the fireflies glowed and projected themselves onto the curtain?"

"That I don't understand," Gamalda said. "But I tell you the magic gift you have is far more powerful than simply having pictures move on the pieces you weave. And far more powerful than my own."

"What is it?"

Gamalda picked up the red and white cloth. "When I

put this on, a feeling came over me. Fear at first. But then that fear changed to caring and courage."

Avielle stared at her.

"Something similar happened when I put on the piece with the starbursts," Gamalda continued. "I felt at first as though I were oppressed. But then that feeling changed—to joy."

"I do not understand," Avielle said.

"Your weavings have got the power to convey virtues or feelings to the person who wears them. Such as these two, which give the capacity to be courageous and to feel joyful. And I expect, as your power increases, there'll be more virtues as well. Perhaps goodness, faith, or trust—even love."

Then Gamalda hesitated, folding up the cloth with the starbursts. "But I suspect there's a danger. The opposite may be possible as well. Bring me the very first weaving you made. When the monster ate you and spat you out in the desert."

Although Avielle hated to touch it, she fetched the black cloth with the splotch of purple and blue, like a terrible bruise that had the tiny silver thread running through it.

"Don't interfere, no matter what happens," Gamalda told her as she put on the cloth. She immediately clutched her hands to her heart and cried out. Tears poured from her eyes. Her shoulders slumped. A minute passed, and Avielle began to wonder if she should snatch the cloth off Gamalda's shoulders in spite of her instructions. Then

Gamalda straightened. A few moments later she blinked and took off the cloth.

"Are you all right?" Avielle asked.

Gamalda nodded, breathing quickly. "It was as I suspected. Fear. Rage. Thirst. Utter despair. But then, a faint hope."

Gamalda stroked the tiny silver thread with her finger. "Your weavings have got the power not only to bestow feelings, but to transform the way people feel. From fear to courage for example, or from despair to hope, from sorrow to joy. You may someday be able to change a soul trapped in darkness back to the light. Oh, Avielle, it's an enormous gift!"

Avielle felt as though bubbles were exploding inside her mind, that she was reaching for the meaning of what Gamalda had said, but as soon as she put her finger on it, it jumped and popped and vanished. She put her hands flat down on the table.

"How can this be?" she asked.

"I don't know. I've never heard of anything like this. Not in all the history of our craft. But I do know that the magic power coming from your Dredonian blood is proving to be a source of great strength for you. Just as we hoped."

"You spoke of a danger," Avielle said.

Gamalda folded the cloth in half, then into quarters, then into eighths, as though reluctant to speak. "As I told you before, the gift of magic power alone does not make a person good or evil. It's how it's used that makes it so. With this gift you've got the potential to wield great power over people. Great power! You've got to learn to use it cautiously and wisely. You could do great evil, if you instill into your weavings such feelings as greed, jealousy, fear, or hatred. I tell you it is even possible that you could grow strong enough to trap others in darkness."

Avielle closed her eyes. She could not believe this was happening.

"The edge you stand on is perilous," Gamalda said. "More perilous than I ever suspected."

That night in bed Avielle thought about evil. She knew that evil came when people turned toward the Malaquasana in their heart. It seemed, however, more complicated than that. What if you were a good person and did only one evil thing, and you did it by accident? Did that make you an evil person? What if you came from a country like Dredonia, where the rulers carried out evil deeds? Did that make all the people of that country evil? She thought about Ogall and Pini; they had not seemed evil at all. In fact, if they spoke truly, they had been fleeing from it.

And what about someone who stood back, did nothing, and watched while someone else was murdered? To Avielle, that person was evil. She was certain of that much anyway.

She suddenly sat up. What about her? She had done nothing while the little girl in red was murdered. She was still doing nothing, while the Black Cloaks murdered people in their beds each night. But if even the wizards of Rhia, with all their spells and power, could not help, what could she do? According to Gamalda, she had the power—great power—to transform people through her weaving. So far, however, she did not know how to use it. "I have to learn more," she whispered. Maybe then she could help in some small way.

But what if she used the power she gained for evil? What if the evil of Dolvoka rose in her blood and she turned toward the Malaquasana? As a princess with such power, and even more as a queen, her opportunity to do that would be very great. *The edge you stand on is perilous. More perilous than I ever suspected.*

Avielle lay back and wrapped herself in blankets until only her nose stuck out. Why couldn't she simply run far, far away from all of this? Run to the Shores of Solill across the western mountains, take a ship, and sail to the long lands of Tenda across the Redstorm Sea? But it would do no good. Dolvoka would be waiting for her even there, because Dolvoka was inside her.

Avielle knew she could not escape this peril. It was written in her blood.

THE BADGE
CHAPTER TWENTY-SIX

"It's the latest news, sweetling," Renatta said, handing Avielle a broadsheet as she sat weaving cloth of red and blue plaid at the downstairs loom the next day. "I thought—considering you're a silverskin—you'd want to read it. I think it's terrible."

Avielle looked at the headline.

LORD GENERAL MALDRECK PERSUADES HIGH COUNCIL TO IMPOSE REGULATIONS ON SILVERSKINS

The High Council, under advisement from Lord General Maldreck, has decreed that due to the threat of Dredonian spies infiltrating the kingdom, all silverskins must now wear badges proving that they are Rhian citizens and thus not spies. The High Council hopes in this way to continue combating the terror that faces us. All such silverskins, with a Rhian citizen to

vouch for their identity, have one week to present themselves at their Neighborhood Council buildings to receive their badges. After that time, all silverskins seen in the city without badges will be arrested as spies. This is so decreed by the High Council.

Signed,

High Councilman Herector

Avielle lowered her hands; the broadsheet crumpled and crackled against her lap. She stared into space.

"Idiots," Renatta said. "It must be because of what happened with the Black Birds."

Avielle nodded.

"It'll be all right, sweetling." Renatta put one hand on Avielle's shoulder. "We'll all vouch for you."

Startled, Avielle looked up. She tried to smile. "Where is Penatta?" she asked. The twins were seldom apart.

"Rotting at the bottom of a barrel, I hope!" Renatta fluffed her hideous pea-colored dress as though admonishing it. "She thinks it's a good idea about the badges. Can you imagine? I snap my fingers in her face, I do."

Avielle recalled that Renatta had not believed the rumors of Princess Avielle's evil nature, but that Penatta had.

"Do the two of you disagree often?" Avielle asked.

"Not much before, but lately . . ." Then Renatta held out her skirt with one hand. "I want a new dress," she blurted. "One of my very own. One that looks different from

Penatta's. Everything we wear is exactly the same. Even our underclothes! I want to be . . . unique. I don't care what Mother says." She hesitated. "You have such beautiful cloth here, my pet. Will you help me pick out something? I can pay—I've two years of wages saved for my dowry. Tinty will sew it up if I beg her—she's a whiz with a needle, though it's not her magic gift—ask her about that disaster sometime. What a riot! Will you help me, dearling? Help me pick something that would look, well, as pretty as a picture on me?"

Avielle folded the broadsheet in half, then in half again, then over and over into smaller and small bits until it was the size of her palm. She dropped it on the floor and ground it beneath her heel.

"I will help you," she said.

"Have you known this silverskin long?" the official sitting behind the desk in the Neighborhood Council building asked Gamalda. Avielle looked at him with distaste. He was round, with folds of fat sinking one into the other, as though he were a slowly melting turtle; and the network of bulging wormy veins on his face made his head look like an overripe cantaloupe. Avielle wanted to give it a swift kick so it would go rolling across the room.

"I've known this young woman since the whirlwind," Gamalda said. "I took her in after all her family were killed."

The official's eyes popped. "So she showed up just after

the whirlwind, eh? That looks suspicious. Nobody can vouch for her before that?"

Gamalda sighed. "I should have said I first met her in the High Hall—where she was an assistant weaver. By great good luck, she was out doing errands the night of the whirlwind. She came to me afterward because I'm a weaver, too. She thought she might gain employment with me. As she has."

"So we have only your word to go on," said the official, leaning back in his chair. It creaked. He poked his pen in his ear and scratched, looking back down at the paper Avielle had filled out.

"Gamalda Calima," he read. "I've heard of you. Magic weavings. A bit of Dredonian blood yourself, though it don't show." He peered at her. "If I had my way all of you with a trace of that cursed blood magic would be suspect. Don't look down your nose at me, woman. It may come to that." He took a round nickel-plated badge off a stack and stared at it. "Number 1446." He dipped his pen, which had lately been in his ear, into the inkpot and wrote the number on the paper Avielle had filled out. "Away with you," he said. "We'll be watching."

"Odious, horrible man," Avielle said to Gamalda as they left the building. She thought of Ogall and Pini hiding in the canyon and knew that if they were found they would probably be killed as spies.

She paused at the bottom of the steps and looked at the

nickel-plated badge. It had the face of a silverskin engraved upon it. But it was grotesque; a parody had been made of the face.

Avielle felt something she had never felt before: sympathy for other silverskins. She had been so busy hating her own skin and the trouble it had brought her that she had never wondered how other silverskins might feel. Now the horrible badges linked them.

"I suppose I must put it on," she said.

"It's a shame upon the kingdom!" Gamalda exclaimed. "A shame. We will live to rue this day. One at a time the authorities will nibble away our freedoms in the name of safety, preying upon our fears."

Later that night, Avielle went up to Master Keenum's room over Mistress Rocat's candle shop for her lesson with Darien.

"Vianna," Darien said. "Come in." As he took her cloak, a fold with the badge on it fell across his arm. He stopped, looking down at it. "Is this . . . is this it?"

"Yes," Avielle said. "The official at the Neighborhood Council gave it to me today."

"But it's hideous! It doesn't look a bit like you."

"What are you speaking of?" called Master Keenum from his chair. He had three rocks in his lap: a small, smooth, slightly pinkish one; a yellow one with crystals poking out; and a gray one that was almost perfectly round.

"Vianna's badge," Darien explained. "Like all silverskins got to wear now."

"Bring it here," Master Keenum said.

Darien gave it to him.

"Hmm," Master Keenum mumbled as he ran his fingertips over it. He pressed it against his cheek, then clasped it between his hands. "Nothing good will come of this. Throw it away, dearie."

"She can't," Darien said, giving it back to Avielle. "It's wrong. All wrong."

"Why do you mind so much?" Avielle asked. "I thought you did not like silverskins."

He half turned away from her. "That was before, well, before I met you. I guess you're all right." Then he hesitated, as though weighing something in his mind. Avielle waited.

"I want to be on the Neighborhood Council one day," he blurted at last. "So I can change things like this. Make bad things right. That's why I want you to teach me to read and write."

"That is wonderful," Avielle said, looking at him standing there so sturdy, straight, and earnest. Grief, fear, or despair would never bow Darien down. She wished she could be like him.

"He's no chance for the High Council, being born in the gutter," Master Keenum said. "But all types can be in the Neighborhood Council. Why, Master Ruskin, the cheesemaker, is, and Mistress Blythe, the bookbinder. Why not our Darien, one day?"

So that was Darien's dream, Avielle thought. And it was possible. The opportunity to better oneself and rise in society was one of the best things about Rhia. Indeed, any child could go from living in the gutter to being a respected citizen on a neighborhood council. As Master Keenum said, rarely did someone like that go on to the High Council, comprised of those of high birth, breeding, and a first-rate education. However, anything could happen. And as Avielle looked at the scraps of brown wrapping paper that Darien had gathered from rubbish bins to practice his writing on, she thought he might have enough determination to be anything.

"I wouldn't let things like this happen." Darien pointed to the badge. "Not if I could help it."

"Then you don't think I might be a spy?" Avielle asked.

Darien laughed. "Maybe you are. I hear you've been poking your nose into all the shops on Postern Street. Stealing secrets from the candles, books, and silver, are you? And Master Lughgor's wondering when you're going to show up at his place."

Avielle blushed. She began to pin the badge onto her dress.

"Don't," Darien said.

"But I am supposed to wear it all the time."

"Not here." Darien closed his hand over hers and gently

took the badge away. "Not here. Now, didn't we leave off at chapter seventeen?"

Avielle crossed Postern Street and approached Master Lughgor's stained glass workshop, *Windows Refulgent*. The boards, painted pure white, had no sign of scuff or stain, as though someone came out and scrubbed them clean each day. The one window, a circle made of stained glass, showed a red rose in full bloom.

When Avielle opened the door, a little bell rang. She stepped into a tiny front room with two straight-backed chairs placed as randomly as though they had been tossed like a pair of dice.

A boy of about sixteen with a pocked face opened a door and came in.

"What can I do for you?" he asked, revealing teeth that leaned to the left.

"My name is Vianna. I have come to see Master Lughgor. Mistress Calima said to say she sent me. I believe the master is expecting me? However, if this is an inconvenient time, I can certainly return another day."

"Ah," said the boy, giving her a curious look. "I'm Smitor. The master told us you'd be coming and to show you right on in."

Avielle followed him through the door into the workshop. The first thing she smelled was turpentine, then coal burning, then something smoky and metallic. The first thing she saw were huge clear, glass windows lining one side of the shop, letting in a haze of light. Master Lughgor had one of the corner shops on Postern Street, so he had windows on both the east and south sides. Smitor led her past table after table scattered with tools, brushes, dishes holding colored powders, large sketches, and pieces of glass in every imaginable color.

She saw an apprentice using a paper shape as a cutting guide on top of a piece of blue glass. She saw another apprentice painting what looked like black swirls on a piece of yellow glass. A third apprentice, a girl, was slipping lead into place between cut pieces of glass. And a fourth apprentice soldered joints of lead together on a small round window—white lilies—which already had its lead in place. That accounted for the metallic smell, Avielle thought. A kiln accounted for the smell of the burning coal.

"The master's here around the corner," Smitor said, "where he can work with the south light. He's having an awful time of it today. He'll be sober tonight."

"What do you mean?" Avielle asked.

"It's like this, you see. It takes him forever to decide what to do next on a window. Once he does, he's so happy he takes a drink. You can always tell he's had a good day if he's drunk at the end of it. If he's sober—nothing got done."

They walked around a frame holding pieces of colored

glass and there, sitting with his back toward them in front of a stained glass window twice the size of a man, was Master Lughgor.

As Avielle stopped and stared at the window, her heart seemed to burst through her chest in wonder at the panoply of light and color that shone before her eyes.

In the middle of the window was the Goddess in a gown of palest gold; she was rising from a huge silver egg that had cracked in two. Her hands pressed against her heart and from them poured a beam of golden light that pierced the darkness—rendered in deep tones of blue glass—which surrounded her. She wore a crown of golden daisies glowing in a halo around her head. Beside her, the Quasana rose like a white prayer into the darkness.

The window, supported by a wooden frame, was not finished; many pieces were missing. Master Lughgor had completed enough, however, so that Avielle could envision the whole. White lines—where Avielle suspected the lead lines would be when the piece was done—formed delicate shapes. Master Lughgor had already painted many of the glass pieces, giving the glass texture, adding to the illustration, and modulating the light.

Avielle looked at the back of the head of the man who had created this marvel. His hair was gray, curled into wild thick locks. The jeweled light coming through the window spattered the floor at his feet like colored drops falling from a rainbow. Smitor announced her.

"It is brilliant," Avielle said to Master Lughgor. "Brilliant."

He grunted. "Might be, one day."

"How do the glass pieces stay up without the lead?"

"They're stuck with wax to a piece of glass behind. So as I can get the colors right. Make changes and so on. Got to get the colors right."

"When do you put the lead in?" she asked.

"Last. When the painting is done. After the pieces are fired in the kiln." He sat with his hands upon his knees, staring glumly up at the piece. "The color around the bottom of the egg is wrong. All wrong." He pointed. "I used dark blues all around and above the Goddess. To show the darkness of the night. Blues should've worked below the egg, too. But it's not right." He shook his head. "Egg has to shine silver in contrast. Background around it still has to be dark. Egg surrounded by the darkness." His cinnamon-colored face sagged. He tapped one finger over and over on the dent at the tip of his nose, and Avielle wondered if that was how the dent came to be there.

She studied the problem he had pointed out. It was almost like a color problem in weaving, except the light added a new dimension.

"Sanguine," she said at last.

"What's that?" Master Lughgor said. He sat like a block of granite. If you were to kick it, Avielle thought, you would make no impression. You would only damage your toes.

"The color you need is sanguine," she said, speaking slowly and carefully as she would to a young child. "A red so deep and dark it will form a strong contrast to the silver egg and set it off. And sanguine will be of the same tonal value as the dark blue pieces of the night. But with the sanguine below the egg it will be almost . . ."—Avielle tipped her head to one side—". . . almost as though the Goddess is rising out of the blood red of the heart."

Master Lughgor turned his head, frowned, and stared at her as though he were trying to remember something.

"The Magnificent Heart," he croaked at last. "How'd you know?"

"What?"

"That's my title for the piece. Smitor!" he shouted. "Get over here."

Smitor came, and Master Lughgor gave him instructions on cutting several pieces of sanguine glass.

"Well now, well," Master Lughgor said. He took a swig from a flask beside his feet, swished it in his mouth, then swallowed. "That's the way to go about it. Care for a drink?"

"Thank you, no," Avielle said.

Master Lughgor looked back at the work. He seemed never to look anywhere else for very long.

"You paint with light," Avielle said.

"The glass is the medium for the light," Master Lughgor explained. "Saracinda!" he shouted.

Saracinda came running up, a brush dabbed with red paint in her hand. "Yes, sir?"

"What is the first rule of a glass artist?"

"A glass artist uses glass to glorify the light of interior space," Saracinda recited.

"That's just so," Master Lughgor said. "Very good. Been studying your Bekins, I see. Off with you."

Saracinda ran off.

"But the true interior space is here." Master Lughgor pointed to his temple. "And here." He tapped his heart. "And I'm the glass. Any real artist becomes the thing that light shines through." He looked up at the Goddess in the stained glass window. "*Her* light."

He leaned back in his chair, heels stuck straight out in front of him in their heavy boots; instead of being laced, the shoelaces wrapped around his ankles several times. He pursed his lips and hooded his eyes, and again had that look as though he was trying to remember something.

"What are you going to paint on her gown?" Avielle asked.

"What? Oh. Flowers. Leaves. Vines. Birds—larks. No devouring Dredonian Black Birds here."

Though she was safe inside his shop, Avielle shuddered.

"What do you think of the war with the Dredonians?" she asked. "What do you think we should do? How do we defeat them?"

The colored light from the stained glass window danced

over him: blue over his cheeks, green upon his chin, red along his forehead, yellow across his wild, gray locks.

Master Lughgor raised his eyes to the window. "We defeat them," he said, "with the Magnificent Heart."

THE BOOK OF THE SORROWFUL QUEEN

CHAPTER TWENTY-SEVEN

Avielle's hands wove on the loom on the third floor. She was deep in a dream trance, walking along the edge of a river. Willow trees swayed on the bank. The river flowed gently, murmuring as twigs and leaves swirled by in the bright water. She saw the silver flash of a fish swimming by.

She came around a bend and saw a stag standing beside a log. The stag raised and lowered its head, rubbing its crown of black, velvet-covered antlers against a snag on the log. Strips of the black velvet sheath hung down, revealing silver antlers beneath.

Avielle went on. The sun was high, and soon she grew hot. She sat down on the rocky bank, unlaced her black shoes, and pulled them off. When she looked up, she saw a white swan swimming toward her; its feathers shone in the sunlight, sparkling as though made of diamonds and pearls. The swan had a human face.

"Light-Bringer," the swan said, "you have progressed this far at last. I am well pleased. I am the Quasana."

Avielle stood and bowed.

"To save your people," the Quasana said, "you must find the full, undiminished strength of your magic power and let it shine forth. So far you have only touched its surface. To go deeper you must find *The Book of the Sorrowful Queen.*" Then he turned and swam away, the river rippling behind him.

Avielle walked on up the bank in her stockinged feet. Then she began to float up out of the dream trance and found her hands weaving at the loom on the third floor.

Later that afternoon, Gamalda put the cobalt blue cloth with stripes of silver and black over her shoulders while Avielle watched, arms crossed tightly, shoulders hunched. After a few minutes, Gamalda took off the cloth and smoothed it with her hands.

"Is it bad?" Avielle blurted. "Did it convey anything terrible?"

Gamalda shook her head. "I felt a shadow, but I've felt that with each weaving you've made. But in each one it grows smaller. Mostly I felt awe and reverence. Your magic is becoming stronger. But that means your responsibility to use it wisely grows greater, too."

The next day Avielle walked through Queen's Square toward Three Alders Street in search of some Linnter's

Liniment for Augum Aslee, who was suffering from a severe case of rheumatism. Usually he would have sent Tinty on such an errand, but Tinty, thinking her magic gift might be doctoring, had tried to magic away the warts on her little finger, and had only succeeded in giving herself a bad cold. And she still had the warts. So Augum Aslee had sent to Gamalda, asking if Avielle would do the errand instead.

Although Three Alders Street was only ten blocks from Postern Street, Avielle walked warily, a tightness in her chest, fearful of being alone in the city—partly because she was afraid of discovery, and partly because of what had happened with the Black Birds. The Black Cloaks might indeed strike again anywhere, anytime. The noon sun shone brightly overhead, however, and she remembered what Gamalda had said and tried her best to put her fears from her mind.

When she reached Queen's Square, she found that many people had come out to sit on the benches to eat their noon meal in the sunshine. Food flowed freely through the city again. Vendors brought their wares to the gates of the city only, where the merchants then picked them up and transported them to their shops. Prices were high, but there was food.

In the middle of the square was a fountain, and in the middle of that stood a bronze statue of a queen, tall and graceful, a crown upon her head, her hair rippling as though in a breeze. Her hands were outstretched, palms forward, as though beckoning to the people in the crowd or offering herself to them, or perhaps both.

As Avielle passed the statue she thought of what the Quasana had said. *"To save your people you must find the full, undiminished strength of your magic power and let it shine forth. So far you have only touched its surface. To go deeper you must find* The Book of the Sorrowful Queen.*"*

Avielle looked at the people eating on the benches. Did the Quasana really think they were her people? Did *she* think they were her people?

A little girl in a red dress climbed up on the rim of the fountain and skipped along the broad edge. Her yellow bonnet, lying back on her shoulders, bounced up and down. Avielle thought of the other little girl in a red dress, the one killed by a Black Bird. She wished she could have saved that little girl. She would have claimed that little girl and been claimed by her. Avielle, in her black dress, stood looking awhile longer, listening to the sound of the water splashing, trickling, roaring, then she went on. At last she reached the apothecary's shop that sold Linnter's Liniment, purchased it, and left.

When she was six blocks from home, a man blocked her way.

"You there," he said. "Stop."

Avielle stopped and looked up at him. He wore green pants and a green tunic with a white circle—the attire of a city guardsman. His black hair looked like a spider had been squished on his head.

"Yes?" Avielle said.

"You're wearing the badge of a silverskin," he said.

"Yes," she said again.

"Silverskins aren't allowed to go veiled. Take it off."

Avielle stared at him. "My pardon, I did not know."

"That doesn't matter. Take off that veil now. Or I'll take it off for you."

Her hands trembling, Avielle picked up the edge of her veil and lifted it back over her head. As the guardsman looked at her face, Avielle felt naked, as though every nerve, every thought, every sensation, was exposed in her skin.

"You're a fair, young looking girl," the guardsman said. "I'll let you off with a warning. But another guardsman might not go so easy. Might take you in for breaking the law. Watch yourself." And he walked on down the street.

Avielle put one hand against the wall of the building, then leaned against it. She wanted to slide down the wall, crouch, pull her knees to her chest, and rock back and forth like Pini had done when he was frightened. The guardsman was only a man, Avielle thought, only a cruel man. She felt every pad of every finger pressing the rough surface of the brick. A cruel man enforcing a cruel law. What was happening to Rhia?

Finally, afraid that she would call attention to herself by

her distress, Avielle walked on, her face bared for all the world to see. She walked as fast as she could, almost running. When she was three blocks from home, she turned a corner, and saw Grig Durdin standing twenty feet away from her.

THE ENDLESS STREAM
CHAPTER TWENTY-EIGHT

Grig Durdin was striding directly toward Avielle, but several people walked between them, so she did not think he had seen her yet. Then he stopped and peered into the window of a butcher's shop.

Avielle turned and fled. He would not recognize her back, gowned as she was in black, her black veil fluttering behind her. She rounded the corner and ran down the block, crossed a street, then ran down another block and another. What if someone from the High Council saw her? Lord General Maldreck or High Councilman Herector? Or some other servant who had survived the whirlwind? She wanted to yank the veil down over her face, but she did not dare for fear of another guardsman stopping her.

At last, taking a long circuitous route, she arrived back at Postern Street. But Avielle realized that even here she was not safe. Indeed, Durdin or anyone else who knew her could walk down Postern Street or come into the shops at any time. She was not safe anywhere. Not from people, not from the Black Cloaks.

Avielle did not knock twice on Augum Aslee's door, as the sign requested; she was too anxious to get off the street. The first thing she heard when she stepped in was a long expletive sneeze that seemed to rock the rafters.

"My nerves, girl, my nerves!" cried Augum Aslee.

"What," Tinty said in a smothered voice, "you want me to put a stopper in my nose?"

Avielle walked toward the back of the shop, making her way around the usual debris, and around a huge pile of musty-smelling old shawls, which had not been there the last time she visited. It appeared that Augum Aslee had been pirating them for yarn.

"Look," Augum Aslee said, wiggling one finger under the battered green hat on his head. "It's that Vianna. Fetched my liniment, did you? Not too quick about it, were you?"

"Here it is." Avielle gave him the package. "I hope you are not suffering too much."

"Joints in these old hands flared up. Can't knit. Only thing that works is Linnter's Liniment."

"How is your cold, Tinty?" Avielle asked.

Tinty blew her nose and wiped it back and forth several times on what looked like one of the old shawls.

"Could be worse," she said in a hoarse voice. "I could've given myself rheumatism and been as crabby as some other people I won't name."

"Enough smart talk from you, girl," Augum Aslee said, "or I won't let you polish my egg dome anymore."

"How is the egg today?" Avielle asked, looking at the blue egg in its spotless glass dome.

"Why do you want to know?" Augum Aslee narrowed his eyes.

"Oh, Auggie," Tinty said between sniffles. "She don't want your egg. She's just asking to be polite-like. It's her way of doing. Her high upbringing."

Avielle looked at Tinty, suddenly fearing she would reveal her secret. But Tinty only winked.

"Polite don't sew the crops nor feed the sow," Augum Aslee said.

Avielle did not know what to say to this.

"Renatta!" Tinty shouted suddenly. "Aren't you done putting on that dress yet!"

"I'm coming now," Renatta called in a muffled voice. A moment later she opened the door to one of the side rooms and walked out.

She wore a dress with a softly draped collar over the scooped neck, a fitted waist, and a skirt that fell in graceful folds, all made of the rose-red nubby silk shot with gold that Avielle had helped her choose that day in the shop. It made her fair skin look like ivory and her lips look as red as a maple leaf in the fall. Her nose, however, was as pointed as ever.

"Oh, Renatta!" Avielle exclaimed. "You look beautiful."

"Beautiful!" said Tinty. "That don't half say it. She looks prettier than a hound dog on the scent of a hare."

Renatta turned in a circle, and the dress whirled out. "You're both sweetlings for helping me. I don't care what ma says. It's time I stood on my own."

"That's right," Tinty said. "Who cares what that old pug dog says."

Augum Aslee had been rubbing the Linnter's Liniment into his hands. "By the look of you, girl, I'd say you don't need that love potion now."

"Love potion?" Avielle asked. "You want a love potion, Renatta? For whom?"

"Smitor," Tinty and Augum Aslee said together.

Renatta blushed. "He's such a darling. I deliver a broadsheet over to the glass workshop every afternoon—stroke of three. He's always there waiting. I think, well I don't know, but I think . . . I still want the potion, Auggie. Just to be sure."

"Oh, all right. Do you have three hairs from his head?"

"No." Renatta's shoulders sagged.

"Well, we'll have to do without. Can't guarantee the magic though. Come here."

Tinty whispered in Avielle's ear. "Nobody ever has three hairs from nobody's head. It's how he gets away with it if it don't work."

"Put your hands on top of the egg dome," Augum Aslee told Renatta.

She did.

"Gently!" he exclaimed. "It's not a brick!"

"All right," Renatta said. "Get on with it."

Augum Aslee put both his hands on the bottom of the dome, a touch that was a caress. "Close your eyes, girl. Picture the egg in your mind and open your heart. When I say these magic words, all the love in the egg will pour into your soul as though you were a magnet. *Avan sodden bounn.*"

As soon as Augum Aslee said the words, Avielle saw a change come over him. He sat up straight, his voice grew melodious, and the way he spoke changed completely. His black eyes glazed over.

"Now, Renatta," he said, "picture Smitor's face. Imagine the essence of Smitor flowing through your heart and out through your veins into every part of your body, mind, and spirit. Now picture yourself doing every kindness you can think of for him. Cooking his favorite dish. Talking things over with him when he is troubled. Bringing him broth—or Linnter's Liniment—when he is sick. Bringing him a candle when all is dark. You're making him happy. Filling him with joy and happiness. Your hands cup his face. You're looking into his eyes with all the love of the egg streaming out through your eyes into his eyes, down into his heart, deep into his soul. Now for the magic words to complete and seal the spell: *arun scoem corum*. Open your eyes."

When Renatta opened her eyes, Avielle could see they were shining.

"So now he'll love me?" she asked.

Augum Aslee slumped back in his chair, hands shaking. He sighed. "Dense as a chocolate torte. But they always are, aren't they, Tinty, girl?"

"Not one in a hundred gets it," Tinty agreed.

Avielle looked from one of them to the other, chagrined, wondering what they meant. She must be one of the ninety-nine.

"Will Smitor love me now?" Renatta persisted.

"I told you, I can't guarantee it," Augum Aslee said. "Not having three hairs from the man's head. Think about how you felt during the spell. Show that to Smitor. Sure as a chicken clucks, the magic spell will probably work."

"But it says on the window you give magic potions. You didn't give me anything in a bottle."

Augum Aslee sighed again. "Give the girl a bottle, Tinty."

Tinty produced a small, empty vial with a stopper in it.

"But it's empty!" Renatta exclaimed.

"Nonsense!" said Augum Aslee. "It's filled with the essence of the egg, the magical love. Put it under your pillow or in your underwear drawer; I don't care. Just look at it every time you need to remember how to love."

Ah, thought Avielle.

"That will be ten tiras," said Tinty.

"Avielle! Avielle! Wake up!"

It was far past midnight the following night, and Avielle

felt someone shaking her. She felt groggy and could not wake.

"Avielle!"

She opened her eyes, squinting at the light; Gamalda stood over her with a candlestick.

"You've got to come with me," Gamalda said, pulling off the covers. "Now. We're in danger. Terrible danger."

Avielle swung her legs over the edge of the bed and stood, still groggy. Gamalda grabbed her hand and led her out of the bedroom. They went through the kitchen, the copper pans on the wall casting flickering shadows in the candlelight, and started running up the stairs to the second floor.

"What is wrong?" Avielle asked, awake at last.

"A Black Cloak is coming toward Postern Street."

They reached the landing. Gamalda threw open the door to the third floor and they started up, taking the stairs two at a time.

"How do you know?" Avielle asked.

"I feel it. I was reading in my room and felt a shadow touch my heart. A great menace coming."

They reached the third floor. Gamalda led her to the magic weaving of the waterfall that poured in a steady stream down the face of the cloth. She set the candlestick on the floor.

"I'm going to try and use my magic to send you into the weaving," she said, "to hide you in the waterfall."

Avielle blinked at her. "How?"

"There isn't time to explain. Listen carefully. You're

going to become part of the water. You've got to *be* water. Imagine yourself falling in an endless stream. You will be nothing but water. No matter what happens, no matter what you fear, no matter what you feel of evil near you, you've got to hold to this. You've got to be water, nothing but water. Do you understand?"

"Yes. But what about you—"

"I'll be fine. Now close your eyes."

Avielle did. She heard Gamalda begin to speak words she did not understand, words that lulled her mind, that flowed in a steady stream, and somewhere in all of it she heard the words, "I love you, Avielle," repeated over and over until they, too, melted into the stream. Every part of her seemed to be slipping and sliding, her limbs dissolving into water; and she seemed to roar and fall and flow endlessly, effortlessly. She knew nothing else.

Then a darkness arched over her. She seemed to hear her heart beating again as her mind wakened; and fear crept into her, fear and dread. Some tiny part of her remembered something that had been told to her long ago, and she started to chant, I am water, only water, water, water. Into her mind came the image of a radiant being pouring the waterfall from a silver pitcher, and the sound of the water was the sound of her singing. Then again Avielle was sliding, slipping, falling, and the singing roar was in her ears, and she was silver, only silver; and she felt the joy of it, and knew she would never stop being water, water that tumbled down the face of the rock and into the pool where she arched up into a fountain of mist.

The shadow withdrew.

An eternity passed where she knew no time, no thought. Then, though she felt no fear or threat, suddenly she felt herself coming forward, emerging from the water. Her limbs solidified. Her heart beat. Her breath rushed in. And she found herself back on the floor crouching on her knees in front of the weaving.

She knelt there for a while, coming back into herself, before the memory of all that had happened returned to her. That evil shadow she had sensed must have been a Black Cloak seeking her. She jumped up. *Gamalda*. Where was Gamalda?

The sky through the window had lightened enough toward dawn that Avielle could see the other weavings hanging on the walls. Could Gamalda have hidden in one of them? Avielle ran from one to the other calling Gamalda's name, but saw no sign of her.

Avielle ran down to the second floor. "Gamalda! Gamalda!" she cried. But there was no sign of her there either. Taking the stairs so fast she almost tumbled down them, Avielle rushed to the first floor, searching. Everything seemed to get in her way, blocking her, stopping her; she bumped into tables, chairs, and walls, then knocked over a lamp that crashed onto the floor. Gamalda was not in the kitchen. Not in Avielle's bedroom. Not in the weaving rooms. Maybe she had fled from the shop. Avielle ran into the front room. The door was open, banging against the wall in the chill wind that blew through the room.

Gamalda lay crumpled on the floor in front of the counter, one arm flung wide, the palm up as though in supplication.

"No!" Avielle screamed and slid onto her knees beside Gamalda, then shook her and called her name over and over again.

But Gamalda was dead.

FRIENDS
CHAPTER TWENTY-NINE

"She gave me a home when mine was destroyed," Avielle said, her shoulders slumping as she finished her speech. "She became my family when my own family was lost."

Avielle was standing in Master Lughgor's shop. Behind her, covered with golden damask cloth that she had woven a month ago, Gamalda's body lay on a table draped in blue velvet. Behind Gamalda's body was the stained glass window of the Magnificent Heart, its jeweled colored light playing across the damask.

"She died to protect me from the Black Cloak," Avielle said to the crowd of people before her. She had chosen Master Lughgor's shop to hold the Pasan, the First Service of Burial, because it was the only place big enough to hold everyone on Postern Street—and Gamalda's other friends as well. The Ocrit, the Second Service of Burial, would be held at the Temple at sunset.

Everyone from Postern Street was there. Master and Mistress Pea—Mistress Pea in a hat piled with artificial fruit; a bundle of cherries kept slipping over her eye, and she kept poking it back. Penatta and Renatta were there in their hideous pea-green dresses. Augum Aslee's love potion seemed to be working because Smitor sat next to Renatta and, during lapses when he forgot this was a somber occasion, smiled at her.

Augum Aslee had come with Tinty, who had dragged a dress out of the dim reaches of their shop; moths had been at the black wool, and the white lace ruff, stained with yellow, was so high around the throat that Avielle wondered how Tinty could swallow. Mistress Rocat had brought tall white candles; they burned in the two silver candelabra stands that Mistress Alubra had brought to flank Gamalda's body. In the front row, Darien sat beside Master Keenum, who rubbed a green rock over and over in his hands. Master Cavenda had managed to tear himself away from his books and sat brooding in a chair in the back. In the very back, pacing rapidly with a preoccupied expression, was Master Steorra. In addition to these were all the apprentices, a few spouses, children, and many friends of Gamalda whom Avielle did not know.

Avielle had been the last one to speak during the service. "Gamalda was the most generous, kindhearted woman I have ever known." And tears began to fall down her face.

The agony of her grief touched the older, black grief that she felt for her family, like a scab that had suddenly been ripped off. When she had found Gamalda, she had rocked her back and forth until dawn speared the sky with red. Then she had covered Gamalda with a white cloth, locked the shop door, and rushed down the street in search of Tinty.

Of all the people on Postern Street she could have gone to, it was Tinty she wanted most. Tinty, who would have looked like an angel in her voluminous white nightgown were it not for the red nightcap split into two points with pom-poms dangling on the ends. Tinty had immediately run to Master Cavenda, who had called the guardsmen. Mistress Rocat, Mistress Pea, and Mistress Alubra had laid out Gamalda's body later that morning. And now, in the afternoon, they were gathered here in Master Lughgor's workshop. It had all happened so fast. Indeed, this time yesterday Gamalda had been alive.

"Let us pray silently now," Avielle said. "And ask the Goddess to bring Gamalda's spirit home." The Pasan was for friends to remember and express their feelings about their lost one. At the Ocrit, Gamalda would be consigned to the Goddess with proper rites. However, Avielle did not think a prayer now would hurt, though she raged at the Goddess in her heart. *Couldn't you leave me anyone!* she shouted in her mind. *You took my entire family. Couldn't you have left me Gamalda?*

After a few minutes she began to cry again, and she felt terribly selfish because her tears were not all for Gamalda; some were for herself.

"I do not know," Avielle said, her voice heavy, "what I shall do or where I shall go, now that I am alone again." Gamalda had left Avielle everything in her will: the shop and her small savings, and though that helped, Avielle still felt lost.

"Blather," said Tinty. "You're not alone. You've got us."

"That's true," said many of them at once. "That's so."

"Why go anywhere?" asked Mistress Rocat in her breathy voice. "Why not stay right here and run the shop?"

"But I'm only an apprentice," Avielle said. "I know so little. I doubt I could keep the shop going."

"Oh, show some spunk, girl!" Mistress Pea said, poking at the cherries on her hat. "Don't go calling failure before you've tried success. If there's anything you need to know about running a business, ask me. I haven't got a head on my shoulders for nothing."

"The girl's a reader," said Master Cavenda. "Anything she needs to know she can find in a book. I'll give her two dozen books for free. Any more at a discount."

"We'll all help you, child," said Master Keenum. "If you need to talk over your troubles, come to me. I will give you a listening stone, maybe Gerdard or Chellan."

"And if she's lonely," said Augum Aslee, "she might as well come see us. Visit the egg. Have tea. Though Tinty slurps so."

"It's a woman she'll need to come to for advice," said Mistress Alubra. The scar on her face was very pink today. "And if I were a less understanding woman I might be hurt that she hadn't come before. Especially after I showed her The Chandelier. And let her try on the crown."

"You let her try on the crown!" Tinty exclaimed, looking at Avielle. Avielle gave a quick shake of her head in warning.

"It suited her well," said Mistress Alubra.

"I'll bet it did," said Tinty, half under her breath.

"Well," said Master Lughgor. "I will provide the girl with coal. For her fire. All winter."

"I'll give her candles for light," said Mistress Rocat.

"Why," said Darien, jumping up, "she'll be like Underfoot! We'll all take care of her!"

"Yes, yes!" cried the others. "Her friends will take care of her."

"That's it," said Master Lughgor.

"He said it just right," whispered Saracinda.

Avielle felt a warmth filling her body as she listened to their words. *Friends?* She had *friends*!

"I will be pleased to contribute as well," called Master Steorra from the back. "Let her come to *Celestial Confabulations* and I will do her birthchart for free. A young woman at such a crossroads must be fully informed as to what awaits her."

"You're so absentminded, you'll forget all about it," scoffed Mistress Alubra.

"I say what I do, and I do what I say. Eventually. Now I must be off. Verge of a breakthrough." And Master Steorra hurried from the room.

"Well," said Master Lughgor. "All seems settled. Good. Very good." He reached into his coat pocket, took out a flask, and took a drink.

"Nobody's asked Vianna what she thinks," Darien said.

"I think you are . . ." Avielle could barely speak. "I do not know how to thank you for your kindness. I will stay. And I will try to be worthy of you all."

Late that night, Avielle lay awake in her room facing the open door that led into the kitchen. The shop was so quiet; oh, there were the occasional familiar creaks of boards settling, a mouse scuttling behind a wall, but there was a great brooding presence of quiet—or was it fear? She should have left a lantern burning. Her legs and arms felt stiff and tense. The words the damada had spoken at the Ocrit played over and over in her head.

"Your fear is great over the manner of this good woman's death. Your despair is great over the darkness that has fallen upon us all. Where does your help come from? From the Goddess Most High. And I tell you she is not only for the strong and the brave, but she is for you, too, the silent, the fearful, the despairing. She will hold you in her arms and comfort you. Know that she loves you. From this comes your help and your strength."

Now, as Avielle lay in her bed, she thought how it had been last night, only last night that such evil had swept through these rooms. Perhaps she should not have stayed here alone this night. Esilia had told her so after the Ocrit had ended. They had stood on the Temple steps in the dusk, cloaks drawn around them against the cold, Esilia's fuzzy hair poking out from under her brown veil.

"You must get someone to stay with you in the shop tonight," Esilia had said. "Or go and stay with your neighbors. From what you told me of their kindness, I'm sure one of them might take you in for a few nights."

Avielle was silent.

"Or I might be able to stay with you," Esilia added. "I'm sure for such a need the damadas would give me leave."

"Thank you, but no. I want to be alone with my grief." In truth, Avielle wanted to be alone to think about Gamalda.

The wind came up, stirring the dry leaves scattered on the Temple steps. Avielle pulled her cloak closer, but it did not warm her. "There is one thing you can do for me, Esilia, if you will."

"You need only tell me," Esilia said, then added under her breath, "Princess."

"I cannot face going to the catacombs to inter Gamalda's body. I still fear the evil there coming from Dolvoka's tomb. And yet, I do not want Gamalda's body to go attended only by those damadas who perform the entombing rites. Will you go and attend Gamalda in my place?"

"I would be honored."

Something creaked in the bedroom. Avielle started, then pulled the covers higher. Somewhere in Tirion, the terror would strike again this night. Someone else would die. Someone else would grieve.

She could die. The Black Cloaks could return. But if they did, she could tell them who she was. Tell them she would send the slaves, relinquish the mines, tell them anything, anything so they would not kill her, too.

Avielle put one hand to her mouth. How could she even think of making such a bargain? Gamalda would have been ashamed of her, ashamed. Gamalda had died to save her; hadn't that taught her anything? The people were suffering. The slaves should be sent and the mines relinquished to save them, not her.

"It has to stop!" she cried. "It all has to stop!"

Then came the voice. *Avielle! Light-Bringer! You are our only hope for Rhia. You must not fail us!*

"But how, how?" she cried to the empty room. "Why do you not tell me how?" Then she remembered the words of the Quasana from her weaving vision:

> ***To save your people you must find the full, undiminished strength of your magic power and let it shine forth. So far you have touched only its surface. To go deeper you must find* The Book of the Sorrowful Queen.**

When Avielle had asked Gamalda if the Quasana had really come to her in the vision, Gamalda asked if Avielle had ever heard of *The Book of the Sorrowful Queen*. Avielle had told her that Esilia had found the title written on a scrap of paper in the High Hall library. Gamalda had said, "Then this is most likely something your mind put together."

But what if that was not true? Avielle wondered now. What if the Quasana really had spoken to her? Really had told her to find the book? If indeed there was even the slightest chance that the book might help, Avielle knew she had to find it. Perhaps it was somewhere in the Temple library; she would ask Esilia to look for it.

"Oh, Gamalda," Avielle whispered, "I need your counsel." She rose from her bed, walked through the kitchen, and climbed up the stairs to Gamalda's bedroom on the second floor. Though the room was dark, a faint light drifted through the window from the street lamp outside. Avielle could see where Gamalda had thrown the bedcovers back when she had rushed out of bed the night before. Her slippers, made of needlepoint worked with roses, sat askew on the blue rag rug. Her book lay where she had tossed it onto the floor.

Avielle sat on the edge of the bed and slid her bare feet into Gamalda's slippers. Then she lay down, put her head on Gamalda's pillow, and pulled up the covers. She smelled the faint scent of cinnamon, vanilla, tea, and wool: Gamalda's scent.

A minute later Underfoot jumped onto the bed. He must have come in through the swinging cat door Darien had made.

"Underfoot!" she cried. "You darling. You always know just when to come." And just when not to come. Thank goodness he had not come last night. After Underfoot curled up by her waist, Avielle rested one hand on his fur and closed her eyes.

"Come back, Gamalda," she whispered. "Come back."

THE VANDAL STRIKES AGAIN
CHAPTER THIRTY

Avielle rose early the next morning, her eyes puffed, her mind dull. The night had not been kind to her; she had slept intermittently, a half-hour here, forty-five minutes there. Once she had thought she heard a banging noise, but it was gone when she woke, and she concluded it must have been part of a dream.

In the kitchen, as she made porridge, she looked at the misshapen teapots lined up on the counter. She ladled steaming porridge into two bowls before she realized what she was doing. She put the pot down and cupped one of the hot bowls in her hands, holding it even though it was beginning to burn.

Someone knocked sharply on the shop door. Avielle dropped the bowl—it clattered onto the counter—and looked at her hands. They were pink, the skin tight, on the edge of being burned.

The knock came again. She left the kitchen, walked through the front room with the heat glowing in her hands, and opened the door. It was Master Cavenda.

"Careful, Vianna!" he said. "Don't get too close to the door or you'll foul yourself."

Avielle stepped back and turned her tired eyes to the front of the door. Someone had stabbed a black-handled knife through the heart of a cow, pinning it to the wooden door. Below, written in smeary, bloody letters, were the words: YOU'LL DIE TOO SILVERSKIN.

Avielle cringed away from the door. She looked right, then left, expecting a black-handled knife to come flying into her own heart. Everything went blurry. She wanted to run, but her knees seemed to dissolve. She felt Master Cavenda's arms come around her, heard Master Cavenda's voice.

A whistling sound grew louder and louder, then suddenly stopped, and another voice was asking, "What's happened? Is she all right?" The sound came from above so Avielle knew she must be down on the floor, though she did not remember getting there. It was Darien's voice. "Let's get her inside," he said. "No," she tried to say, "I can walk." But either she did not say it, or they did not listen.

Then she saw thick bars above her, and she was behind them, and she could not get out. She tried to breathe. A moment later, Avielle realized she was lying on her back on the sofa in the front room, looking up at the oak beams in the ceiling. "It's all right, Vianna," said a voice. Was it Darien? Master Cavenda? "No one will hurt you." That was not true. Someone had hurt Gamalda; she had died in this very room. "You're safe now, Vianna, safe." Then she could speak.

"I am not safe," she whispered. "I am not."

Darien cleaned up the mess. He would not let Avielle touch it, go near it, or see it again. Mistress Pea and the twins rushed over from next door as soon as Master Cavenda told them what had happened. Avielle was still on the sofa, though she was sitting up now, returned to her senses. To her surprise, Mistress Pea plopped down beside her and gathered her up in her arms.

"Poor girl, poor child, poor pet, as if you had not suffered enough." Avielle began to cry. "There now, that's good. You let it all out." And Mistress Pea rocked her back and forth like a tree in a gale. "Make the girl some tea, Penatta. Don't just stand there like a useless stump." She stroked Avielle's hair. "There, child, there. We shouldn't have left you here alone last night. Idiots we are. Tonight you'll stay with us. Renatta and Penatta can squeeze one more into their bed. No, Vianna, don't protest! I've made up my mind, and I'm a woman to be reckoned with."

Darien came back, his face grim. "We'll catch whoever did this, Vianna, I swear it." For a brief wild moment, Avielle wondered if he could have done it. After all, he had almost hated her when she had first come to Postern Street. He had changed, however. She considered everyone else on Postern Street but could not think of anyone who might dislike her enough to do such a thing, nor could she bear the thought that any of them would have.

After she'd had her tea, and everyone had left, Avielle stood in the shop rubbing her fingers over and over the chain attached to Gamalda's spectacles. She thought of how Gamalda's hands had always been moving, touching everything.

Avielle wondered what to do next. She did not have the heart to wait on customers or to weave cloth for the shop, and she was afraid to weave on the third floor without Gamalda's guidance. So she decided to close the shop for the day and visit everyone on Postern Street to gain comfort from her friends. First, she visited Tinty, Augum Aslee, and the egg. Tinty had tried to magic up a rose and had succeeded only in conjuring one giant thorn. Next, Avielle went to see Mistress Rocat, who showed her how to dip candles. Avielle was glad to help; indeed, she wanted to help all her friends, as they had helped her.

As she and Mistress Rocat worked, they discussed the war. "Do you think the slaves should be sent?" Avielle asked her.

"Not a one," Mistress Rocat said in her breathy voice. "If you'll excuse my saying so."

"Isn't it right to sacrifice some people so others will be safe?"

"Only if you are willing to be one of those sacrificed. Are you?"

Avielle did not answer.

Next she went to see Mistress Alubra, who let her watch her work on The Chandelier. However, Avielle's eyes kept turning to the silver circlet on its stand across the room. Though made for a princess, it could easily be a crown for a queen.

Renatta, Penatta, and many others might think a queen's life was all about silk gowns, jewels, and balls, but Avielle knew a queen's life was mostly about duty. And her most important duty was to act for the good of the people. And a queen, Avielle thought as she looked at the diamond on the circlet, did not think of her own safety.

An hour later, Avielle visited Master Cavenda.

"Have you read the book I gave you," he asked her. "The book on the history of Dredonia? Or are you still a teacup?"

"I finished it a week ago," she said.

"And do you still think all the people of Dredonia are evil murderers? That we should kill them all before they kill us?"

"No. I think they are oppressed by the Brethren of the Black Cloaks." Avielle thought of Ogall and Pini in the canyon, the little boy rocking back and forth with his face pressed against his knees. Were they cold? Did they have enough to eat?

"Good," Master Cavenda said. "You have progressed."

"I am looking for a book," Avielle said. "It's called *The Book of the Sorrowful Queen*. Do you have a copy of it?"

"*The Book of the Sorrowful Queen*," he repeated. "Let me see. We've had several queens with special appellations. Queen Soria the Wise; Queen Alanea the Knee-cracker; Queen Josina the Joyful; and Queen Treasha the Scatterwit—among others. But no sorrowful queen that I know of."

"Oh," said Avielle, sitting on her hands and leaning forward. Then she had a thought. "Would you like me to do a little dusting for you?" she asked.

"What? And disturb the peace of those poor little mites who have lived quietly upon the shelves for fifty years? Evict them from their places of residence? Cruel, cruel girl." He stood up. "Start at the top and work your way down. Duster's in the back somewhere in a bin labeled *Why Bother*."

Avielle dusted for two hours, climbing a ladder to reach the top shelves, until she was thoroughly begrimed. And she had made only the merest dent. As she worked, she kept her eye out for *The Book of the Sorrowful Queen*. Master Cavenda had so many books that it was possible he had overlooked it on some shelf in the nether regions. Finally, she washed her hands and face in the sink at the back and went along to Master Lughgor's shop.

Master Lughgor let her watch him paint a panel of the Goddess' foot stepping on the edge of the egg as she rose out of it.

"One step," he said, "She didn't know what she was stepping into. Yet, she did it. Took the first step. What courage."

"Of course," said Avielle. "She is the Goddess. She fears nothing."

Master Lughgor shook his head. "Courage isn't fearlessness. Courage is something you have in spite of fear. Who knows what she feared stepping into all that blackness."

When Avielle reached Master Keenum's late in the afternoon, he gave her a blue rock with pink crystals, Colonna, a comforting stone. She recited poetry to him as he spun, then helped Darien with an essay he was writing.

As she walked toward home, she felt as though she were floating on a sea of tea; everyone along the street had given her tea. Avielle considered going to *Celestial Confabulations* and seeing Master Steorra, but she knew him least well and something else stopped her besides. She was not certain she wanted him to cast her birthchart, because she was not certain she wanted to know her future.

That night Avielle ate dinner with the Peas, a rollicking, screechy dinner where everyone reached for everything at once—elbows nudging, teeth chomping, cries of "pass it here," spoons dripping red sauce on the tablecloth, food flying from platter to dish to mouth, and knives spreading butter as thickly as though it were the mortar between bricks.

Afterward Avielle spent the night in bed with Renatta and Penatta. Renatta snored like a thunderstorm.

THE CROSSROADS
CHAPTER THIRTY-ONE

The next morning was blue and misty, and clouds with a silver sheen passed over the city. Avielle stood looking up at them, after throwing birdseed from the birdfeeder into the street.

The Peas' door flew open, and Renatta came running down the street.

"Vianna!" she cried, waving a broadsheet. "The latest news!" And she thrust the broadsheet into Avielle's hands. Avielle read the title, then the story.

THE BRETHREN OF THE BLACK CLOAKS IMPOSE DEADLINE

The Brethren of the Black Cloaks have sent a message to the High Council giving them four weeks to give up the slaves and mines, or another devastating calamity will strike Tirion. Our wizards are split on the veracity of this threat. Some do not believe the

Black Cloaks will have regained their former strength by then, but some do. The question is, what will the High Council do now? They have been deadlocked over whether or not to send the slaves. Now they must make a decision one way or another.

"It's terrible," Renatta said. "What's to be done?"

"I do not know." Avielle remembered how Master Steorra had said her life was coming to a crossroads; indeed, all of Rhia was coming to a crossroads, and an hour later she decided to consult him at last.

Three times Avielle walked back and forth down the block, each time pausing in front of *Celestial Confabulations*, each time passing it again. The shop, painted red, had a midnight blue door; it was arched with a point at the top that seemed to direct one to other worlds in the great celestial scheme.

Earlier, Avielle had written a note to Esilia asking her if she would she be so kind as to check in the Temple library for *The Book of the Sorrowful Queen*. The library was vast; the book could easily be sitting somewhere in the dim reaches.

Mistress Alubra came down the street with a wicker market basket on her arm.

"How is The Chandelier coming along, Mistress Alubra?" Avielle inquired.

"Steadily, steadily," Mistress Alubra said, fiddling

with a button on her cloak. "I'm certain it will be finished next month."

"Marvelous," said Avielle.

"Any more . . . unfortunate incidents?"

"You mean the vandalism?"

"Yes."

"No, thank goodness," Avielle said. And she thought of the terrible words YOU'LL DIE TOO SILVERSKIN; indeed, they seemed inscribed upon her brain.

Mistress Alubra patted her cheek. "You're too fine a girl to have had such trials in your life. If I were a less discerning woman, I wouldn't see those gray shadows under your eyes. But I do. You be sure to get enough rest. And if you need anything, come to me." She sniffed. "Mistress Pea couldn't help a mouse." And Mistress Alubra walked on with a strange kind of waddle because she was wearing shoes with three-inch heels.

Avielle started down the block again. After five more minutes, she at last mustered her courage, put her hand on the doorknob of Master Steorra's shop, and went inside.

Bells of every timbre and note of the scale jingled above her; indeed, an entire string was set above the door to ring when it opened, as though the proprietor of the shop might not notice a single chime. Star charts plastered the walls, along with prints of the moon in all its phases, paintings of the planets with their names and characteristics, and pictures of the constellations. Avielle saw hers, the Light-Bringer, carrying the sun in one hand and the moon in the other, her hair of stars sweeping out behind her like a cloak.

Several tables with dinged and scuffed legs stood here and there around the room, as though they had been quickly pushed aside to get to something else. And the books! Every table was heaped with them, some closed, some open, some flung on their stomachs as though in disgrace. Papers covered with tiny writing—and what looked like arithmetical and geometric problems—lay scattered over everything, the books, tables, chairs, and even the floor.

"Who is there?" Master Steorra charged into the room. He had one pen behind his ear and another in his hand.

"It is I, Vianna," she said.

He stopped abruptly, almost tripping over one of the tables, then picked up a sheet of paper from the floor and began to read it. He frowned.

"This equation makes no sense," he said, jabbing it with his finger. "All night plucking it from my mind, and it makes no sense. Not a jot, not an iota." He crushed the paper into a ball and threw it back over his shoulder. Then, with his head tipped back and his eyes on the ceiling, he began muttering numbers. His silver-rimmed spectacles slid down to the tip of his nose as though contemplating an escape.

Avielle wondered what to do. "Master Steorra?" she tried again.

He blinked at her. "You—still here?"

"As you see."

He lifted his arms over his head and stretched like a cat. Indeed, he was so rubbery that Avielle suspected he could bend all the way backward and do a flip, like the acrobats in the market. He straightened, then rumpled his jet-black hair.

"I have no time to talk to you—on the edge of a breakthrough that will show the Royal Academy scientists a thing or two. Strumpets!"

Avielle knew, of course, about the Royal Academy of Science. It was where the most learned men and women in Rhia went to study and discuss the sciences.

"Who did you say you were?" Master Steorra asked.

"Vianna. Apprentice to Gamalda . . . who died."

He thrust out his jaw and wiggled it from side to side. "Terrible thing, that. Wish I had heard that foul thing attacking her. I would have rushed over right away."

Avielle wondered if that were true. She would never know.

"During the service for her at Master Lughgor's," she began, "you said you would do my birthchart for free, because I was at a crossroads, and must be as fully informed as possible about what awaited me."

"Did I say that? Did I?" He hummed, looking at the ceiling. "I don't recall."

"Mistress Alubra said you were so absentminded you would forget all about it. Then you said, 'I say what I do, and I do what I say. Eventually.'"

"Oh. Yes. It comes back to me now. But this is not a good moment. Come back later."

Avielle nodded, left the shop, stood outside the door, waited a minute, and then went back in. The bells rang out again. Master Steorra was staring down at another piece of paper in his hand.

He looked up at her, mouth open.

"You said it was not a good moment," Avielle said. "Perhaps this is a better moment?"

Master Steorra's eyebrows flew up, then he frowned. He took off his spectacles folded them up, and tapped them against the side of his nose.

"I believe this is a much better moment," he agreed. He hurried over to the front door, locked it, and flicked the sign over to CLOSED.

"Never good to be interrupted in the middle of doing a reading," Master Steorra explained as he put his spectacles back on. He walked over to a small, square table in one corner of the room, grasped the edge, and tipped it. Down slid books and papers and a scratched metal ruler, all landing in a mess on the floor.

"Have a seat," he said and pulled up a battered chair for her.

Avielle sat. Master Steorra grabbed a sheaf of paper, a pen, a ruler, a pot of ink, and a compass from a shelf, then sat down across from her.

"Date of birth?" he asked.

"The first day of Mara, in the year 3620."

"Ah, the first day of spring. Significant. Interesting. Possibly prophetic. Time of birth?"

"Dawn. Six forty-three."

"Excuse me now while I do some calculations. I must find your rising sign, as well as which planets were in which constellations and houses at the time of your birth. You understand that a birthchart is a kind of picture of the sky at the moment of your birth?"

Avielle nodded.

"Good, good, hate a dense customer—takes hours away from my scientific work. When I am finished with the chart, we will interpret its meaning."

As he worked, Avielle looked at the signs of the zodiac painted on the ceiling. There were the three fire signs: her own Light-Bringer, as well as the Phoenix and the Arrow. There were three earth signs: the Tree, the Mountain, and the Snake. There were three air signs: the Dragon, the Lark, and the Artisan. Last there were three water signs: the Dreamer, the Chalice, and the Fish.

Next, she looked at a painting of the six planets that revolved around Alamaria: Hycath the Hunter; Kikitt the Shrew; Findamora the Sorrowful; Demord the Demon; Ylisynn the Fearless; and Lashata the Lover. With the sun and the moon, these comprised all the heavenly bodies that revolved around Alamaria. Alamaria was at the center of the cosmos.

Master Steorra muttered as he worked and was never still. He sat up in his chair, then leaned back. He swiveled and crossed his right leg over his left, then did the same thing on the other side. With a little sniff, he tapped his spectacles. He shook out both legs as though he were doing a little dance. At last, after this amusing ballet—Avielle thought he should have charged admission— he jabbed the center of his pen into the center of the paper and twirled the paper around it. He had drawn several concentric circles with strange symbols inside them.

"Your birthchart is extraordinary, fascinating," he said at last. "Now let me see if I can explain it. Your sun sign is the Light-Bringer—that is the constellation the sun was in at the time of your birth. Very good, very good—a sign of intensity, spirit, intuition, light. Your rising sign, the Artisan, was the constellation coming over the eastern horizon at the moment of your birth. This is the face you show to the world. Quite appropriate because you are a weaver.

"Now look at this." He tapped his finger on the paper. "Your chart is in what we astrologers call a bucket pattern. Picture all the signs or constellations of the zodiac in a circle—as I have drawn here. Now see how all the planets are clustered on one side of the circle and how this one planet alone stands out on the other side? That planet is Lashata the Lover. This is your Ruling Planet and it is dominant in your chart. It means your capacity for love is enormous, tremendous, unparalleled. That is true about you—past, present, and future.

"Love, eh?" He smiled slyly.

Avielle tried to hide her face by looking down at her hands. How could this be? Her mother had said she was incapable of a deep and abiding love.

"You said you could warn me about my future," Avielle said.

"Yes, yes." Master Steorra scribbled away, making more calculations, sometimes scratching the pen against his chin and leaving blots. Then he slowly raised his head and stared across the room. He lay down the pen with exquisite care, aligning it perfectly beside the paper. He put the compass beside it so it, too, lined up exactly with the paper.

"I . . . ," Master Steorra began, then stopped. Interlacing his fingers one by one, as though all the world depended on his precision, he folded his hands on the table. "I have never seen readings so dire," he said at last. "Are you certain you wish to know?"

Avielle crossed her feet and pressed her ankles together. She closed her eyes then opened them. "Yes," she said. "I must know."

"It will begin on the afternoon of the second day of the month of Novasenna," he said. "And come to full force at dawn on the third day. On those days Hycath the Hunter and Demord the Demon will both be in the constellation of the Light-Bringer and in the House of Death."

An arrow seemed to strike Avielle's heart. "Is this as terrible as I think it is?"

Master Steorra nodded. "Some great evil awaits you. You may die. Or fall into some kind of darkness."

She could not speak.

"But do not despair; there is hope."

Avielle splayed her fingers over her birthchart. "Tell me!"

"On that same day Lashata the Lover and the sun will be in conjunction. A powerful combination of light and love. So do you see now the crossroads at which you stand?"

Avielle sat back. "I do," she whispered.

"Now then." He stood up and pulled down his stained cuffs, his brisk, busy self again. "I must get on with my work. It is critical. Important. Imperative."

She stared at him. How could he deliver a fate so dire and expect her simply to walk away? Her throat seemed to swell, her head to ache, and she felt small and insignificant, like crumbs on a plate, before all these forces arrayed about her.

"I will fall into darkness," she said. "I will fall."

"You may," he agreed. "It is entirely within the realm of possibility. Come now, child, do not be downcast. I must be getting on with my great treatise, *The Starry Messenger*." He scowled. "I will show those old relics at the Royal Academy of Science! Refuse to see what's in front of their eyes. But my telescope, oh yes! My telescope will change all that." He paused. "Oh bother, are you still here? Still upset?" He sat down again, took off his spectacles, and waved them in the air.

"Look, child. You have the sun on your side and that means the Goddess is a powerful ally."

Avielle wiped her tears. "I do not understand."

"The Goddess dwells in the sun."

"That is wrong," Avielle said. "The Goddess dwells in Alamaria."

"Ridiculous! That is based on the old idea that Alamaria is the center of the universe, and that the sun revolves around Alamaria. But that idea is false. Utterly, absolutely, completely, totally false." He put both elbows on the table and screwed up his face. "The truth—and what the old relics at the academy refuse to admit—is that the *sun* is at the center of the universe, and Alamaria revolves in a circle around it."

All the star charts on the walls, all the papers with equations scribbled on them, all the books, all the pictures of the constellations blurred before Avielle's eyes. What Master Steorra had just said went against everything that she had ever been taught.

"And it means, Vianna," he said, "that light is at the center of the universe. Thus the Goddess is there, too."

Avielle had always believed that the Goddess dwelt at the center of the universe; that was nothing new. However, to learn that the sun was at the center was an idea with ramifications so immense she could barely grasp them. The

Goddess had to dwell at the center of the universe; therefore, she had to dwell in the sun.

"You are certain?" she asked.

Master Steorra nodded. "All this will be made clear in *The Starry Messenger*. Then I will no longer be called a fool and forced to do astrology for a living when I should be teaching at the Royal Academy! Away now, child, away!"

Avielle walked home, her steps slow, her mind brimming.

COMING HOME

CHAPTER THIRTY-TWO

Early the next morning on the third floor, Avielle threaded the loom with white thread, as she always did to prepare for one of her weaving visions. When she finished the threading that afternoon, she sat down slowly on the bench before the loom, still uncertain whether she should attempt this without Gamalda.

Avielle looked across the room at the weaving of the waterfall that had saved her life. She remembered the roaring sound of the water as she had flowed with it, remembered the sound of Gamalda's voice that had flowed with it, too. And Avielle knew that Gamalda would have wanted her to continue seeking the full strength and goodness of her Dredonian magic power, in spite of the danger that she might use it to do harm, in fact to avert that danger. *The edge you stand on is perilous.* It seemed even more perilous in light of what Master Steorra had said yesterday.

Avielle put one hand in her pocket and felt the note

Esilia had sent. She had written that she would look for *The Book of the Sorrowful Queen* in the Temple library.

Avielle looked down at the loom, and though her hands were shaking, she picked up the shuttle. She began to weave and chant until her mind sank down into the dreaming trance.

Wearing her white petticoat and chemise, she walked along a path through a forest of redwood trees. She passed among the giant trunks, since the branches began high up in the air. Rays of sun like the tines of a fork shone crosswise through the trees and fell onto the forest floor.

When she reached a clearing, Avielle dug a hole in the earth. When it was deep enough, she stepped down into it and buried her legs in their black stockings. She touched the bag of pearls hanging from her neck, then straightened and stretched her bare arms over her head, pointing toward the sky.

Avielle took root and grew into a tree. There among all those redwoods, she shone silver, with silver bark, limbs, and leaves that glistened in the sun. She did not grow as tall as the redwoods, and her leaves fell each winter and grew back each spring, but there she stood—steadfast, wholehearted, joyful.

The trees murmured to one another in their creaky way, spinning tales of rain, of sun, of wind, and of earth. Families of squirrels made nests among Avielle's roots; she felt glad that she could shelter them. They tore off strips of her old black stockings to make nests for their babies until at last there was only one thread left, zigzagging up and down like a black crown.

The next morning Avielle did not want to rise from her bed. Sometime during the night she had pulled the covers over her head until only her nose and eyes remained exposed to the frigid air. Now, when she breathed, her breath hung in the air as though asking a question—where is the fire that will warm me? Avielle felt something move under the sheets in the crook of her knees.

"Underfoot!" she exclaimed. "How did you sneak in here, you lazy creature?"All she heard was a faint meow.

Avielle got up at last, threw on her quilted dressing gown, and went to the kitchen stove to stir up the fire that she had banked last night. When it was crackling, she went back to her room to fetch her clothes so she could dress by the stove. Her eyes fell on the book on her bedside table: *A Past and Present History of Dredonia*.

As she pulled on her hose, petticoats, and black dress before the stove, she wondered if Pini and Ogall still lived in the canyon, and if so, how they fared this cold morning. How long had it been since they had slept in a real bed? *We hunger . . . each night colder . . . can you help? Pini is so small.*

Later, after she had eaten, Avielle swirled the tea in her cup, looking down at the brown liquid. She remembered how in her weaving vision she had sheltered the families of squirrels and how wonderful that had felt. She set the cup down, picked it up, and then slammed it down, making the china ring.

"All right!" she said. "I will do it."

First, she found two old woolen cloaks, both brown, that Gamalda had meant to donate to a charitable society; Avielle had not yet found the time to take them herself. She shortened both and ran a quick hemstitch along the bottom. Next, she found the largest market basket in the shop and began packing it. In went the folded cloaks, two pairs of mittens, four loaves of bread, a block of strong cheddar cheese, half a dozen apples, and a blanket covering everything. She wished she had time to make clothes for the boys; she suspected theirs were threadbare by now.

They might not even be in the canyon any longer, she told herself; after all, it had been three weeks. Then she felt ashamed at the relief that possibility brought.

An hour and a half later, Avielle was walking through the canyon, breathing in the scent of the pine trees. The day was clear and cold; and though it was midmorning, frost lingered like a guest who did not know he had worn out his welcome. It was the tenth day of Octal, and most of the leaves had fallen from the aspens, leaving their bare branches as white and fragile as an old woman's hair against the blue sky.

As Avielle walked she thought about the vandal who had stabbed the cow heart to the front door, and the bloody message, YOU'LL DIE TOO SILVERSKIN. Darien had made her bars to place against the front and back doors for extra protection, but she still did not feel safe. Avielle wondered if the vandal meant only to scare her, or if he really meant to harm her. And she wondered what he might do next. For days now she had slept poorly, always listening, always starting awake at the slightest noise.

When she reached the meadow with the massive boulders lying about like giant's teeth, Avielle looked for the golden glorionnas that had carpeted the hills on her last visit. Instead, she saw a sight so beautiful she nearly dropped her basket.

Frost coated the entire north-facing hill with sparkling silver light. Each blade of grass, each leaf on each bush, each bud, each petal of each flower, was silver; all were shining as though some enchanted spell had brought the stars down to lay quivering on the hillside.

Avielle began to climb the hill, clambering around the rocks, her black skirt trailing through the frost. She paused and looked up at the sun, as much as she could without being blinded. Was it really at the center of the universe as Master Steorra claimed?

Avielle started forward again, listening for the sound of Ogall's flute, for how else would she find them in all of the rocks and rills in the canyon? After an hour of fruitless searching, she was nearly ready to give up; the boys must have traveled on. Then she thought of calling them. Why not? Why wouldn't they come? Who else would know their names?

"Ogall!" she shouted. "Pini! Where are you?" Her voice echoed off the rocks. "Ogall! Pini!" she shouted again and again. "It is I, Vianna!"

She heard the sound of bushes crackling, of small stones skittering. She turned eastward. Ogall was running toward her down the hill some distance away. He came closer and closer, skirting rocks and wild rose bushes, until at last he stopped before her. He was not even out of breath.

"What you doing!" he cried. "Do not scream our names so. Brethren will hear! They will come!"

"I am sorry, but I did not know how else to find you. Where is Pini?"

Ogall pointed. "Back over hill. We find a cave to shelter." He hesitated. "Why you come? You bring soldiers?"

"No!" Avielle held out the basket. "I brought you food."

His eyes lit up. "Bread?"

"Four loaves. And cheese, too."

Ogall jumped into the air. "Come, take you to Pini. He will be full of happiness."

When they reached the cave, just a small hollow in the hill, Avielle saw a fire ring outside it—nothing burned in it now. She followed Ogall inside the cave. Pini lay on a pile of fir boughs and grass, which functioned as a pallet large enough for the two of them. More boughs lay over him—makeshift blankets. In one corner of the cave was a huge pile of nuts. A log made a bench to sit on, another, split in half, made a table. On it was a cleaned fish. This was how they lived, Avielle thought, and her hands dug into the handle on the wicker basket until they hurt.

"Look, Pini," Ogall said. "Remember Vianna? She come to see us."

Pini, his silver hair matted, his neck a stick, took one look at Avielle and curled into a ball.

Avielle knelt on the dirt and began unpacking the basket.

"First, there is a blanket to keep you warm," she said, spreading it on top of Pini. He put his hands over his head.

Avielle lifted out the cheese, the loaves of bread, and the apples and put them on the makeshift table. Ogall grabbed one of the loaves, broke off a piece, held it out to Pini, and said something in Dredonian.

Pini opened his eyes. He saw the bread. His hand darted out, and he snatched the bread, shoving as much of it into his mouth as possible. He chewed with his cheeks bulging.

"Careful," Avielle said, "he will choke."

Ogall broke off another piece of bread, began to eat it, then checked himself.

"You wish some, Vianna?" he asked.

"No," she said. "Thank you, but I am not hungry."

As the two boys worked away at the bread, cheese, and apples, Avielle took note of how terribly thin they were. Indeed, they seemed to be all sharp corners—elbow bones, wrist bones, anklebones, and knee bones sticking out from their torn trousers. Dirt crusted their clothes, which were really only holes held together by thread. And the boys smelled terrible.

She took out the cloaks she had shortened for them.

"Be warm!" said Ogall, first laying one of the cloaks over Pini, then wrapping the other around himself.

However, even as she saw their joy, Avielle knew that her gifts bestowed only brief comfort; four loaves of bread, some cheese, and the cloaks were not enough.

"You cannot stay here like this, Ogall," Avielle said. "You will never survive the winter. You must go home, or go somewhere else."

"Never go home. Brethren take Pini. Kill me for stealing him from evil school. Think to go south, to warmer place, but Pini too weak to walk so far."

Avielle looked at Pini crunching an apple, juice running down his chin. He and Ogall needed help. But they were Dredonians. Her muscles tightened. Then Pini looked at her and Pini smiled.

"Come home with me," Avielle said.

THE GLORIONNA SUN DAISY
CHAPTER THIRTY-THREE

Avielle waited until dark to lead Pini and Ogall out of the canyon and onto the road that lead to Tirion. Avielle had wrapped the boys in the cloaks she had brought for them—she had overestimated Pini's height and his cloak dragged on the ground—and instructed them to draw up their hoods. That way, she hoped, no one would see they had silverskins and demand to know why they were not wearing their badges. After a mile, they entered the southern city gates.

Although it was dark, people still thronged the streets, since the Black Cloaks did not begin roaming until after midnight. Then you would not see a soul, not even a guardsman, healer, or midwife; anyone sick or injured would have to wait until dawn. Though Avielle went unveiled according to the law, she hoped the dark would protect her from being recognized.

"Stay close," Avielle whispered to Ogall, as they wove their way through the crowd. "Keep your heads down."

Pini stumbled just as a guardsman came toward them. Avielle grabbed him and turned him to face a baker's shop window. She pointed at the cookies and pies, as though showing them to an eager little boy, as indeed Pini was when he saw the food. The guardsman passed.

When they at last reached Postern Street, Avielle lurked on the corner, uncertain what to do. What if some of her neighbors were out on the street? They would certainly question her about her two followers.

"Walk several paces behind me," she instructed Ogall. "If anyone comes up to speak to me, continue past, go around the block, and come into the shop with the red and gold cloth in the window. I will be waiting." And she started down the street.

Their luck held; no one she knew passed them. She fumbled with her key, opened the shop door, pulled Pini and Ogall inside, and then locked the door behind them.

"Hurry," she said. And she led them to the third floor.

"Pini will not look away from the magic weavings," Ogall told Avielle the next day when she climbed to the third floor with an armful of new clothes for them to wear. With the ugly badge pinned onto her cloak, Avielle had walked unveiled to a shop ten blocks away to make the purchases, so no one from Postern Street would see her and wonder why she was buying boys' clothes. It had been a risk, for Lord General Maldreck, Grig Durdin, High

Councilman Herector, or someone else who had once seen her at the High Hall might have recognized her. Fortunately, no one had.

"Pini like this weaving best," Ogall added, pointing.

Pini was sitting on the floor before Gamalda's weaving of the forest that changed from spring to summer to fall to winter over and over again. Each time the picture changed Pini clapped his hands and laughed.

"I haven't heard him laugh in much time," said Ogall. "He call it shining magic. Pini ask—you weave these, Vianna?"

Avielle shook her head and explained to him about Gamalda, then told him how she herself was just learning to make magical weavings. After Ogall told all this to Pini, Pini clasped his hands around his ankles and asked Ogall something.

"He want see your magic weavings," Ogall said.

"Perhaps later," said Avielle, stalling. She did not want to show them her mangled attempts or have them discover the feelings that went with them. "You two need baths before you put on these new clothes. And remember, you must stay very quiet. No one must know you are here."

She filled a washtub with hot water for them—lugging the pots of water all the way up to the third floor. After that, she brought them food, then told them she had to work for the rest of the day.

All afternoon, while she waited on customers, she

jumped at every strange sound she heard, fearing it might be the boys.

"I'll take three yards of this white linen," said a young woman whose waist was cinched so tight in her corset that Avielle thought it a wonder she did not snap in two. Avielle cut the cloth, wrapped it in brown paper, and tied it with blue ribbon, just as Gamalda had always done. The shop was still doing well, for Gamalda had left a large supply of cloth. However, although Avielle was adding to it bit by bit, she was still selling cloth faster than she could make it.

Late in the afternoon, when the midday rush was over, Master Steorra hurried into the room.

"Vianna—fine day," he said. "I need a good length of cloth for a suit. A tweed might do. Brownish. Something that looks learned. Have to look an authority when I present my treatise to those relics at the Royal Science Academy."

"Then you have finished it?" Avielle cried. "You have finished *The Starry Messenger*?"

Master Steorra turned a little sideways to her and swung one leg back and forth. "Well, finished, but not, let us say, *legible*. I took it to the Peas, but they will not print it. Not for any amount of money. Say they cannot read it. Haven't they eyes?" he grumbled.

Avielle thought. "My handwriting is very clear—I was taught well. What if I transcribe it for you? You can read me the words, and I will write them down."

He turned toward her, pushed his recalcitrant spectacles up, and peered at her through them, as though he were just seeing her for the first time through his telescope.

"You would do that for me?" he asked.

She smiled. "Of course, it is the very least I can do after you were so kind as to do my birthchart."

"I did your birthchart? Hmm. I can't recall."

"Hycath the Hunter and Demord the Demon in the sign of the Light-Bringer and in the House of Death?" Avielle reminded him. "And the sun and Lashata the Lover in conjunction?"

"Oh yes. I remember now." He pulled on the end of his nose. "But that's all still a few weeks away. You should be able to finish transcribing *The Starry Messenger* before your fate descends upon you. Come after work tomorrow."

"I will be there at six o'clock," she said.

That evening, after the shop was closed, Avielle took a tray with bean soup, apples, and fresh rolls from Waterbee's Bakery up to the boys. She ate with them.

"Pini still wants to see your weavings," Ogall said when they finished their meal.

Avielle hesitated. She did not want to bring fear or sorrow to them, but even when she explained the nature of the magic, Pini still insisted on seeing the weavings. She brought the most significant out of the chest and placed them on the floor in the order in which she had created them.

Pini put them on one by one and many emotions passed over his face. When he finished, he spoke rapidly to Ogall.

"Pini say you have great powerful magic," Ogall said. "But most you not know yet. He says he teach you more, good magic, if you want."

"What can he teach me?" Avielle asked.

Ogall spoke to Pini, then turned back to her.

"He say you not need loom to weave, that first thing to learn. Second thing, harder thing, is what you weave not even need to be made of thread."

Avielle stared at Pini. "How can this be?"

"I not know," Ogall said. "But if Pini say it so, it so."

Pini cupped his hands together. They began to glow brighter and brighter, until a ball of light grew between them. He raised his hands to his lips, blew gently, and the bubble of light floated up and hovered in the air. He laughed.

Avielle watched the light. Any magic Pini taught her would be Dredonian magic, and she still feared it. But wasn't it what she had been seeking all along? To embrace pure Dredonian magic, to find the deepest power at the heart of herself? And her explorations of this had not led her wrong so far; although she had suffered fear, sorrow, and rage, she had also found courage and the ability to care about people. There was good in the Dredonian part of herself, something she had not known when she had begun all this with Gamalda two months ago. *Gamalda had known.*

Yet the evil of Dolvoka still lurked inside her, and if Avielle entered totally into Dredonian magic, the risk of that evil coming forward through her weaving would be greater than ever. But everything she had learned had prepared her for this next step; once again, to go deeper was the only way to go forward. She needed all the magic she could learn, so that when she stood at the crossroads, when the power of Demord the Demon and Hycath the Hunter was unleashed, the evil of Dolvoka would not overcome her. Avielle had to risk everything so she could stand with Lashata the Lover and the sun.

Then she remembered how in her vision the Quasana had said she had only touched the surface of her magic power, that its full depth remained to be discovered. And she heard the voice that haunted her mind. *Avielle! Light-Bringer! You are our only hope for Rhia. You must not fail us.*

Avielle turned to Ogall. "Tell Pini I wish to learn."

Early the next morning, as the pale pink light of dawn crept through the big windows on the third floor, Avielle sat cross-legged on the yellow rug with a pillow between her back and the wall, as Pini had instructed. He rested his hand on her left knee, about to teach her to weave without using her loom, but still using thread. Yet, there was no thread laid out on the floor before her. Ogall had explained that the thread would appear by magic.

Avielle felt slightly ridiculous, and her muscles tightened.

"Take comfort, Vianna," Ogall said, sitting on her other side. "Pini never lead wrong."

Avielle wished she were as certain.

"Before we begin, Ogall," she said, "I need to ask you a question."

He nodded.

"Do you think the Brethren of the Black Cloaks will keep their promise? To end the terror if we send them the slaves? And give them the mines?"

"No," Ogall said. "Evil has no . . . what word . . . honor?"

"What will they do with the slaves, if we send them?"

"Slaves have terrible lives. Work deep in dark mines in mountains. Never see sunshine more."

Avielle bowed her head. Was there, then, no way out of this woe that had fallen upon Rhia? There were fewer than two weeks left before the Black Cloaks' deadline. What new terror would they unleash upon the city?

Avielle turned her attention back to Pini as he began to speak in Dredonian. His voice was a murmur, rising and falling, a chant that rippled through her mind. Avielle closed her eyes. She seemed to be carried on the chant, wandering up and down white-capped mountains and deep green valleys. The words penetrated so deeply into her mind that they were no longer words, but existed in a realm beyond words. And she knew them, understood them, and part of what they told her was to think of one bright, shining thing.

She saw the hill in the canyon covered with glorionna sun daisies waving in the wind, then all the beauty of one sun daisy alone filled her mind. The petals, flame-shaped, were gold and radiant. Darker golden shadows showed where the petals overlapped. From the amber-colored center grew hundreds of tiny spikes powdered with yellow pollen.

Avielle took the strands of the flower—the petals, the spikes, the pollen, the golds—and wrapped them around her fingers. She seized a strand of green stem and another of pale green leaf, and wrapped those around her fingers, too. Then she began to dance, play, and sing, weaving the strands in and out of each other. The sun daisy burned bright in her mind, and she could smell it, see it, and taste it. There was a note in the singing, a pure high note that seemed beyond all knowing, above all knowing, and all knowing. Avielle thought she was hearing the faintest echo of the voice of the Goddess.

However, beyond all this, a shadow loomed. She could feel it beyond the circle of the sun daisy. It came to her, a strand in her hand that she did not want to weave, but could not drop.

When the sun daisy was complete and glowing in her mind, slowly the dancing stopped, the weaving stopped, and the singing stopped. Her hands grew still. Avielle became aware of Pini's hand patting her leg. She opened her eyes.

There on the floor before her lay a weaving. In the center of it was a glorionna sun daisy, glowing, vibrant in satin thread, the petals distinct around the amber center. But one petal—half hidden behind the others—was black and serrated at the tip, like a crown.

A LEADER
CHAPTER THIRTY-FOUR

Over the next few weeks, Avielle continued to practice weaving without a loom with Pini. She also spent what time she could spare from the boys, and from transcribing *The Starry Messenger,* with her friends on Postern Street. Usually she visited after the workday had ended, and sat with them talking and drinking tea, eating toast, or munching cookies.

She learned that Master Alubra, who worked at a bookbinder's shop in the market district, loved music, particularly waltzes. She learned that Mistress Rocat's husband and child had both died of red-eye fever five years ago. She learned that Master Lughgor thought Saracinda, in spite of her wispy ways, would be one of the greatest glass artists of the next generation. She learned that Master Cavenda wrote novels that he never showed to anyone; that Tinty feared mice; that Master Keenum had a penchant for toffees; and that Master Steorra thought children should be free of schooling until they were ten years old, to better develop their imaginations.

One subject was on everyone's mind: the Black Cloaks' deadline. Indeed, although there was no hint of a decision yet from the High Council, rumors flew through the city, a different one each day.

One dark and rainy morning Darien stopped by the shop. "Master Keenum has a bad cold," he said. "He snuffled and coughed half the night. And I've got me a job in the south part of the city. No jobs all week, then all of a sudden—bang! Sniffles and work. Both at the same time." He shook his head. "I'll be away long past nightfall. Would you look in on him, Vianna?"

"I would be happy to," she said. Later that afternoon, after she had taken lunch to the boys, she stood at the stove, making ginger-cabbage soup for Master Keenum. As she stirred it, she wondered what to do about the boys. She could not keep them on the third floor of the shop forever. Besides, there was so little for them to do there. She had given them books, but they could not read Rhian and so could only look at the illustrations. She had also given them paper and colored chalks, and taught them the game knight-on-a-stick. Fortunately, Underfoot had discovered them and provided hours of entertainment with bits of string, balls, and wadded-up paper. At night she was teaching them to speak Rhian. In their new clothes the boys looked like Dredonian Rhians, but Ogall's accent would give him away instantly. She had told him if they were discovered he should stutter and act like a scatterwit, and Pini should act mute.

Pini. Were the weavings she wove without the loom his magic or hers? When she had asked, Ogall had assured her that the magic was hers, that Pini simply led the way. The next step was for her to find the way herself. How she wished Gamalda had been here to see this magic. How she would have loved it.

"Oh, Gamalda," she whispered, as she stirred the soup, "I miss you so much. And you, my Rajio."

When the soup was done, Avielle took it to Master Keenum's.

"Come in and be welcome," said Master Keenum's creaky old voice when she knocked.

Avielle went in.

Master Keenum leaned back on three pillows, propped up in his bed like a king on a throne, covered with a pile of quilts.

"It is I, Vianna," she said, putting the soup pot down on the table. "I have brought you some ginger-cabbage soup. Gamalda's recipe. Excellent for a cold."

"Kind of you, sweet dearie," he said. "It's cold enough today to freeze even one of Augum Aslee's socks. Hot soup will be quite the treat. Just so." He sneezed into a large purple handkerchief.

Avielle filled a chipped blue bowl with soup and took it over to him. He was turning a highly polished pink rock, veined with white, over and over in his hands.

"Here is the soup," she said.

Master Keenum hesitated. "Oh, yes. It's just that I can't bear to put down Omalia even for a second. She's my newest treasure. Comes from the wild Nanara Mountains in the east. Her magic fits into mine like a cat into a lap." He had a fit of coughing.

"I really think you should eat this soup," she said. "It will ease your tight chest."

"Oh, very well. Hold Omalia for me."

Avielle took the rock and gave Master Keenum the bowl and a spoon. She drew up a chair beside the bed and fiddled with Omalia while he ate. She thought she sensed something coming through the rock, a kind of presence, but she might only have been imagining it.

When he finished, he handed her back the bowl. "Now, give me Omalia, sweet dearie," he said.

Avielle put the stone into his hand.

"Omalia has great power," he said. "The greatest of any stone I have ever known—for one who knows how to hear. And I do, dearie, my hearing is first-rate. Omalia goes down, right down to the truth about someone and plants her thumb on it. There's no getting away then! She doesn't play games like my lovely, cryptic, little Lidel, who only gives snippets and snappets." He turned toward the room. "Do you hear me, Lidel?" he shouted. Then he leaned forward and pointed one finger at Avielle. "Omalia put her thumb on you when you held her, sweet dearie, and she says you're a leader."

"She is wrong." Avielle laughed. "I am no leader."

"Omalia doesn't lie," Master Keenum said, his voice severe. "Perhaps you aren't a leader yet, but you'll lead; and not only that"—he sneezed—"you'll be a mighty leader."

"You cannot be a leader," Avielle said, forgetting to be cautious in her bitterness, "if your people hate you."

"No one hates you on Postern Street," he said.

"Then who smears hateful messages across my door?"

"Bah! One vandal is of no importance. You're welcomed here, for your kindness and your goodness."

Avielle tried to organize her thoughts. "You cannot be a leader if you are afraid to put yourself at risk of death."

"So you're afraid to die, who isn't? But when it comes to the moment"—he nodded—"you might throw yourself in front of a carriage to save a drunkard and a wife-beater. How can you know until it's staring you in the face? So that's no reason." He coughed. "What else? Come to the heart of it, dearie. I think I want a second bowl of soup."

There was a silence.

"I stand at a crossroads," Avielle said, "and may fall into darkness. Should I try to lead, I might do great harm."

Master Keenum rolled one of the quilts, an orange one, in his hands. "Now it seems to me that a crossroads goes four ways. So you also might stop great harm, stop those foul Brethren of the Black Cloaks dead in their tracks if you lead your people, Princess Avielle. You may save Rhia."

Avielle made a strangled sound in her throat.

"Your words gave you away, sweet dearie," Master Keenum said. "That and other things. But don't be afraid. I swear by rock and stone that I'll keep your secret. But Omalia never speaks wrong—unlike some other rocks I know!" he shouted across the room again. He turned back toward Avielle. "You'll be a leader. And a mighty one. Whether for good or ill I can't say."

That night Avielle sat up late in the kitchen drinking lemon tea, going over all that Master Keenum had said. She thought she had given up being a princess, but all fate seemed to be pushing her to take up that mantle again, or rather, to take up the mantle of being a queen. *You might stop great harm . . . if you lead your people, Princess Avielle. You might save Rhia.* The only way to do that was to stop being afraid of what might happen to her if she came forward and claimed the throne. For if by some miracle the Brethren of the Black Cloaks did not kill her, and she became queen, she would send the slaves to Dredonia and give over the mines in order to stop the terror, in order to save Rhia.

And then Avielle saw herself standing on a tower, a black crown upon her head, her dyed black hair streaming behind her in the wind. Below, tens of thousands of people—ready to follow her commands—knelt beneath a great black magic net that she had woven. On either side of her were spears set in the stone floor, and on each spear, a head. Behind her stood a Black Cloak, not threatening her, *standing beside her.*

"Please, no," Avielle whispered as her teacup slipped from her hands and fell onto the table. *You'll be a leader. And a mighty one. Whether for good or ill I can't say.* Tea dripped down the tablecloth onto the floor, staining the white cloth brown. And Avielle remembered what Gamalda had said: *It is even possible that you could grow strong enough to trap others in darkness.*

Avielle heard a sound coming from the front of the shop. She stood up, thinking one of the boys had risen, and went into the front room. No one was there. The noise came again—it was coming from the front door. Her scalp tingled and the backs of her arms felt tight. She felt no sense of dread, however, so she did not think it was a Black Cloak. What if it were the vandal? It could be dangerous to confront him, but she wanted to know who he was, and she wanted to tell him to leave her alone.

She crept toward the door, lifted the bar, put her hand on the latch, and yanked the door open.

"Penatta!" she cried. For Penatta stood before her with a brush dripping with red paint in one hand and a pail of red paint in the other. "You?" Avielle asked, incredulous. "You are the vandal?"

Penatta just stood there scowling.

"But why?" Avielle asked. "Why?"

"Because you're a silverskin," she said, "and you're probably a spy. You silverskins are nothing but Dredonian puppets. You all should be banished. And if you won't leave the country, you should be killed—or you would if I had my way."

"But—"

"And you've taken Renatta away from me. She talks to you now. Instead of me. She wants to dress different from me. Be different. I miss her. I hate you!" And Penatta threw the pail of red paint at Avielle: it splashed over her, trickling down her face, her hair, her dress. Then Penatta ran away.

Avielle stood, trembling; she felt covered in blood. She found a clean place on her sleeve and wiped the paint out of her eyes; it smelled of turpentine. When she could see again, she shut the door, locked it, and replaced the bar. She stripped off her clothes, not wanting to drag the dripping garments through the shop. Not letting her mind think, she concentrated on making a neat little bundle out of her clothes, putting the paint splatters on the inside. With the outside, she wiped her face and hands.

Later, however, as she washed her hair, the thoughts broke through. Penatta had written the words YOU'LL DIE TOO SILVERSKIN on the window. Penatta had stuck the knife through the cow heart on the door. Avielle remembered with a shudder that she had shared a bed with Penatta at the Peas right after that incident. *She could have throttled me,* Avielle thought, *throttled me in my sleep.* So much hate living right next door, and she had not even known.

As Avielle scrubbed her face and hands—she could not

seem to get all the paint out, especially from her hands—she wondered what to do. Should she tell Mistress Pea? Tell anyone on Postern Street? Would Penatta stop, now that Avielle had caught her? Or would she grow even bolder?

BEAUTIFUL BEYOND WORDS
CHAPTER THIRTY-FIVE

The next day Master Keenum's cold grew worse, settling into his frail old chest. Avielle received a note from Darien saying that his job had been extended for a week, and he would be staying on. Unfortunately, he had sent no return address, so Avielle could not write back to tell him to come home. She called a healer, who left herbs for tisanes and poultices to be administered every four hours. After much thought, Avielle gathered the people of Postern Street together to organize them into shifts to take care of Master Keenum.

"I'll cook for him," Mistress Pea said during the meeting in Gamalda's shop, where they were all crowded together.

"No," said Mistress Alubra. "I shall. Everyone knows my soups are nourishing for the sick."

Avielle mediated between them until both were, if not satisfied, at least mollified.

"Now I think we have everything arranged," Avielle said at last. "Does everyone know what to do?"

They all nodded.

Master Steorra waved his spectacles. "I do not mind taking time away from my research for such a fine, for such a worthy, for such an exceedingly humanitarian cause."

Tinty stayed after everyone else had left, and Avielle told her what had happened with Penatta.

"I doubt she'll do anything more," Tinty said, "now that you've caught her at her dirty tricks. Beastly little coward. I've a mind to blacken her eye. Maybe both of them. Serve her right."

"No," Avielle said. "No more violence."

Tinty left, grumbling.

When Avielle took up porridge to the boys the following morning, the room on the third floor was cold, a sign of winter's impending arrival, although it was only the first day of Novasenna, the middle of fall. There was no fireplace on the third floor. The boys had blankets enough to be warm, but they could not stay under blankets all day. So after lunch Avielle closed the shop and walked to Augum Aslee's to buy some magical warm socks.

When she reached the shop, she knocked twice on the door as usual, as the sign requested. No one answered, however. She heard a strange sound coming from inside, and stood, puzzled. Was it—could it possibly be—barking? She stood for a moment, undecided, then put her hand on the doorknob and went inside.

"Hello?" she called.

"Quick, you idiot, close that door!" Tinty cried.

Avielle did, then looked around in amazement.

Puppies romped and rolled and ran all over the room—brown ones, white ones, black ones, yellow ones, spotted ones, and all combinations in between. They chewed on paper they had pulled off chairs; they nosed among overturned tables; and they scampered about with balls of wool in their mouths. Tinty stood in the middle of this chaos looking rather dazed. Augum Aslee, his knitting thrown over one shoulder, stood behind his chair clutching the dome that held the egg.

"What happened?" Avielle cried as she waded through the puppies toward Tinty.

"Thought my gift might be juggling," Tinty said glumly.

Avielle stared. "What does that have to do with puppies?"

"Watch." Tinty picked up three apples on the table.

"No, don't!" cried Augum Aslee. But it was too late, Tinty had already begun to juggle. She threw the apples into the air, and they whirled in a circle—one, two, three—one, two, three—faster and faster. Then each apple began to shimmer with light. A moment later the apples turned into sparkling forks, then into books, then into fish as silver as steel. Last, the fish turned into puppies, and the puppies flew out of Tinty's hands and jumped onto the floor where, yelping, they joined their brothers and sisters.

"You see," Tinty said with a sigh. "Me and my magic going bidderly-winks again. Could be worse, I suppose. Could be elephants." She scratched her nose. "What're we going to do with them all?"

"Turn them into the street!" Augum Aslee cried. "You wretched girl." His mop of red hair fell over his face; his nose poked out like a meatball in a bowl of tomato sauce.

"Oh, but they would starve!" Avielle exclaimed.

"Well they'll starve here, missy. I can't be feeding a gaggle of dogs."

Tinty sat down cross-legged on the floor, and the puppies pushed and crowded over themselves to pile into her lap and lick her fingers.

"I'll find homes for every one of them," she said. "I swear it on my name, Tinty. If I don't, you can all start calling me Tinitia. And I won't say a word against it."

"It'll take weeks to find them all homes," Augum Aslee said. "No one's going to come in for business when they can't walk across the floor. And what about poop, I ask you that? Have you looked at the corner? It's already beginning to stink in here. And that black one's chewing on a pair of my magic socks."

Avielle took the socks away from the puppy, then could not resist scooping him up and petting him.

"No, there's only one thing to do," Augum Aslee said. He paused, parted his hair, and looked at them with his mournful black eyes.

"What?" Avielle and Tinty asked together.

"We'll have to get a wizard to change them all back."

"A wiz?" Tinty said. "Fancy. You won't get no wiz to come in here. Too snotty by half."

Augum Aslee cradled the dome around his egg. "They'll come," he said. "If . . . if I give them my egg."

"No!" Avielle clutched the puppy so hard he whimpered.

"Not your egg!" Tinty cried. "And it's all my fault! Me and my rotten magic. I won't let nobody take your egg—you loving it so. I'll fight them."

"Tinty," Avielle said, "what if you tried to change the puppies back? Maybe you could try juggling them and they would change back into forks or something."

"Yes!" Augum Aslee cried. "Now forks would be useful."

"You're both daft," Tinty said. "I'm not juggling no puppies. What if I dropped one and broke it? Live puppies is better than dead ones."

But Avielle thought Augum Aslee did not look so certain of that.

Up on the third floor that night, wearing Augum Aslee's magical socks to keep them warm, Pini and Ogall asked Avielle to sit back against the wall to try for a fourth time to weave without the loom. This time Pini intended to teach Avielle the chant, and then she would sing it herself in the hope that it would lead her down to the deep powerful place of magic inside her, from which her weaving came. Avielle tried not to think of the black net she had seen flung over the people of Rhia.

"I'm ready." Avielle shifted her shoulders, then relaxed them.

"Pini says," Ogall explained, "this time, instead of think of one good thing, think of all good things. Especially when darkness presses close."

So Pini taught her the words of the chant, and when she had learned them, she closed her eyes. Soon the words became a ribbon, a silver ribbon that seemed to flow through a valley between white mountains covered with snow, a joyful ribbon that whispered: think of all good things. She thought of the goodness of Gamalda taking her in after the whirlwind; and Avielle seized that thread. She thought of the goodness of the people of Postern Street watching over her after Gamalda had died; and Avielle seized that thread, too. She thought of the goodness of Master Steorra reading her birthchart, of Mistress Alubra letting her help with The Chandelier, of Mistress Rocat talking with her, of Mistress Pea comforting her; and she seized those threads, also.

She added the threads of Tinty's friendship, Master Keenum's advice, Master Cavenda's wisdom, and Augum Aslee's generosity in giving her free magical socks. She did not forget Master Lughgor telling her about the Magnificent Heart. And there was also Darien, who had overcome his prejudice against her. And she did not think only of their kindness to her, but also of their kindness to one another.

All of these threads, all that was good, kind, and bright, Avielle wove together as the chant in her mind grew to a roar. Her power flowed through her, stronger than ever before, yet, there was a deeper power she could not quite reach. It was as though a dark blanket—although now threadbare and shot with holes—still covered it.

Then the chant softened, and her hands dropped. As she swayed, exhausted, she heard Pini exclaiming. Avielle opened her eyes and looked at the weaving on the floor before her.

The weaving showed hands clasped together: brown, black, white, and silver. Hands that were rough, hands that were smooth, hands that were young, hands that were feeble, old, big, and small. All were raised. And in the center, two brown hands held up the silver bowl of the Goddess used in the Sacrament of Love.

"The Goddess," Avielle whispered, and felt something swell in her heart. The cloth was about six feet long by six feet wide. Avielle reached for it, pulled it over her shoulders, and felt . . . safe. *Safe*. For the first time since the High Hall had fallen and all the terrible things that had happened since, for the first time in her life, really, Avielle felt safe.

"Ah . . . ," said Pini, patting the cloth. He smiled. Then he spoke to Ogall.

"Vianna," Ogall translated. "Pini say what you weave

here is beautiful beyond words. He say, too, you can go deeper into magic even more. He say you ready to weave without thread."

"Without thread?" Avielle asked. ""What does that mean?"

Ogall asked Pini, then turned to Avielle. "All Pini say is weave different kinds things together. But he no not how to teach you that. Must learn yourself."

Avielle stroked the cloth with one hand. She decided she would make it into a cloak so she could wear it around herself and feel safe.

Early the next afternoon, the second day of Novasenna, when Avielle was just knotting the last stitch in the cloak's hem, a messenger came with a letter from Esilia urging Avielle to come to the Temple. Avielle put on the cloak, pinned on the hated badge, closed the shop, and started toward the Temple.

She found as she walked with the cloak swinging from her shoulders that she did feel safe, but not blindly so. She knew that dangers still existed. Indeed, she knew someone might recognize her as she walked through the streets unveiled, but she was not cowed now by the threat of danger. The bright thoughts, the thoughts of all good things, gave her the strength to live with the dark thoughts. She felt safe from despair. It was as if at last she understood Gamalda's words: that true safety exists only in the mind and spirit, exists in how you look at the world. And she felt held up, embraced, protected, by all the hands on the cloak and by the Sacrament of the Goddess.

When Avielle arrived at the damadas' cloister behind the Temple, the old damada with the face like a raisin waved Avielle in. "Damada Esilia's room is the tenth on the right."

Avielle walked down the hall and knocked on the tenth door.

"Come in," a voice called.

Avielle opened the door, then shut it behind her. The room was tiny, hardly more than a large closet, and the white walls were bare of everything except for a small painting of the Goddess in her incarnation as a young girl. Esilia sat on the edge of her narrow bed. Instead of her novice robe and veil, she wore a plain blue dress. Avielle was startled to see that her brown hair had been cut short around her ears. Her robe and veil lay folded in her lap, and her hands crossed over them, clutching them tightly. An open crate beside her feet had a few clothes and books packed inside of it.

"I'm leaving the Temple," Esilia said, staring at the wall.

"Leaving?" Avielle asked, astonished. "Why?"

Esilia just sat, her face unmoving.

"But, Esilia," Avielle said, "you've wanted to be a damada for so long. Ever since you were little."

"I don't believe in the Goddess anymore. I can't believe in a Goddess who would let so many evil things happen. So

I don't belong here." She looked up at Avielle and seemed to notice her at last. "You're wearing a new cloak," she said. "Did you weave it with magic?"

Avielle nodded.

"Let me see."

Avielle held out her arms and turned around so Esilia could see the entire cloak.

Esilia lay her veil and robe on the bed, stood up, picked up the edges of the cloak, and held it out.

"But this is . . . it's . . . it warms my heart," Esilia said. "All these hands clasped together. And the sacrament! This came to you through magic?"

"Yes." And then words came out of Avielle from a new place inside her. "Esilia, I do not believe the Goddess let the Brethren of the Black Cloaks destroy the High Hall, or let them send the Black Cloaks, or do any of the other terrible things that are happening."

Esilia looked up. "You don't?"

"No. Because the Goddess is all the good things that happen. All the kind things. She has nothing to do with the dark, terrible things, Esilia. The Goddess is what you have always thought, the center of all that is bright and good. I've found a way to hold those things inside myself, to keep me safe on the inside, where it counts. Maybe you can find faith that way, too. This cloak can help." And she flung out her arms, embraced Esilia, and wrapped the cloak around them both.

Esilia stood quite still for several moments. Then Avielle felt her relax.

"I understand what you are saying," she said. "I can feel it coming through your cloak. Goodness. Kindness. Make me believe, Avielle!" she cried. "Make me believe in all that is good and bright."

"Believe in people helping one another, holding out their hands to one another, trying to better the world, even in the face of darkness. It is happening. I tell you, Esilia, I have seen it happening every day."

"I can believe in that," Esilia said.

Avielle reached down, picked up Esilia's brown veil, and shook it out. "This is another of the bright things. Faith itself."

"Yes."

Avielle draped the veil over Esilia's head. "If you can believe in all that is good and bright, then you can believe in the Goddess."

"Because they are the Goddess," Esilia said.

Avielle nodded.

Esilia held each side of the veil. "All right," she said, "you—or your magic cloak—have convinced me. I'll stay one more day. The damadas say to take faith one day at a time."

"But was this why you sent for me?" Avielle asked. "To tell me you were leaving the Temple?"

"No, no, I almost forgot. I was working in the library—in the old chests again—I don't know why I always end up there—and I found this." She pulled out a bundle of clothes in the crate, sorted through them, and pulled out a book bound in red calfskin. "It's *The Book of the Sorrowful Queen*."

Avielle's heart leaped. At last!

"But Avielle . . ." Esilia hesitated. "I don't know how to say this . . . but I must tell you, the name of your great-great grandmother is written on the inside of the front cover—Queen Dolvoka Coroll."

Avielle's hands, which had been reaching for the book, fell back to her sides. It could not be. It could not! Why would the Quasana have told her to find this book if it had been owned by Dolvoka, or worse yet, written by Dolvoka? How would such a thing help Avielle to find the full depth of her magic power? It was ludicrous! She stared down at the front cover, which was smudged and worn.

"I knew the damadas would destroy it if they found it," Esilia added, "and I thought maybe . . . you'd still want it. I haven't had time to read it—I didn't want anyone to catch me with it. Do you want it?"

Avielle did not move. Just when she had begun to feel safe—this. *Tell her to take it away,* a voice whispered inside her. *Take it away.*

"Are you all right, Princess?"

Avielle put out her hand, which trembled. Esilia gave her the book. The calfskin cover felt cold and slick against Avielle's skin.

BRIMMING WITH MAGIC
CHAPTER THIRTY-SIX

Avielle left Esilia and walked slowly home through the streets—the red book tucked inside her dress pocket like a burning coal. Just as Avielle was about to turn the key and open the door into *Wind Weaver,* Tinty shouted and waved at her from across the street.

"Over here, Vianna!" she cried. "Over here. The wiz is coming!"

"What?" Avielle called as Tinty, dodging carriages, zipped across the cobblestones.

"Haven't you got ears?" Tinty said, stopping before her. "You'd think a princess would have ears. The wiz is coming! To change the puppies back. Might already be there." And she grabbed Avielle's hand, pulled her across the street, and over to Augum Aslee's shop.

"Come in fast," Tinty said, "so the puppies don't get out."

They went in and slammed the door behind them. The room stank so much Avielle nearly turned and ran out again.

A man stood looking at Augum Aslee's egg in its glass

dome. Avielle saw at once that he was a young man who could easily have been comfortable at court in the High Hall. He wore a deep blue doublet trimmed in velvet, with black trousers below. Although his black boots were plain, they were exquisitely made. He had a certain understated elegance that Avielle found pleasing. He was not what she had expected a wizard to look like. But what had she expected? The stuff of children's tales? Perhaps a pointy hat, a magic wand, and thunder and lightning following his every footstep?

The man turned to look at Tinty and Avielle. His brown hair, sleeked back along his head as though he had just been swimming, matched his brown eyes, which surveyed them both keenly before going back to rest on Tinty. She set her legs wide apart and folded her arms over her chest.

"I am Wizard Telindor," said the man. "Are you the girl responsible for"—he waved one hand at the puppies—"all of this?" he asked Tinty.

"That's right," Tinty said, staring him down. "It's my fault and not Auggie's. So you better not take his egg or you'll have me to deal with. I'll pay you for your services—I pay my debts, I do. I'll be your servant if you want and work it off that way. But you're getting that egg over my dead body."

The wizard smiled. "I will keep that in mind. But why don't you start by telling me how this happened."

Tinty, surprised, uncrossed her arms and thrust her hands in her skirt pockets. "It happened like this . . . ," she began. The man listened without interrupting. When Tinty finished, Avielle spoke:

"She has been trying to find her magic gift, and she is having a terrible time."

"There have been other such . . . incidents?" the wizard asked.

"Save us, yes." Augum Aslee rolled his eyes.

"Tell me about those, Tinty," the wizard said.

"You going to lock me up or something?" Tinty put both hands on her hips.

The wizard laughed. "Not today. Now tell me what mischief you have been up to."

So Tinty told him about her mishaps with her hair; the type at the Peas; the pastry crowns at Waterbee's Bakery; the spinning at Master Keenum's; the rose and the thorn; the warts and the cold; as well as a few other "incidents" that Avielle had not heard about.

"I see," the wizard said. He turned to Augum Aslee. "I will gladly make your puppies disappear. But I want something instead of your egg."

Augum Aslee's face brightened. "A love potion? A lifetime of magical socks?"

"No. I want your apprentice."

Avielle looked at Tinty.

"What'd you say?" asked Augum Aslee. "What'd you say?"

"Man's daft," Tinty said. "Even if he is a wiz."

"You see, Tinty," the wizard said. "You have not been able to find your magic gift because your gift *is* magic. All of these 'incidents' you describe show magic power in many different ways. You are brimming with magic. You simply do not know how to use it. If you become my apprentice, I can teach you to be a wizard."

Tinty tipped her head to the left, then to the right. She closed her right eye. She closed her left eye. Then she opened them both.

"Me?" she said at last. "A wiz? Go on."

"Yes," said the wizard, and he smiled. "I am glad to have found you. There are very few Dredonian Rhians with the ability to become wizards. And in this dark time we need as many as we can get. Will you come?"

Tinty pursed her lips. "There are conditions."

The wizard raised one eyebrow. "Yes?"

"First, let me see you change the puppies."

The wizard said, "*Mya, abercam solatum metara*." With a flash of blue light, the puppies vanished.

"If you wouldn't mind," Augum Aslee hinted, "the poop and the odor in the room?"

This time the wizard did not speak, but merely made a gesture with his hands. Avielle breathed in the clean scent of mountain air.

"That's all right then," Tinty said, letting out a deep breath. "The second condition is that you won't under any condition ever call me Tinitia."

"You have my promise," the wizard said.

"And last, you got to wait until I find somebody to take care of Auggie here. His head's too crammed with stuff. He can't remember to do nothing but polish his egg."

"I agree to your terms, Tinty," said the wizard. "They are all quite sensible. Shall I come back for you in a week?"

"That'll do fine."

The wizard bowed and left.

Tinty turned toward Avielle with a slightly dazed expression. "You got any money? I need a crisscross cinnamon crisp bad. Maybe a dozen." Then her face lit up. "Hey! When I'm a wiz, I can just magic them up. Pull as many as we want out of thin air. That'll show that fat old Waterbee."

Later that afternoon, after Avielle had checked on the boys, she sat at the kitchen table tapping her fingertips against a pot of hot tea. Beside it sat an empty brown cup. Beside that lay *The Book of the Sorrowful Queen*. The title was worked in gold on the red cover.

Avielle poured the tea into the cup and smelled the delicate fragrance of vanilla and plum; the tea was the last of the blend Gamalda had made. Avielle picked up the cup, blew on the tea, then sipped—too hot. The cup clinked when she sat it back on the saucer. She looked down at the book, looked away. Tried the tea again. This time her hands trembled; a little bit of the tea sloshed onto the table.

She knew all the reasons why she did not want to open

the book, and all the reasons why she had to. She looked at Gamalda's misshapen teapots on the counter. *You are not her,* she heard Gamalda say in her mind. *Do you understand me? Listen well. You are not her.*

Avielle slipped one finger under the book's front cover, flipped it open, and drew her hand back as though fearing it might be snapped off. And there it was, her great-great grandmother's name written in a bold elegant script across the vellum on the inside cover:

Queen Dolvoka Visnae Coroll

Avielle traced each letter with her eyes; here was the writing of the woman who had haunted all her days. Seeing her handwriting made Dolvoka more real than she had ever been before, more real even than the painting of her, because her own hands had written these letters. It was the same handwriting as that on the labels of the vials in the Chamber of Wings.

Avielle found that she was breathing too fast. She picked up her cup of tea and took a sip. What would she see when she turned the page? Monsters? Beasts? Perversions? People mutilated? Horrible incantations? Spells calling for the heads of babies? At last Avielle turned the page, then sat back and grabbed her teacup with both hands to keep it from falling.

On the page was an exquisite pen-and-ink drawing of a

meadowlark, colored with watercolor washes. The outlines and details were rendered in black ink, the mass of the body painted in white, yellow, and a soft gray-brown. Avielle knew it was a meadowlark because she had seen paintings of them before. However, this painting was like nothing she had ever seen. Indeed, the artist had taken the utmost care with every detail, and the bird did not seem to simply represent his species, but also seemed to be a live, particular bird, perhaps a friend of the person who had painted it.

All around the drawing, and on the opposing page, were notes written in the same bold elegant script as Dolvoka's name. These contained facts about the bird's physiology; its mating, migratory, and nesting habits; its food; its dwelling places; and other such facts. At the very bottom Dolvoka had written, "The meadowlark's melodious song, the sweetest of all birdsong, fills my heart with praise to Her."

Avielle put her teacup down and swallowed hard. She ran her finger over the gilt edges of the book again and again, read the words again and again, and looked at the beautiful painting again and again. But she found no evil, only joy. How could this be?

She turned page after page. She saw paintings of ducks, herons, jays, robins, wrens, eagles, swans, and more, all rendered with the same exquisite care. She thought of the scrap of burnt paper Esilia had found in the library in the High Hall with the words "cobalt," "vermilion," and "black" written on it. Perhaps it had been a list of the colors Dolvoka had needed. Had she painted these in the days before she turned evil? For it was obvious from this book that she had loved birds, loved them passionately. Indeed, how could she have destroyed something she apparently loved so much? How had she come to hate them? What had happened? It must have been something terrible.

Avielle turned the last page, hoping to solve the mystery, and saw more writing in the form of a long poem. The words were blotted and smudged, almost written in a scrawl, quite different from the careful writing throughout the rest of the book. Avielle was about to read them when someone came bursting in through the front door.

"Hello there!" a man called. "Hello!"

Avielle stood and walked into the front room, where she saw two guardsmen. Her heart skipped. Had they discovered who she was?

"Yes?" she asked. "How may I help you?"

"Under order of the High Council," one of them began, "all citizens must participate in a lottery to determine whether they will be sent as slaves to Dredonia. You must come with us now and take your place in the line. Is there anyone else in the shop?"

"No," Avielle whispered. "No."

"She's lying," one of the guardsmen said to the other. "Search the place." And he pushed Avielle out the door.

THE LOTTERY

CHAPTER THIRTY-SEVEN

The guardsman led Avielle into the center of Postern Street, where the guards had gathered everyone who lived or worked there. At last, she thought, at last the High Council had come to its senses and was going to send the slaves and stop the terror. They had certainly waited long enough to make their decision; tomorrow was the deadline the Black Cloaks had imposed before unleashing yet more terror upon the city. Avielle felt as though a great weight had been lifted from her shoulders. Now she would not have to decide whether to become queen and risk doing some evil to the people. She would never have to step upon the crossroads.

Nor, if truth be told, would her own life be in danger any longer. For surely now that the Black Cloaks had what they wanted, they would leave Rhia. Doubt whispered in her heart, however, as she remembered that Ogall had said the Brethren of the Black Cloaks would not keep their promise. *Evil has no . . . what word . . . honor?*

Tinty ran over and stepped into the circle beside Avielle.

"You should tell them," she whispered, "tell them you're the princess!"

"And be killed by the Black Cloaks? No, thank you. Besides, the High Council is only doing what I would have done anyway."

"You would have sent the slaves?" Tinty's mouth opened wide.

"Yes."

"Then you're a ninny." Tinty crossed her arms. "Look. There's Mistress Alubra coming out—think she'll make a good slave? And the Pea twins—instead of ink stains on their aprons it'll be dirt. Oh, here comes Master Lughgor! Think what a fine slave he'll be, bent double, walking in those dark old mines. Never seeing the light he loves no more."

"Stop, Tinty," Avielle cried. "Stop."

Tinty, however, would not stop. "Here they are dragging Darien down the stairs. Oh, he's young. He'll work long and hard in the mines for years. They must have let Master Keenum off when they saw he was blind and old. But who'll take care of him? Look! It's Master Steorra. He won't be talking to the Royal Brains at that academy of his down in the dark."

Avielle felt her heart sinking under the weight of Tinty's words. She had not thought when she had wanted to send the slaves that maybe some of them would be her neighbors, people she knew, people who were her friends.

The guardsmen had blocked off both ends of Postern Street so no one could flee and no conveyances could pass through. Avielle had never realized how noisy the street had been until now, when it was quiet, ominously quiet. Then she saw Pini and Ogall stumbling out of the shop, pushed along by a guardsman. "Here," she shouted, "over here." They came running toward her. If the Black Cloaks took Pini, they would sense his power and take him back to the terrible school where they taught evil magic.

"Who are those boys?" Darien asked her.

"Friends," said Avielle.

"She's been hiding something," said Tinty. Then she screwed up her voice in imitation of Mistress Alubra. "If I were a less tolerant woman, I would be outraged." But her voice was shaking.

When everyone—shopkeepers, apprentices, and their children—was ferreted out of the shops, one of the guardsmen stood in the center of the circle and began to speak.

"Each of you will reach into the basket and pull out a stone," he said. "White stones remain free. Black stones will be sent as slaves to Dredonia."

A guardsman with a bristling mustache, holding the basket high so no one could see inside, began to walk around the circle, pausing before each person. Most drew white stones. The first to draw black was Master Lughgor.

No!" Avielle cried as a guardsman pulled him out of the circle.

Several apprentices drew the next few stones—one drew black. The basket came closer, to Penatta and Renatta. Both drew white stones. Renatta sobbed with relief and turned to Smitor, who had also drawn a white stone. Master and Mistress Pea drew white stones also, as did Mistress Alubra. Master Steorra, however, picked a black one.

"Should have consulted the stars about myself," he said. "Idiot. Nincompoop. Dimwit."

Then it was Darien's turn. He stood feeling the different stones. Avielle wondered if he had learned from Master Keenum how to discern the nature of a stone.

"Draw one!" the guard exclaimed at last. "Or we will take you."

Avielle held her breath. Darien drew out a black stone.

Mistress Rocat pulled a white one.

Master Cavenda white.

Ogall white.

Augum Aslee white.

Pini pulled black.

"No," Avielle cried, reaching for him. "Don't take him! He is too little. He can do no work."

"Step back!" the guardsman told her. "You're next."

Avielle's thoughts grew wild. Her throat jammed with fear as she put her hand in the basket, which was brown wicker, slightly frayed. It seemed so simple a thing to hold one's destiny. She groped, she grasped a stone, she pulled it out. White. She was safe.

Tinty was the last to choose. She stood with one hand on her hip, her head cocked. She reached in, drew out a stone, threw it up in the air, and caught it.

A black stone gleamed in her palm.

Dazed, Avielle left the street and walked back through the door of *Wind Weaver*—the guardsmen had left the door open. Sobs burst from her throat. Tinty had not cried, not Tinitia Bottledown, who would never be a wizard now. Tinty. They had taken Tinty. And Darien, Pini, Master Lughgor, and Master Steorra. Avielle entered the shop, passed through the front room, and went into the kitchen, where she grabbed the pot of tea she had made earlier and flung it across the room; it crashed against the wall, then made tinkling sounds as the pieces fell to the floor.

Her arms ached. Her entire body felt squeezed, as though a rope coiled around her from head to toe and someone was pulling it tighter and tighter. All this time when she had thought Rhia should send the slaves, she had never truly thought about what it would mean: that real people would be chosen.

She had been stupid, ignorant, blind.

Someone came up behind her. Avielle whirled around, but saw only Ogall.

"I go now," Ogall said.

"Go?" asked Avielle. "Where will you go?"

"To be with Pini. I not let him be slave alone."

"But when the Black Cloaks sense his power they will send him to their school. And you will be a slave at best. At worst they will kill you for stealing him."

"I not let Pini go alone," Ogall insisted. "I love Pini."

Avielle clasped her arms around him.

"Good-bye, Vianna," he said. "Many thanks for care taking of us. Pini say so, too." Ogall turned and walked out of the kitchen. The front door clicked shut.

Avielle sank down on the kitchen chair. Through her tears she saw the cloak of hands she had made hanging on its hook beside the back door. She saw now what a selfish creature she had been. For although the cloak had kept her safe from despair, it had not kept her friends safe from harm. She should have tried to weave something that would have kept them safe, though what it would have been she did not know. Instead, she had thought only of her own safety. She should go and join her friends, as Ogall had, but that would not save them, and she desperately wanted to save them.

But how? The greatest wizards of Rhia had been unable to defeat the Black Cloaks, and Avielle was only an apprentice weaver struggling to find the full power of her magic gift. She turned her head, and her glance fell on the last page of *The Book of the Sorrowful Queen*, the page she had been about to read when the guardsman had burst into the shop. Avielle leaned forward and began to read the writing, scrawled as though whoever had written it had been in a hurry.

No! It cannot be!
Death rains from the sky,
Beat of wing and heart stilled by my cursed hand.

On corridors of wind, my beloved birds,
you flew in the light of dawn.
All destroyed. May I be cursed!

I only wished to send my spirit out with you,
whom I love above all things,
to soar in freedom on the arms of the wind,
free from these prison walls I hate.

But it was a spell wrought in grief and despair
by a heart forlorn.
And so it turned to a howling shriek.
And what I loved more than my life, I murdered.

Empty sky, my empty heart descends,
down
down
down into the darkness of my tomb
where I shall suffer grief beyond death.
In darkness shall I wait for wings
to beat against my bones.
In darkness shall my ears be strained.

In darkness shall my heart await.
Hear my voice! Come home! Come home!

In agony I shall burn,
until one day the daughter
of my daughter of my daughter
seeks my tomb at last.
Light-Bringer!
The power you seek,
The Power Beyond All Powers
that Opens the Magnificent Heart,
the key waits upon my tomb.

Only when you find the Magnificent Heart
will the land be healed of the darkness unleashed upon it;
will the sky be filled with wings again.

From my bones in my tomb I shall call them,
from the light beyond death I shall call them,
until my call is a Power Beyond All Powers
to fill the sky with wings again.

This night I slay myself.

The words blurred before Avielle's eyes. Her hands were clutching her chair; she could feel the sides cutting into her palms. It seemed to her that she sat that way for an hour, then two, then three. It seemed to her that all her life was now divided in two—to the time before she had read these words and to the time after. Her life—*she*—was forever changed. For what she had thought all her life, what had shaped all her life and her own self, might be false. Her breath came fast and shallow.

If Dolvoka had not meant to kill the birds, if it had really been a terrible accident, a spell gone wrong, did this mean Dolvoka was not evil? She had committed an evil act, yes, but she had not been motivated by evil. If this were true, then Avielle could not have inherited any evil from her. However, Avielle thought, as she looked at the scrawled words, even if there were no evil taint in her blood, there was still a kind of taint inside her. It had been put there by those she had lived with in the High Hall; it had been put there by Avielle herself, put there by her fear of Dolvoka that had been inside her for so long that she could not simply extract it by reading a few words on a page.

And yet, as each day her magic power had deepened, and as each day she had lived among her friends on Postern Street, she had moved farther from Dolvoka's shadow. But not yet far enough. One last thread of shadow remained.

Avielle drummed her fingers on the table. Dolvoka had named her—*daughter of my daughter of my daughter. Light-Bringer*. The Quasana and her ancestors had called her Light-Bringer, too. How had Dolvoka known? How had she foreseen that a darkness far greater than the loss of the birds would hang over Rhia?

Avielle read part of the passage again. *The power you seek, the Power Beyond All Powers that Opens the Magnificent Heart, the key waits upon my tomb.*

Avielle looked up. "Power," she whispered. She did indeed seek power, the power to free her friends from the terrible fate that awaited them as Dredonian slaves. What was the Power Beyond All Powers? She had to find it, had to seek the key to it in Dolvoka's tomb whatever the danger, whatever her fear. She had no choice.

Coldness stole over her, and the walls of the kitchen grew close. What if Dolvoka were luring her to some great evil? Avielle closed her eyes and thought of the excited sound of Master Steorra's voice as he talked about Alamaria circling the sun; thought of Pini, Ogall, Darien, and of Tinty's magical mishaps; thought of the spots of color dancing around Master Lughgor as he contemplated the window of the Magnificent Heart. How odd that he, too, had spoken of the Magnificent Heart.

Avielle opened her eyes. She had no choice.

She would go to the tombs, and she would go now before her courage waned. Avielle stood up and put the book in her dress pocket. She was about to walk out of the kitchen, when her cloak with the hands woven upon it caught her eye. Avielle picked up the cloak, threw it around her shoulders, and fastened it. Perhaps it would provide some protection, keep her mind from crumpling under the fear she would undoubtedly feel in the tombs.

The silver badge with the ugly Dredonian face was pinned to the left shoulder. She unpinned it and dropped it on the floor.

Let anyone try to stop her. Let anyone try to stop her now.

THE SIGN OF THE SCEPTER
CHAPTER THIRTY-EIGHT

Avielle walked eastward through the city. In some places the lottery was underway, and she heard the cries of those taken and of those bereft. Guardsmen herded lines of unlucky people through the streets. Avielle overheard them say that the slaves were going to be held in Queen's Square before Lord General Maldreck and High Councilman Herector turned them over to the Black Cloaks at dawn.

This was what she had wanted so the terror would stop. But this, Avielle saw now, was terror, too. She felt ashamed. And yet, what else was to be done? If she could not help her friends, if she could not find some power in Dolvoka's tomb to save them, then she would join them and go as a slave to Dredonia.

People stared at her in wonder as she passed, and she could imagine how she must look to them: a silverskin with black hair—with two inches of silver at the crown of her head, for it had been two months since she had dyed it—wearing a strange cloak over a black dress. Odd indeed. However, her resolve did not waver, nor did her footsteps falter.

Then Avielle remembered what day it was—the second day of the month of Novasenna. *It will begin on the afternoon of the second day of the month of Novasenna,* Master Steorra had warned. *And come to full force on the morning of the third day. On those days Hycath the Hunter and Demord the Demon will both be in the constellation of the Light-Bringer and in the House of Death.* Sweat broke out on Avielle's forehead, since she was going to the tombs, a place of death. However, there was good, too, she remembered. The planet Lashata the Lover and the sun were in conjunction. She stood at the crossroads after all. Would she fall into shadow or stand in the light?

Soon, as she approached the eastern edge of the city, the buildings grew farther apart until she at last walked through the gate. Axillian Road began to wind gradually up through the two low hills dotted with salal bushes. After a quarter mile, her steps grew slower and slower; ancient holly trees flanked each side of the road, their red berries like drops of blood. The path ended in massive oak doors set in the side of a hill covered with sweet grass. Avielle had reached the catacombs of the city.

The catacombs, the tombs of the dead, sprawled in a vast underground network beneath the hill. Tunnel after tunnel and chamber after chamber lay filled with those who had died since the time of Queen Soria the Wise, who had

had the catacombs excavated from natural caves over five hundred years ago.

The arched oak doors were bound in silver and adorned with carvings that showed the Goddess in her form as Great Mother, giving birth as the dead were reborn to walk the Paths of Light in the Otherworld.

"Do you wish to enter?" asked the Door Warden, a wizened man who limped forward from the little gatehouse near the doors. "Five tiras for a torch."

Avielle hesitated. She felt an ache across the back of her shoulders, as though something were pressing her down. Here lay those whose bodies had been recovered from the fall of the High Hall; here lay those killed by the Black Cloaks and the foul Black Birds; here lay Gamalda; and here lay her darling Rajio.

"Yes," she said, "I wish to enter." She gave the Door Warden five tiras. He counted them out, then handed her a torch.

"If you lose your way, young mistress," he said, "look to the right side of the doorway of each passage or chamber. Follow the carving of the ringed snake with its tail in its mouth. It'll lead you out again, if you keep your eyes sharp. And you'd better keep three eyes open, if you take my advice. The torch will burn for a little more than three hours. Don't chance to cut it close or you'll be plenty sorry. It's not a pretty thing to be lost in the dark among the dead. And some have, mind you, some have."

"How do I find the royal tombs?"

"Follow the sign of the scepter cut beside each passage. Remember this, though. Loot or disturb the dead and you'll find punishment quick all right. You'll be shut up alive in the blackness to die."

"I want . . . I wish to find the tomb of Queen Dolvoka. I know it does not lie in the royal tombs. Do you know how I can find it?"

The old man cupped his chin in his hands and shook his head wildly.

"No! No!" he exclaimed. "Don't seek such a dark road! That way is buried deep. It's not known, not on any of the lists, no indeed, young mistress. All I know is this. The legend says it begins somewhere in the royal tombs. But I'd advise against such rashness. For you'll find no signs marking any passages to the Cursed One, nor any back if you do—Goddess save us!—find her. You'll surely be lost."

"Thank you," Avielle said.

He limped over and pulled the iron ring on one of the oak doors; it opened slowly, creaking on its hinges. A blast of musty air issued forth. Avielle did not move. As she looked into the mouth of Death, a horror came over her, for she felt as though the flesh were already stripped from her body, as though she were already nothing but bone. Then she thought of her friends, her friends who would be on their way tomorrow to live in the darkness of the mines.

At last, taking a deep breath, Avielle passed into the

darkness. Holding the torch high, she walked down a tunnel that branched into eight other tunnels, all of which had different signs cut into the right hand side. She followed the tunnel cut with the signs of the fish, arrow, and scepter. It opened into a low chamber where deep niches were cut out of the blue-gray stone. In them lay many bodies wrapped in shrouds that gleamed white in the light from the smoky torch.

She went on into the next chamber and the next, always following the sign of the scepter. She knew that the royal tombs lay deep inside the oldest part of the catacombs. The weight of the earth above her seemed to press down on her so that it was an effort to take each step. A chill crept between her clothes and her skin, making her shiver. She could smell the ancient cold; it smelled of stone, dust, and bone. She pulled the cloak close around her, and felt some of her fear—but not all—lift. She wished she could find the place where Gamalda lay—the Door Wardens kept an extensive list of the location of every body—but she did not have time, not if she were to save her friends this night. She would return to visit Gamalda another time—if she did not go as a slave to Dredonia.

Avielle walked deeper and deeper into the maze of the catacombs, entering chamber after chamber, always following the sign of the scepter, until at last she reached the oldest part of the tombs. At the entrance, white marble columns worked with golden filigree supported a high archway. She held up her torch. Written in gold across the top of the archway were the words: *The Chamber of the Kings and Queens of Rhia.* And beneath those: *May the Goddess Protect Them.*

As Avielle entered the room of her ancestors, the ceiling soared out of sight, lost in shadow. In some of the niches lay piles of dust and bones with the glimmer of gold rings and jewels. All of the cloth had long since rotted away. In other niches lay bodies wrapped in shrouds covered with brocade. Names were carved above the niches; she saw Queen Kykalassa, her grandmother; Prince Askan, her great uncle; Princess Trisarna, her great aunt; King Oldon, her grandfather, and many more.

Then she came to the last filled tomb—beyond it, the niches lay empty. As she looked at them, she began to tremble so much she feared her bones would crack. In one of those niches she would lay one day, if she ever revealed her true name. She read the words inscribed in the stone above the last filled tomb: Prince Rajio Islion Coroll. Avielle knelt. Rajio lay wrapped in a shroud of white silk—she could see where his nose made a bump. Drawn up to his shoulders was a coverlet of blue and gold brocade.

Where was Dumpkins, his stuffed lamb that he had dearly loved and slept with every night? It should be here in his tomb with him. Maybe it had been lost in the rubble of the whirlwind. And that seemed somehow more terrible than his death, that he would have to sleep here forever without his beloved lamb. Avielle decided that if she lived and remained free, she would make another just like it and bring it to him.

"Rajio," she whispered as she knelt beside him. "Oh, Rajio." Although she wanted to take his body in her arms and press him to her heart, she knew better. He would be stiff and rigid, nothing like the soft, warm little boy who had sat on her lap. After awhile she began to sing to him, all his favorite songs—the one about the three ships that sailed to the moon; the one about the cat who cornered two mice and could not decide which one to eat first. She told him the nursery tale he had liked best: "The Tale of the Seven Troublesome Geese."

Finally, she stood up, her knees aching from being on the stone floor for so long.

"I must find Dolvoka's tomb, Rajio," she said. "Let your little spirit guide me since I do not know the way, and I may be lost. I am afraid, Rajio." She lingered for a moment, however, since she could not bear to leave him, so cold, so lonely. "Good bye, Rajio," she said at last.

Avielle turned and walked all around the edges of the royal chambers, looking for any door or opening that might be the beginning of a passage to Dolvoka's tomb. However, even after making the circuit of the rooms several times, she found nothing. She sighed in frustration. It had to be somewhere; there had to be something she was not seeing.

Statues were set among the tombs: some scattered about

the rooms, some against the stone walls, some carved into the walls. In the middle of one room was a white marble lark, the symbol of all of Rhia. Avielle wandered, looking at the statues. There were bears standing on their hind legs; fish swimming; a dolphin leaping; a deer grazing, and there were birds—many birds.

An accident, Avielle thought. Had Dolvoka's curse really been an accident?

Where was the secret way? Where? Where? It had to begin in the tombs of her ancestors. And then came the voice, stronger than she had ever heard it before, echoing off the stone. *Avielle! Light-Bringer! You are our only hope for Rhia! You must not fail us!*

"Then show me the way!" she shouted. The words, however, only echoed and faded.

As she walked, Avielle traced her fingers over a duck, a wren, an owl, an eagle, and a jay. She stopped suddenly, stepped back to the eagle, and held the torch closer.

The eagle had no wings. They had been stricken off so that the bird was a mere stump, only a body and a head. Avielle pressed her hand against her stomach. This had to be a sign of Dolvoka; it had to be. The eagle stood about four feet tall. Avielle felt all around the edge of it, pried and pulled, but it fit snuggly against the wall. The intense eyes carved of stone looked out at her over the hooked nose. The statue must have been magnificent, once.

Magnificent.

"I seek the key to the Power Beyond All Powers that Opens the Magnificent Heart," she said. "I seek the way to Dolvoka. Let me pass."

Nothing happened. Avielle tapped her foot and looked at her torch. Three hours the Door Warden had said it would burn. She had used an hour of that already.

She tried again. "I am Princess Avielle Reginnia of the House of Coroll. Let me pass!"

Again nothing happened.

Avielle sighed and shook her head. "Poor old thing," she said, "down here in the dark where you would never fly across any but the skies of the dead. Even if you had wings." And she touched the place where she thought the eagle's heart would be.

A shrill creaking noise filled the air, shattering the silence of the tomb. Suddenly a door appeared in the wall behind the eagle. It swung open, revealing a dark passageway within. Avielle gripped her torch and stepped inside.

DOLVOKA'S TOMB
CHAPTER THIRTY-NINE

Avielle walked down the sloping passageway, her footsteps making the only sound. The walls, illumined by the torchlight, were not black, but a dull, dead gray. She began to think it was all a dream, as though she were weaving on the third floor of the shop. For how long she walked, she did not know, only that the path went steadily down. Once she thought she smelled new-mown grass, but the scent was quickly gone.

At last, she entered a round hall ringed with seven open doorways, open except for one flanked by a beast whose breath stank of excrement. Avielle stopped. It was the same chamber, the same beast, as in the very first weaving vision she'd had.

"No!" she cried, remembering the pain of being eaten by the beast. She backed away.

The beast watched her, its seven red eyes glowing above its snout. It still had human hands with long pointed nails like claws, and its left hand was still bleeding, just as it had been before. It lifted its hand to its mouth, licked it, and then roared in pain. The beast made no move to come forward, however; and indeed, Avielle recalled that in the weaving vision it had not seized her until she demanded that it let her pass. Perhaps Dolvoka's tomb lay through one of the other chambers? But which one? She could not try six different passageways; her torch would not last long enough. Her eyes went back to the monster's bleeding paw. Blood dripped on the stone floor. Poor thing.

"If you please, sir"—for she did not know what else to call the beast—"if you please, I can bandage your sore hand."

She could not be certain, but the creature seemed to nod. So Avielle reached down and tore off two long strips of her petticoat. She folded one into a compress, then looked warily at the beast.

"I'll need to come close to you in order to bandage your hand. Will you hold it out please?"

The beast did so.

Swallowing hard, Avielle walked toward it, holding her breath. The beast's hand felt rough and slimy. She pressed the compress along the cut and blotted the blood. Then she wound the other strip of petticoat around and around the beast's hand and tied it in a knot.

"There," she said. "Hold your hand up in the air. That will help stop the bleeding."

The creature grunted and complied.

Avielle stood, uncertain what to do next. Would it eat her now? Should she back away? Run into one of the other chambers?

Then the beast stepped sideways, unblocking the passageway. That, Avielle guessed, was the way she was meant to go. She walked toward the passageway slowly, ready to run in case the beast changed its mind. But it did not accost her. At the threshold she turned.

"Thank you very much," she said, and then ran into the passageway.

Now the tunnel was wider, and the black rock, speckled here and there with mica, sparkled occasionally in the torchlight. Avielle looked at her torch anxiously, but it did not seem to be burning down so quickly as the Door Warden had predicted. The tunnel branched, and branched again. The Door Warden had been wrong; there was a sign to guide her—the sign of a black crown cut into the stone. Then the tunnel stopped, and she found herself in a hall with a row of soaring black marble pillars supporting a vaulted ceiling made of stone. She walked between them, feeling dwarfed by their size.

Then she saw it. Where the pillars ended there was a black marble sarcophagus that shone in the torchlight.

Dolvoka's tomb.

Avielle stopped. She felt a pain in her heart, and her hands and lips were cold. She pressed her legs together in order to stay on her feet. Here was the source of all the evil in her life, of all that had haunted and tormented her since the day she was born. She could not move, could not take another step.

She put one hand to her chest, as though expecting a bag full of pearls to be hanging there, but of course there was nothing.

"The people gave me pearls," she said at last, and took a step forward. "I brought bells out of a lantern," she added, and took two more steps forward. "I rescued a baby." She lifted her foot and put it down ahead of her. She was getting closer and closer to the sarcophagus. Now she kept walking steadily as she spoke: "I turned rocks into stars. I grew into a silver tree and sheltered families of squirrels. I became a glorionna sun daisy. And the hands reaching up in the Sacrament of Love." And, slowly, she kept walking toward the sarcophagus.

"I am facing it, Gamalda," Avielle whispered. "I am facing it."

When she had almost reached the sarcophagus, she saw a stand for a torch and put her torch into it. Then she looked at the sarcophagus.

It was about seven feet long, with no carvings, only a thin molding where the lid fitted to the sides and another at the bottom. The black marble—so cold, so smooth, so forbidding—seemed utterly inhuman. How, Avielle wondered, could it contain a heart that had once beat; eyes that once looked upon the world; a body that had once walked, run, and born children? It seemed polished by silence, yet there was something about it that seemed to be waiting and listening. There was no plaque, no name, nothing to indicate who lay inside. But Avielle knew.

Her lips would not form the words she wished to speak.

"I have come, Dolvoka," she said at last, "as you foretold. I am the daughter of your daughter of your daughter, the one you named Light-Bringer. You promised me power if I came, the key to the Power Beyond All Powers that Opens the Magnificent Heart. I have come for it now, to save my friends. I beseech you, give it to me."

There was no answer.

Avielle took the book bound in red calfskin out of her dress pocket. "You wrote that the spell was an accident," she said. "That you did not mean to kill and curse the birds of Rhia. Is this true?"

There was no answer.

Avielle closed her eyes. She felt no evil; despair, yes, and grief, but not evil. Evil was the feeling that came when the Black Cloaks were near. There was none of that here. Only a great heaviness, a great weariness.

She opened her eyes, then opened the book to the last page, where Dolvoka had written her lines of despair.

"The paintings in this book," Avielle said, "and these words at the end of it are the only real things I have of you. The rest are stories, legends, probably lies." And suddenly a light dawned in Avielle's mind. "And in that way we *are* the same, for stories and lies were told about me, too, all of my life. We are the same, but in a way I never imagined. So . . . ," she paused. "So, I choose to believe what lies before my eyes. I choose to believe that while you did an evil thing by accident, you were not evil. You did not mean to kill the birds of Rhia."

Avielle slipped the book back into her pocket. "And if you were not evil, then there has never been any evil taint from you that could rise in my blood. There is only what I carry from my own self."

She placed her hand on top of the sarcophagus; the cold seeped through her skin. "You said your spirit waits here until the birds come home again. Give me the key, give me the power to help my friends, and I do not know how or when, but I shall do everything I can to bring the birds home again."

Silence.

Avielle sighed. There was nothing for her here. The scribbling of a madwoman in an old book had led her into folly. The only thing left for her to do was to leave the catacombs and join her friends in their enslavement. She slipped the book back into her dress pocket.

"I pity you, great-great grandmother," Avielle said. "And I forgive you." She took off her cloak and laid it over the black sarcophagus so that the silver bowl of the Goddess in the Sacrament of Love showed on top. Then Avielle picked up the torch and began walking back down the hall flanked by the rows of marble pillars.

A roaring sound came from behind her, and Avielle spun around. A beam of golden light shot up from the sarcophagus through the cloak to the ceiling far above. The beam turned, and inside it a white feather whirled gently round and around as though stirred by a breeze.

Avielle ran to the sarcophagus, put her hand in the golden beam—the light skittered and played over her skin—and plucked out the feather. It felt warm, but not hot. A white pinion feather, about ten inches long, perhaps the feather of a swan. The Quasana? There did not appear to be anything magical or extraordinary about it at all.

"How do I use this key?" Avielle asked.

The shaft of golden light shone silently. Avielle bowed.

With the feather in one hand and the torch in the other, Avielle walked away down the hall. When she reached the last pillar, she looked back. The beam of golden light still shot up from the sarcophagus.

"Good-bye, great-great grandmother," she said. "Thank you. I will bring the birds home if I can."

Avielle returned through the maze of corridors, always following the sign of the ringed snake with its tail in its mouth. She never came again to the round hall with the beast and the seven open doorways.

At last she came to the arched doors that led out of the catacombs. Pink and yellow streaked the dawn sky and stroked the bellies of the clouds with lavender. She had been in the tombs all night, and yet her torch still burned. Indeed, when she gave it to the wizened Door Warden, he stood gaping at her.

"Thought you was lost in the dark," he said. "Was going to get up a search."

"Thank you for your concern," Avielle said, "but as you see, I am fine." She strode along the Road of the Tombs between the ancient holly trees, and though she only carried the white feather, she walked as though she carried a silver sword.

Avielle headed toward Queen's Square. She would not let her friends go into the darkness of slavery. She would save them or she would die.

QUEEN'S SQUARE
CHAPTER FORTY

As Avielle approached Queen's Square, she began to slip from doorway to doorway; she did not know what kind of power the white feather might have, but she doubted it would make her invisible. She also did not know what kind of guard might have been set up around the perimeter of the square.

The streets were deserted. Milk carts should have been rattling about this early in the day, as well as scullery maids sweeping the stairs and servant boys busy with their small jobs. But there was no one. Everyone seemed to be in hiding. Even the lamplighters had not come out to quench the lamps.

Then Avielle heard a din, a kind of muffled roar, which grew louder as she approached the square. The next moment, dread came over her. It seemed as though a great stone had been dropped upon her shoulders, and she bowed beneath the weight of it. She guessed it meant a Black Cloak was near. She wanted to run away, but she thought of Tinty, Darien, and the others, and kept going.

She hid behind some camellia bushes, peered around

the corner of a building, and saw that the din was coming from the people who filled Queen's Square. It had once been a place of joy and celebration, but no longer. Now it was filled with lamentations: people weeping, moaning, and calling for mercy. Indeed, there must have been more than five thousand people, most sitting down. Guardsmen had erected sawhorses around the perimeter to make a pen to imprison the people. On the far side, across from Avielle, stood three Black Cloaks; it was her first sight of them.

They were tall, perhaps seven feet tall, and their cloaks—hanging in ragged, knotted strips—shrouded them from head to toe. Their hoods were drawn far forward, and where they should have had faces, there was only a cave of darkness broken by glittering eyes. The air seemed to wither as they passed through it, and the earth itself seemed to cringe away from them.

Avielle slipped back behind the camellia bushes and leaned against the building, panting, clutching the feather. Help me, she thought, help me. Where would she find the courage to do what she had come to do?

One step, Master Lughgor had said of the Goddess stepping out of the egg. *Didn't know what she was stepping into. Yet she did. Took the first step. What courage.*

The clip-clop of horses drew near; a carriage was coming down the deserted street. Avielle crouched down behind the camellia bushes as it passed. Through the carriage windows she saw the faces of Lord General Maldreck and High

Councilman Herector. What business did they have here? Then she remembered what she had heard in the street yesterday. They were going to release the slaves to the Black Cloaks at dawn today.

Dawn. It was dawn on the third day of Novasenna, the time Master Steorra had warned that the forces of darkness would come into full strength against her. It did not matter. She had to try to save her friends.

With the white feather clasped in her hand, Avielle slipped out of the bushes, and stepped around the corner of the building into Queen's Square. And though her heart pounded, though she felt dizzy and sick, though she was more afraid than she had ever been in her life, she walked toward the slave pen and the Black Cloaks.

No one noticed her. All eyes were on High Councilman Herector as he shouted his speech to the slaves.

"Good citizens, you are giving your lives, so that your fellow citizens may be safe from terror. So they may live. The High Council and all the people of Rhia praise you for your great sacrifice. Know that your fellow citizens will never forget it. We will build a monument in this spot to honor you. May the Goddess protect you." He turned to the Black Cloak who hovered nearby. The other two were now at the far end of the pen. "Take them," High Councilman Herector said, "and the mines, and end the terror. Begone and leave us in peace."

A murmur rippled through the crowd, and Avielle knew

it was because the people in the pen had at last noticed her. She had almost reached the carriage where Lord General Maldreck, High Councilman Herector, and the Black Cloak stood, when the Black Cloak, turning to see the cause of the commotion, saw her.

Though she could not see his face hidden deep within his hood, Avielle staggered from the force of the menace turned upon her. She felt as though hands seized her throat, squeezing the life from her as a harsh voice whispered to her of death.

Avielle looked away, clasped her arms around herself, and at last straightened.

"I am Princess Avielle," she said in a trembling voice. "And I have come for my friends."

"Princess?" asked High Councilman Herector. "Princess Avielle?"

"It cannot be," said Lord General Maldreck. "She was killed when the High Hall fell."

"I was not killed," she said. "I have been in hiding."

"You are an imposter," said Lord General Maldreck.

"But remember the coachman's story, Maldreck," High Councilman Herector said. "He swore he saw her leave the High Hall before the whirlwind." The Councilman stepped closer to Avielle and peered at her. "It is she," he added after a moment. "Though her hair is dyed black—look, you can see the silver roots—I recognize her beyond any doubt."

"Princess," the Black Cloak hissed. "We have been seeking you, but you have eluded us. Now we will deal with you as we dealt with your execrable family."

"You hold six of my friends here," Avielle said, averting her eyes. "I command you to free them."

"You have no right of command," Lord General Maldreck said. "The High Council rules Rhia now."

Avielle ignored him.

"What do you wish in exchange for my friends?" she asked the Black Cloak.

"In exchange?" the Black Cloak laughed. "We will take them and crush you. You are a worm. There is nothing you can offer us."

Avielle's thoughts raced. There must be something she could offer, something they wanted; she tried to recall everything she knew about Dredonia or had read about Dredonia and the Brethren of the Black Cloaks.

And suddenly she felt something coming, something rising like a dark wind, a dark tide, sweeping all before it. It came from the deepest, blackest place inside her, the thing she had feared from her earliest days, from the earliest whispers that had dogged her through the rooms of the High Hall. And now it was here at last, seizing her by the throat. She felt the shadow of the wing of the Malaquasana, the teeth of Demord the Demon, and the arrow of Hycath the Hunter.

"It would be unwise of you to kill me," Avielle said

slowly and distinctly. "For I can be a great asset to you."

"You are nothing," the Black Cloak said. "How can you help us?

Avielle turned as cold as a marble statue. A heavy crown seemed to rise upon her head, a crown of obsidian, black as a night without stars or moon.

"I would rule Rhia as a subkingdom to Dredonia," she said in a terrible voice. "I would command that my people convert to the religion of the First Foundationalists and worship the First One."

The people at the front of the slave pen cried out.

"Princess!" exclaimed High Councilman Herector. "You must not do this."

"I have the power. I am the leader of Rhia by right of birth." *You'll be a leader. And a mighty one. Whether for good or ill I can't say.*

The Black Cloak hesitated. "And all that you ask in return is the lives of six slaves?"

Avielle nodded.

The Black Cloak laughed. "So be it. You shall be as a puppet in our hands."

A murmur ran through the crowd, as the news passed from one person to another. Avielle could see them look upon her with hatred. But why should that matter? Had they not always looked upon her with hatred?

"Call forth the six that you would save," the Black Cloak ordered.

Avielle turned toward the crowd and began to call. "Tinty. Darien. Pini. Ogall. Master Steorra. Master Lughgor. Come forth."

The crowd picked up the names and shouted them until six people all grouped together stood up and began making their way to the front. At last they climbed over the barriers and stood before Avielle and the Black Cloak. She looked upon their dear faces.

"You are free to go," she said. "Go home now to Postern Street."

They looked at each other, then back at her. None of them moved.

"We heard your terms," said Master Lughgor.

"You're out of your blinking mind." Tinty crossed her arms over her chest.

"You can't sacrifice the good of the entire kingdom for the six of us," Darien said. "You're an idiot, Vianna, if you think we could live with that."

"Your name would be cursed by the stars themselves," said Master Steorra.

"Worse than that evil great-something grandmother of yours," Tinty added.

Avielle stared at Tinty. It was true. If she did what she espoused here, her deed would be far worse than what her great-great grandmother had done, because it would be intentional. Rhians would curse Avielle's name for a thousand years because of the darkness she would spread over the land. She would be the Cursed One. There would be no redemption. But none of that mattered.

"We are waiting!" the Black Cloak said.

"If you would have me rule as your puppet queen, you will wait while I speak to my friends!" Avielle shouted at him.

"You have one minute," the Black Cloak said. "Then I will kill you all."

"Go home!" Avielle exclaimed, turning back to them. "I must save you. Go! I command you as your princess."

"You're not our princess." Tinty put her hands on her hips. "Not like this. We know you. You'd never get up to anything wicked."

"You're in there somewhere, Vianna," Master Lughgor said. "Come back to us, child, from whatever dark place has hold of you. We want the girl Gamalda loved."

"We want the girl who taught me to read," said Darien. "Even when I was mean to her. And the girl who brought Master Keenum his soup when he was sick."

"That's right," Tinty said. "I want the girl who helped me when I mucked up my magic. And who helped Renatta get a dress of her own. Though what she sees in Smitor I don't know."

"And I would be most pleased to see the girl who transcribed my treatise," said Master Steorra. "Damn those relics."

"You're the kind, loving Princess of Postern Street," Tinty said, "and we want you back." She scuffed the toe of her shoe against the ground. "Because . . . bother, you're dumber than a chicken if you don't know we love you."

The others nodded.

Love? Avielle felt the word wash over her.

"And we all knew who you were, of course," said Master Steorra. "All except the Peas. We didn't tell them. Couldn't be trusted—well, perhaps Renatta."

"You knew?" Avielle gasped.

Master Steorra nodded. "A very simple, a rather simple, an exceedingly simple deduction."

"You all knew who I was and yet you loved me, and love me still?"

They all nodded.

Then it seemed to Avielle as though their hands lifted her, as though their faith and their trust and their love shone through her, piercing every part of the darkness that lay upon her. Avielle felt the black crown crack and fall into pieces, which shivered away into dust and were no more. "It is gone," she whispered. "It is gone at last."

She turned toward the Black Cloak.

"I will wait no longer!" he screamed.

"I withdraw my offer," Avielle said in a loud clear voice. "I will not cast this kingdom into darkness. May the Goddess give us the strength to stand against you in the face of whatever terror you cast upon us." She looked at her friends. "I am sorry I cannot save you. Farewell. May the Goddess protect you."

The Black Cloak screamed again. It stretched out its hand and let out a burst of green light that struck Avielle in the throat. Pain seared through her as she fell to her knees. The Black Cloak came closer, one arm raised to strike again. At that moment, Avielle heard a sob. Pressed against the edge of a sawhorse was a girl wearing a red dress. Her brown hair hung in two braids down to her waist; some of the hair had come loose and straggled into her eyes. She was weeping and shrinking back in her terror of the Black Cloak.

Avielle looked at the faces beside the girl: a woman clasping her face with both hands; a man in a white linen shirt clutching a woman in a green hat; a boy with his knees drawn to his chest; and other faces down the row, face after face, all stricken with terror, all without hope.

She had been horrifically selfish, Avielle thought as she looked at the despairing people she had been about to cast into darkness in order to save her friends. These people needed her, too. She remembered that High Councilman Herector had once blithely written that they must all go marching bravely on in the face of terror, and she had wondered about those like her who were too frightened or too full of despair to go on. She had wondered who spoke for them. She should have. She should have spoken for them. Now it was too late. She had failed them. Tears spilled down Avielle's cheeks. *I wish I could have saved them,* she thought. *I wish I could have saved them all.*

The white feather flashed in her hand and began to glow brighter and brighter. Avielle threw it at the Black Cloak in the second before he struck her down.

THE MAGNIFICENT HEART
CHAPTER FORTY-ONE

Everything turned white, a soft glowing feathery white, in a deep silence. Avielle drifted in this softness, this whiteness, her thoughts still filled with the faces of the people she had seen. The feathery whiteness grew more brilliant, as of crystals and diamonds afire in sunlight. I should have saved them, she thought again and again, and her heart filled with the feather, filled with compassion, which were one and the same.

Avielle prayed: *Goddess most high, help me to use this key of compassion to find the Power beyond All Powers that Unlocks the Magnificent Heart. Please! I must find it so I can save my people.* Yes, Avielle thought. Yes. My people.

Then, into the great silence, into the feathery whiteness, into her heart, fell three words sung by a voice of gold:

AVIELLE OF RHIA

The whiteness began to dissipate, and Avielle found herself scattered into pieces that flew as high as an eagle over the land, and she could see every rock and rill; every flower; every farm; every hill, town, and tower. She saw a child spinning with her arms held out, looking up at the sky. She saw a man crouching on his knees with his face in his hands. She saw two men laughing together. She saw a woman sobbing in a sheet hanging on a clothesline. She saw a boy hiding, whimpering in the closet of an old house while a man with a club searched for him. She saw a man and a woman all in white walking down the steps of a Temple, their arms clasped around each other. She saw an old woman sitting next to the bed of a dying man who could not stop coughing.

As Avielle floated above the land and saw these her people, she felt her compassion growing until she could no longer contain it.

I will speak for you, Avielle sang upon the wind. *I will speak for all the people of Rhia because I love you.*

And then she heard it. A kind of thrumming, a beating, a whooshing on the air. From the north, east, and west they came. Like a warm wind from the south they came. From rivers and trees and lakes they came. In flocks over mountains they came. From dream, thought, and memory they came. Rising from ponds and nests they came. Out of thickets and sweet grass they came. They came and they came and they came! Birds coming home to Rhia. And they gathered her spirit upon their wings and flew with her to Tirion.

As they approached the city, Avielle began to weave, not with her hands, not with her mind, but with her heart and spirit. *What you weave not even need to be made of thread.* She took the strands of the river. She took the strands of the mountains and trees. She took the strands of the rising sun. And the strands of earth she took and the strands of stone. She wove the strands of the white birds who were glad to help her. She gathered threads from the depth of each pool, from the flight of each butterfly, and from the roar of each river. And last of all, she took every look of joy on every face she had ever seen. All of this Avielle wove into the cloak, and its magical cloth was the Power Beyond All Powers, which was love.

Then suddenly she was kneeling before the Black Cloak again, and the din of the crowd was loud in her ears.

"She awakes! She awakes!" Avielle heard the people cry. "She is not dead!"

Without effort, without thought, Avielle rose to her feet, and as she did, saw that she had changed. Now her dress was shining silver. Now her hair was silver as the moon, and glittered. Her magic cloak of white birds and sparkling light blew twelve feet behind her.

"I am the Queen of Rhia," she called to the Black Cloak. "And I banish you from my kingdom forever. Begone! You shall prey upon my people no more."

The Black Cloak screamed. "I shall see that you stay dead this time!"

As he came toward her, Avielle lifted her arms as though she were a giant bird stretching her wings. Light flowed through her, possessing her, until she swept one arm forward and the magic cloak, too, swept forward and coiled around the Black Cloak. He fell screaming upon the ground, then shriveled up into a black mist that drifted away. The second Black Cloak came charging forward, and Avielle vanquished him in the same way.

She crouched on her heels, panting, exhausted, her power almost spent. But there was still the third Black Cloak, who had been on the far side of the pen, and he was approaching her now. What else could she do?

The Black Cloak came closer and closer until he stood before her. He hurled a clot of darkness that fell over Avielle and the magic cloak like a coating of foul soot. Her light diminished. Terrible pictures filled her mind. She saw Rhia on fire, the starving people in chains. She saw a battlefield littered with bodies being savaged by the Black Birds. She saw ragged children working in mines, whipped by Dredonians. Her heart begin to freeze with despair.

"You have killed my brethren," the Black Cloak cried. "I will crush you."

Avielle turned her eyes toward the rising sun, where the Goddess shone, where the planet Lashata the Lover stood too near it to be seen, in conjunction. Then she heard a roar: the people cheering her, calling her name: "Avielle! Avielle!" Strength filled her, and she staggered to her feet. Her hand rose to her chest as though feeling for a bag of pearls hanging from her neck. She begin to spin. The magic cloak whirled and the edge of it spun around the Black Cloak again and again. Eddies of blue light ran up him until he, too, vanished.

Avielle stood, panting. The birds who had formed her magic cloak flew into the trees on the edge of the square, and the rest of the cloak disappeared. She turned toward the crowd of people, whose mouths were open in astonishment.

"Avielle!" they shouted. "Slayer of the Black Cloaks! Avielle!"

Avielle held up one hand, but they would not stop. A minute passed, and then another, until at last they all fell silent.

"You are my people," Avielle said. "I will give my life to save and protect you. But we cannot allow a single person to go as a slave to Dredonia, for if we allow this blackmail we become slaves to fear—"

"But if you do this," interrupted Lord General Maldreck, "the terror will not end."

"Then we must live with it," Avielle said, "until we find another way to defeat it. Because a greater terror is giving in, sending our people to be their slaves." She paused. "And I don't believe this slave tribute will end the terror. Evil has no honor. What will the Brethren of the Black Cloaks demand next, having seen that we will bend to their will? More gold? A larger tribute of slaves each year? More children to crawl through the narrow passages of their mines? The rule of our country itself? No, we cannot give in to them."

"If you do not wish me to be your queen," she added, "I will retire to some obscure part of the country and never trouble you again. But if you do wish me to be your queen, I will try to be a wise, just, and compassionate ruler. I will be queen not only of the proud and strong and fearless, but also the queen of the despairing, the queen of the frightened, the queen of those who cannot march bravely on. I will be the voice of all my people. And we will restore to Rhia the worship of the Goddess in her light and glory, with all the love in our hearts, as she deserves to be worshiped." She hesitated, waiting while people passed her words back through the crowd. Then she shouted, "What say you?"

The crowd began yelling again.

"Queen Avielle!"

"She brought the birds home!"

"She slayed the Black Cloaks!"

"Queen Avielle!"

"The birds are home! The birds are home!"

"When word spreads of what you have done here this morning," said High Councilman Herector, "no one will question your allegiance, though your skin is silver. You are heir to the throne of Rhia. Will you come with us now and take up your rightful place as queen of your people?"

"I will come," she said.

At dawn the next morning, Avielle stood absolutely still beside the window high in the White Tower of Cialaya. A bird hopped along the windowsill. She had just released her mother's meadowlark from its cage, the cage and bird that had miraculously survived the whirlwind.

"Go little one," Avielle said. "Fly free." She looked over at Dolvoka's book of birds lying on the table. "We brought them home, great-great grandmother, you and I together, we brought back Rhia's heart."

Avielle leaned against the windowsill. From this height she could see far over the city, even to the pile of rubble that was the ruin of the High Hall. She knew that yesterday's triumph was only one victory in a long battle. The Brethren of the Black Cloaks would return. But she and her people would face their evil together, and they would defeat it.

And for a moment, for one shining, magnificent moment, even as Avielle looked at the rubble of the High Hall, she did not wish for revenge against the Brethren. Instead, she wished them the beauty of bird flight, she wished them true strength, she wished their hearts to be opened.

On the windowsill, the meadowlark burst into song, then spread its wings and flew toward the sun that was rising over Rhia.